Healing Creek

a Love Story

By Jaclyn M. Hawkes

Spirit Dance Books ™

Other books by Jaclyn M Hawkes

Journey of Honor
The Outer Edge of Heaven
The Most Important Catch

Rockland Ranch Series Books
Peace River
Above Rubies

Healing Creek

a Love Story

By Jaclyn M. Hawkes

Spirit Dance Books ™

Healing Creek

By Jaclyn M. Hawkes

Copyright © August 2013 Jaclyn M. Hawkes

All rights reserved.

Published and distributed by Spirit Dance Books.LLC

Spiritdancebooks.com 1-855-648-5559

Cover design by Roland Ali Pantin

Cover copyright © Spirit Dance Books LLC

Printed in USA

First Printing August 20

Library of Congress control number 2013946199

ISBN: 0-9851648-3-6

ISBN-13:978-0-9851648-3-6

Dedication

This book is dedicated to the unsnivelers. To all those wonderful salt of the earth individuals who never whine. The ones who find their lives turned upside down and simply get up the next morning and keep on swimming, without ever railing at why whatever had to happen to them. God bless them for their strength of character, and for the fact that they never suck the life out of everyone around them. I'm so definitely not there yet, but I aspire to be.

It's also dedicated to my husband. He *is* one of the unsnivelers and a truly good man. I'm so grateful for him. He's not a romance novel cover model. Honestly, the idea would embarrass him. But he could be. And he's definitely great romance novel inspiration.

Jaclyn

Chapter 1

Monet McLaughlin-Johnson knew her life was due for a massive upheaval. She had known it for a while. What she didn't know was the upheaval would show up on Wednesday, just before dinner.

When her doorbell sounded, she rinsed her hands from the broccoli she was preparing, and dried them on a hand towel as she went to answer it. She had no sense of impending marital doom. Funny, you'd think you would have an inkling about something like that—especially when you're a professional marriage counselor.

Opening the door, she looked out at the pretty teenaged girl standing there with a tiny baby bundled in a blanket in her arms. The girl seemed nervous and Monet glanced back out to the street, wondering if the girl had car trouble or something. There was an older model Nissan pulled up in the driveway, but other than that, nothing seemed amiss and Monet looked back at the girl in confusion and asked, "Can I help you with something?"

The girl nodded wordlessly, and Monet opened the door wider. "Come in. What is it that you need?"

Hesitantly, the young mother asked, "Is this Frank Johnson's place?"

Monet nodded and said, "Yes."

The girl closed her eyes for a moment and then seemed to square her shoulders as she stepped up into the house. Still confused, Monet motioned into the nearby living room. "Please. Have a seat. Frank should be home any time now. Can I get you something to drink? Water? Soda?"

"No thanks." The girl shook her head sadly and added, "But that's real nice of you." The baby began to fuss and the young women sighed as she dug into the blanket for a pacifier she placed in the baby's mouth. Instead of sitting, she began to gently bounce the baby and make tender shushing noises, and Monet looked from the girl to the baby and back, wondering why the girl was here.

And why she was looking for Frank Johnson's place? The girl was an enigma, but Monet had long ago quit being jealous of other women with Frank. This last year of trying to help people with struggling marriages had only helped to harden her against the vulnerability of being hurt by a man as chronically unfaithful as Frank. She just didn't care anymore.

She and Frank were married in name only, and realistically that was only because Monet couldn't face being a divorced marriage counselor. To her, that was just too ludicrous to be professional. Although, in principle it didn't make much difference when realistically their marriage had long ago failed.

She'd thought she had also gotten over being surprised. As she looked at this hopelessly nervous new mother, she began to wonder if Frank had finally broken the last straw. Surely he wouldn't have been foolish enough to have had unprotected sex with a girl this young, would he? She barely looked out of high school.

At this troubling thought, Monet asked politely,

"What was it you needed Frank for? Is there something I could do for you?"

The girl only shook her head as her eyes filled with tears and she said, "No. Only Frank can help me. If he will. Are you his housekeeper?"

Monet considered that for a moment. In a way, that was an excellent description of her role here in her own home. Their marriage had been on the rocks from nearly the very first, although Monet had used all her training, as well as all of her patience to try to hold things together as well as she could. Still, when Monet had caught Frank cheating for the third time in the first two months of her marriage, she hadn't needed a master's degree in psychology to know that it might be hopeless.

The psychologist in her knew that Frank had a problem—a very large and deep-seated problem. But, if she were honest with herself, there were times in her most private thoughts, where she tried not to delve, that she wondered what was wrong with her that she wasn't enough for her husband.

Then, several of months ago, when a college friend had brought her attention to the reality that Frank's profile was on a dating website, and had, in fact, been placed there six weeks before they'd gotten married, Monet had given up completely. This marriage was toast before they had even made their vows. She knew she was good, but she couldn't fix issues that deep.

The website had been Christian, of all ludicrous things, and Frank's profile had been thick with self-righteous blarney. These last weeks, Monet had been simply going through the motions, both in her marriage and in her professional life. She and Frank were roommates. Nothing more.

She had failed in her marriage. She knew that.

Now she just had to come to terms with how to meld the years she'd spent becoming a certified marriage counselor, and the deeply held religious beliefs she had about marriage vows, with the ugly reality of that failure. So far, she hadn't been able to face any way to resolve it. Maybe the teary eyed young woman standing there in her living room was the long sought answer.

Resolutely, Monet led the girl to sit on the couch, then sat beside her and quietly said, "I'll bet Frank will help you. Can I ask you a question?" She met the girl's eyes and went on gently. "Is this Frank's baby?"

The tears spilled over to roll down the young woman's cheeks as she closed her eyes and nodded yes. Monet looked at her, and all she could think to do was put a gentle arm around her shoulders and say, "She's beautiful." She gave the girl a small uncomfortable pat and added. "She's a very beautiful baby." And she was. God help her.

Monet took a deep breath and stood up. *Well. Alrighty then.* She took another deep breath. Maybe trying for a more eternal perspective would make walking away from six years of college, and the practice she'd built up over the last year, feel more doable. At any rate, now it was out of her hands. Frank had a baby with a teenager. *Holy Copernicus.*

Two years later

Pulling the Ranger and trailer into the hay barn, Monet glanced at her watch and then stepped up onto the hay stack to begin tossing bales down onto the trailer. The photo people were due to show up here in less than half an hour. She would just have time to drop the bales in the alleyway of the main barn before she would need to be available to assist them in whatever it was they were doing. The man who'd set up the appointment had said they would be shooting photos for book covers with the stables as the setting. It sounded simple enough.

Monet flicked a hand at the dust motes dancing in the sunlight in the alleyway and glanced out the barn door at her facility lazing under the blue western Washington sky. Rich dark wood and stone barns were surrounded by neat wood fences and lush green pastures dotted with horses. The creek meandered throughout, and behind it all were her house and her parents' house, with the foothills and crags of the mountains in the distance.

Healing Creek Stables was a beautiful location and they had people take photos occasionally. It had even been used for a backdrop for wedding invitations once. Monet loaded eight bales on the trailer and climbed back in the Ranger to head to the main barn. They were paying her two hundred dollars for the use of her facility and she could be accommodating for that kind of money, just as long as she finished in time for her ten o'clock clinic.

Twenty minutes later, she heard a car and glanced up from the hay she was feeding to see a fire-engine red Ferrari purr up the lane between the cedar rail fences and pull to a stop in front of the office. A surprisingly big man climbed out considering the height of the car. He reached

5

back inside to retrieve a fashionably squashed straw cowboy hat, then stood and slowly looked around. Dark hair tousled over the collar of his shirt. When he saw her standing inside the long barn looking his way, he raised his chin in a miniscule nod and then glanced around again.

This was definitely the model. He had to be. He was all but heart stoppingly gorgeous and exuded confidence like he owned the place as he surveyed the various barns, paddocks, and pastures. Sunlight glinted off his sunglasses and the chain at his throat and Monet began to wonder just what kind of a book cover they were shooting to need Adonis, the mythical ultimate male's help.

Even from this distance she could tell his cowboy boots and belt were some kind of exotic snakeskin and that he either truly bucked heavy bales of hay for a living or spent an inordinate amount of time weight training. She shook her head and laughed to herself as she cut the strings of the bale of hay she was feeding. *That hat is pathetic.* Hopefully he was an amiable pretty boy. She might be earning every cent of that two hundred bucks if he was arrogant.

After looking around for a few moments, he walked across to the oval paddock and leaned on the top rail to watch the broodmares and foals grazing just inside. Monet felt a hint of pride. It didn't matter what breed of horse you preferred, or if you even knew anything about them—those seven mares and their foals were glorious. Not only were they champion stock, but they were sleek and shiny, and exuded spirit. They were her pride and joy.

As she watched, while she fed the last few stalls of yearlings, the nearest broodmare put up her head and ambled over to where the man stood at the fence, obviously hoping for a bite of carrot or apple from the brawny stranger. Tying off the last of the baling twine, Monet tossed it into a barrel in the alley and headed that way, stopping to grab an apple out of the bin inside the tack room door.

At the fence, she handed the man the apple with her left hand, and extended her right. "Monet McLaughlin. You must be with the book cover people. And this is Summer Storm." She indicated the mare. "Give her the apple and she'll be your life long friend."

He pushed his sunglasses onto the top of his head, revealing eyes the color of the moss on the creek bank. "Nick DeGrassi. It's a pleasure. You've got a beautiful place here." Turning back to Summer Storm with the apple, he added, "A guy can always use a life long friend."

Summer Storm took a dainty bite of the apple and then took a step toward Monet and pushed her nose into Monet's hair in a gentle snuffling hello. Without even realizing it, Monet put her hand up to pet the mare's head and rub her ear as she said, "Who can't use a life long friend? Please, make yourself at home here. I'll be working there in that largest barn if you need anything. I'll get horses or tack as you need them. Just let me know."

He nodded. "Thank you. The others should be here shortly. Is there any place we shouldn't go?"

Turning to walk back to the barn to finish feeding, Monet shook her head. "You should be fine. Don't get into any stalls with horses. And close any gates you open. But other than that, we're a pretty safe operation. We have to be. Most of what we do here entails working with children. It was good to meet you, Mr. DeGrassi."

While this Nick had been early, and wandered around exploring, the other three people were more than twenty minutes late. They stood talking for several

7

minutes while a rather effeminate man fussed with a busty young woman's long blonde hair. Then he dusted her shoulders and chest above her tight white tank top with some kind of makeup, touched up her face, and insisted she sip a bottle of water. When she appeared to be sufficiently primped, they headed toward Nick, who was out near the oval paddock again, the photographer carrying a huge bag of gear while the assistant carried his own gargantuan bag.

They took a number of photos of Nick and the girl beside the paddock as Monet occasionally glanced over, then Monet was floored as the photo shoot seemed to degenerate into overt touching and clothing began to come off. First it was Nick's shirt and then the young woman's jeans, leaving her in a ridiculously short pair of Daisy Mae denim cut offs. Monet hadn't seen the actual change of clothing, but it must have occurred right there in the stable yard, because the young woman hadn't had time to go anywhere else to switch clothes. Apparently, the book covers were of the trashy romance genre.

Monet shook her head and rolled her eyes as the young woman wrapped both legs around Nick's waist and he held her up with his hand squarely on her pretty little hind end, as the photographer directed them from behind the camera. From where Monet worked, the photographer seemed frustrated with the young woman, who only seemed to get uptight as the photographer got more worked up. *It would seem the female model was a little stiff with Mr. Italian Adonis holding her fanny. Poor girl.* Monet grinned as she worked. These people were unreal.

Upon emerging from the barn alleyway near the foursome, Monet paused to watch the spectacle. Nick actually had the top button of his jeans undone, with his thumb hooked into the waist band, and was looking down at the girl with an expert sultry gaze. The guy was good. Insanely good. For a nasty model he had the technique down to a T. It was almost frightening to know men could stage this kind of thing. The girl, on the other hand, looked more and more stiff and amateurish, and the photographer was getting grumpy as he got more impatient.

Just when Monet was going to move on to pulling the tack for her clinic, she felt her eyes widen as hottie Nick put a hand out to stay the photographer, then he turned to the girl and unleashed even more charisma. He put his head down next to the model who had begun to tear up, and apparently whispered something to her, because she looked up at him and gave a hesitant smile. He put a hand gently on her neck and pushed it up into her hair and leaned even closer to say something again and Monet saw the girl literally begin to melt into him. He rubbed her bare shoulder tenderly with his other hand, kissed her temple and spoke again. He put the hand to her cheek, rubbed a thumb over her top lip and nuzzled his mouth against her forehead as he continued to whisper.

Monet's eyes widened even further. Within the space of about three seconds, he had the girl so loosened up that Monet half expected the rest of the clothes to come off, as the blonde looked up at him in worship mode, and the photographer grinned at the makeup guy.

Dang, he was unreal! In a way it was fascinating, and in a way it was awful. She'd never actually witnessed such a thing. Not even in her own bedroom, although her ex-husband had turned out to be an amazingly prolific womanizer to ladies he wasn't married to, bless his heart.

Watching Nick was like watching a snake charmer. And although the girl was obviously old enough to realize just what her line of work entailed, Monet pitied her. If that had been her little sister, Monet would have wanted someone to arrest the guy. Heck, if that had been her big sister, Monet would have still wanted him arrested. He was like the seduction wizard. Who needed alcohol or drugs to make someone unaware, when you had chemistry that potent?

With another glance at the master of allure at work, Monet began to carry tack to the hitch rack in front of the small arena. If he wasn't flat out beautiful, he'd be disgusting. Beautiful, he was frightening. These guys were going to have to be through before her seven-year-old autistic students came in another hour and a half. The last thing those little girls needed to see was Nick, the Romeo, plying his craft.

The saddles were ready, and she had gone back in for halters and bridles when Nick himself put his head in the door. "Excuse me, Monet, but would it be too much bother to use a horse in our shoot?"

Monet shook her head, even as she was wondering what kind of kinky pose they would involve her poor defenseless horse in. "No, not at all. Any preference of color?"

Without a hint of a smile, Nick said, "Any color but neurotic blonde. The modeling agency sent me a drama queen today. Easy going is more important than color. Got anything really patient?"

She smiled. "Most horses are incredibly patient. Which is why I prefer them to neurotic blondes." Drily she added, "I'm surprised you're bothered. You seemed to have her so well in hand. Literally."

He gave a half-hearted chuckle, but didn't really smile. "That was a good one. Touché."

"Sorry, but it seemed so apropos. I'm just getting ready to saddle a black, a buckskin, and a red dun. Would any of those colors work?"

"What color is red dun?"

"Strawberry blonde. Or strawberry gold. That's what my niece calls it. Which works perfectly to avoid the blonde word."

"And this strawberry gold horse is willing to cooperate without whining?"

Smiling, Monet said sweetly, "All strawberry gold beings are the very paragon of cooperation."

He finally smiled and frankly, it was stunning. "Perfect. Can I help you get it ready?" It was no wonder this man made his living by romancing women.

She shook her head with an apologetic grin. "I am absolutely sure that I don't need your style of help, Romeo. But thanks for the offer. Do you want her saddled? The horse, I mean."

Evenly, Nick said, "That was crude."

"You're right. I apologize. Please forgive me."

"You're forgiven."

"I'll saddle the dun and if you don't need the saddle, we can take it back off."

Nick smiled again. "You are the absolute paragon of cooperation. Thank you."

When Monet appeared with the horse, they were shooting under the overhanging roof. Nick had the blonde backed up in a stall doorway, her tank top and a black bra strap hanging off one shoulder and him kissing her neck. It was definitely your classic trashy romance novel look with Nick all rippling brown pecs and shoulders, and the girl's chest fairly bursting out the top of her marginal shirt. It was sickeningly tacky, but Monet had to hand it to them. Since Nick's whispered caressing pep talk, they were able to crank out what was probably a boatload of steamy photos like it was their job. And weird as it was to watch, it was definitely Nick's job. Even if he did have to occasionally coax his cohort into relaxing into their intimate roles.

As Monet looked on while she prepped for her clinic, it still almost freaked her out a little to watch Nick handle the girl he'd deemed neurotic. Monet wouldn't have believed they weren't a couple if he hadn't said something. For the camera, he seemed to be smitten by the girl. Knowing it was all acting made Monet's already cynical heart shrivel even further.

Maybe the whole male race was like this. Maybe it wasn't just that she had been a blithering fool in trusting her husband before she had learned better. Maybe her brother and her dad were the only honorable, caring, trustworthy men on the planet. It made her stupid mistakes in life seem less damning, but it also made any hope of finding the happily-ever-after of her parents' marriage seem less plausible than ever.

Just minutes before the girls for her clinic were due to arrive, and after several more suggestive photo settings, the book cover crew began packing up their gear. If Monet hadn't already been spooked by Nick's ability to charm on command, she would have been completely blown away to watch him literally straighten up from holding the female model, pull his shirt back on, button it up, tuck it in and turn to lead the dun over to where Monet had just put two yearlings on the horse walker to exercise.

He hardly even waved to the blonde who was herself straightening her shirt, but watching every move he made with big puppy dog eyes. Nick may have been able to flip the switch, but the young woman was obviously a little tangled emotionally. And who could blame her? Even in this era of Hollywood celebrity shows, men who looked and seduced at the level of Nick the

Italian Adonis were fatally rare.

In a completely professional voice, Nick said to Monet, "You were absolutely correct. This is a very patient horse. Thank you for your help. You have a fabulous place here. It's very calming. It has peace."

Monet shrugged. "I didn't do much. And I'm glad you felt comfortable. Were you able to get the shots you needed?"

"Not as many as I had hoped, but the others want to call it a day. It's enough for now." He glanced out at the stable surrounding them again. "Would you mind if I looked around some more before I go? It's been awhile since I've been near horses much and I'd forgotten how they fascinate me."

Monet turned the walker on and clicked her tongue to get the horses moving, then said, "Look all you want, as long as you keep your clothes on and your hands to yourself. There will be children here for the balance of the afternoon, so you'll need to be G-rated from here on out."

Nick grinned and chuckled. "If you insist, Ms. McLaughlin. You'll think I'm a saint."

Out loud, she amiably said, "See that I do, Mr. DeGrassi." But in her head, she thought, *Not a chance, Mr. snake charmer. But you can always try.*

At dusk that night, as she was in her office doing the day's books, Cade, the twenty-year-old college student who lived over the tack room and helped with all the odd jobs stopped in the doorway and said, "Do these look familiar to you?" He held up the jeans with the sparkles on the back pocket that the neurotic blonde had been wearing when she'd first arrived that morning. "I found them hanging on the corral fence. It's lucky the horses

13

didn't chew on them. Are they yours? They're Armani. "

His face behind his glasses was confused and Monet laughed. "They're not mine. In the first place, I don't spend four hundred dollars on jeans, and in the second, I most definitely don't undress at the corral. They belong to a model who was here this morning."

"Some model undressed at the corral this morning?"

Monet shook her head disbelievingly and laughed again. "Actually, yes. It was quite shocking."

"And I missed it. I miss all the good stuff. What should I do with them?"

Pointing to the chair near the door, Monet said, "Leave them here. I'll try to get hold of the girl. If she doesn't come get them, you can put them on E-Bay and buy a text book with the money. If she does come, you can meet her. Although I don't think she was marriage material."

Drily, Cade said, "Not if she was undressing near the corral." He grinned. "But she might be great NCMO material!"

Placidly, Monet replied, "Yes, I'd imagine she'd have no problem with worse than making out without commitment. Stop it. You're trashing my faith in the males of the species and it has already been stomped today. Go lock the main gate and find Sherlock, would you? He wandered through here awhile ago, but I haven't seen him lately."

"He's in the north paddock with the broodmares. I fed him when I came in about a half hour ago."

"I left some rib bones from dinner on the counter in the tack room for him. When he comes back through, see that he gets them if you're still up. Would you?"

The typically cheerful student gave her a salute and

14

a grin. "Will do. See you tomorrow."

Monet closed down her spreadsheet and rolled her neck for a moment, then unlocked her desk drawer. She got out her purse to find the phone number from Nick DeGrassi's check so she could let someone know about the designer jeans. There actually wasn't a phone number on the check, just a website. Imagesofromance.com. *Oh, brother.* That sounded even more questionable than the shoot had been. And the shoot had been questionable enough.

She pulled up the website and shook her head in disbelief. The banner across the top said it all. Images of Romance.com, starring international model Nicholas DeGrassi, featured on more than 1300 book covers. The Baron of romance!

Good heavens! Thirteen hundred! She scrolled down through a number of the images and was amazed. On the first page Monet counted twelve different girls he was posed with. There were twenty four pages with a hundred photos per page. No wonder Nick had the seduction thing down. He *was* a machine!

Some were images of Nick and the girls in all kinds of settings. Some were just of Nick. He was posed as everything from a knight, to a James Bond type, to whatever those European Lords or Earls were called. There were a few of other male models, and some were actual book covers with the text and designs already added. There were even some pictures of just back drops of castles or the ocean. Actually, both the photography and cover designs were surprisingly good—for covers and photos that consisted mainly of muscles, six pack abs and voluptuous bosoms anyway.

Monet wasn't a connoisseur of male models, or trashy romance novel jackets, but these seemed like beautiful bold designs with rich colors and textures. They were balanced and read easily and if she had had a penchant for that type of racy literature, she would have been intrigued. At the very least, it was definitely a beefcake show of epic proportion. She had never even conceived of such a website, but apparently there was quite a market for this kind of thing. Thirteen hundred was near unbelievable. And he *had* been driving a Ferrari. You would have to sell a lot of book covers to pay for an exotic Italian sports car.

After searching for a phone number for long enough to become almost a bit scandalized, Monet simply sent an e-mail from the "contact" section at the bottom of the site explaining about the jeans, and then called it a night. It had been a long day, aside from the fact that she now had scantily clad Adonis Nick tattooed inside her eyelids. He had been all but lewd in some of the photos, but he was definitely attractive.

Chapter 2

When the birds outside her bedroom window began to chirp and sing in the dark of early morning, Monet turned over with a small groan and then yawned. Crud, she had even dreamed of that blasted gorgeous snake charmer model in some kind of animal skin loin cloth. He'd been wielding a machete through a tropical paradise on his way to a very private waterfall. Geez, what did that say about her? Apparently she was still a human female, in spite of being schooled by marrying 'Frank the perpetually unfaithful Johnson'.

She should know better. And she did. At least she did when she was wide awake.

She dropped to her knees beside her bed to say her morning prayers, and then climbed back under the covers to mentally go over her day. Chores and a private clinic in the morning. Lunch with her parents, and then working the two year olds and paperwork for the duration. Oh, and the feed store was sending a load of grain sometime mid afternoon.

Getting up, she showered, did her hair, and dressed in her typical attire of form fitting riding breeches, soft riding boots, and a cotton button down blouse. She opened her fridge to consider what to have for breakfast and added grocery shopping to her mental list. Settling for wheat toast with fresh strawberries and a glass of milk while she read a chapter from the book of Luke open beside her plate, she watched the chickadees and finches flit from bird house to bird feeder outside her kitchen window. Still no baby bird heads popping up inside any of the houses that she could see. It should be any day now.

Walking out the kitchen door, she shooed one of the barn cats from the top of the milk box and said, "You stick to the barn, Patches, and leave my momma birdies alone." Sherlock, the dark chocolate Newfoundland that kept watch over the whole operation, peeled himself off the top step of the deck to come up to her with a sedate wag. She gave him a pat and said, "Good morning, Sherlock."

On the way to the stable office, she stepped off the stone path to pull the odd weed from her collection of tomato seedlings basking in the south beds against the house. It was that time in April when everything grew faster than she could keep up with, even with her mother appearing from time to time with her pruners. It was time to hire the neighbor boy down the valley to help again.

At the gate from her yard to the stable yard, she stopped to look all around. Everything looked under control so far. Horses were grazing in several different pastures and the hired hands, Miguel and Cal were already mucking out in the east barn.

A ringing neigh sounded from her left and she frowned for a moment. If she had known how aggressive Herb Bertoldi's new horse was going to be, she would have never agreed to let him board it here. Not many horses were true outlaws, especially not the European warmbloods, but that stallion was a fiend. A very large fiend. She made another mental note to have Herb move it to one of the stalls with runs before he went out of town next week. She didn't want any of her staff having to deal with it more than simply feeding it and stall care while he was away.

When she saw that Miguel already had the younger horses on the walker, she smiled and headed for the tack room. It was a delightful morning. Perfect for schooling the jumpers over the hunt course.

Nick DeGrassi slowed to turn into the rocked entry gate of Healing Creek Stables. He was just in time to look left and see the ultimate genteel scene of a rider in classic English tack and dress take a beautiful white horse over a jump beside the winding lane. The horse landed gracefully and galloped on toward the next jump and Nick looked around to take in the brilliant green pastures and deep blue sky set off by the stately fence lined road. This place was worlds away from the traffic he had left behind just fifteen minutes ago on I-5. It felt like stepping clear out of the rat race. The peace here was amazing.

He slowed even further, watching the lovely slender rider in the form fitting clothing. He worked around scantily clad women most days and it had become sadly stale to him. But, even though the woman on the horse was much more modestly dressed than he had grown accustomed to, there was something about her. Some innate grace. Or confidence. Class. Something aside from her bone deep beauty that he couldn't put his finger on, but it was there, and even from this distance, she was thoroughly attractive in a completely different way from most women. It was almost surely that Monet from yesterday, although it was hard to tell with the riding helmet covering her hair.

She hadn't been overly impressed with them yesterday. He had known that. Who could blame her? What he did wasn't exactly curing cancer. Still, she had been helpful and professional for the most part as she assisted them throughout the morning. He didn't know when he had ever recognized such a marked difference between the kind of girl Monet was and the kind of girl that model had been. It was as if Monet had an aura of light or something, and he didn't even believe in all that baloney. It had been a surprisingly striking contrast.

Driving slowly up the lane, he finally stopped altogether to watch the rider jumping the horse. When she eventually finished the course and began to walk the bridle path, Nick drove on up the last of the road to the buildings. He'd come here in answer to the e-mail about some jeans, but he could admit that that was just an excuse. Yesterday had been therapeutic to him. Made him feel more alive than he had felt in years. He hadn't even realized he was feeling a bit burnt out until he'd felt enthusiasm yesterday.

He'd forgotten how much he enjoyed working around horses although he had only ridden a handful of times. And he couldn't soak up enough of the out-of-doors here. When he picked up the jeans, he was going to see about taking some kind of rides or riding lessons. Whatever it was he had felt here affected him, and he wanted more of it.

When the jumping horse appeared to be headed his way, he sat in his car and watched them. They were an incredibly beautiful pair and he wished his camera wasn't packed away in his trunk. They would have been striking subjects.

It did indeed turn out to be Monet. She rode up to a nearby hitch rail and dismounted. After looping a rein around the horse's neck, she removed the horse's bridle, slipped a halter on, tied the horse to the rail and then took off her own helmet and shook out her shiny deep brown hair. She had incredible hair. Falling well over her shoulders, it reminded him of rich dark chocolate.

As he got out of his car, she began to loosen the saddle. He put a hand on it as he stepped up beside her and asked, "Can I carry this for you?"

Turning to glance up at him, she said, "Hello, Mr. DeGrassi. No. I've got it, thanks. It isn't heavy." She picked up the saddle and headed into the barn with it. He tagged along and she asked, "Is there something I can help you with?"

When she continued into the tack room, he paused at the door and said, "I came to get the jeans you e-mailed me about. But I'm glad I had to come back. It's beautiful here. Do you ever rent the horses out?"

She shook her head, put the saddle on a rack and draped the pads over a nearby bar. "Not just for rides. We do give lessons. Do you have children who want to learn to ride?"

"I don't have any children. But do you only take children? Am I too old to learn to ride?"

She glanced him up and down briefly. "No. There's no such thing as too old. I typically work with challenged children, but sometimes I just give riding lessons. What do you have in mind? What type of riding do you want to learn to do?"

That was a good question. One he hadn't given any thought to. He didn't even know what types of riding there was. Knowing that Western saddles had saddle horns and English didn't and usually jumped something was about as much as he knew. After considering, he said, "I don't know enough to even be able to answer that. I just

know that there's something about horses that is very . . . "
He hesitated, trying to think of the word. "Therapeutic maybe?"

With a minimal nod, Monet gave a small smile and said almost as if she was reciting something, "The outside of a horse is good for the inside of a man. Or woman."

He nodded his own head. "Yes. Who said that?"

"Will James. An old cowboy philosopher who had it right. It's true. That's why we use them with the kids. They're far easier for the kids to communicate with. Especially the autistic ones. What's your goal?"

He looked at her blankly and she added, "With riding lessons. What do you want to accomplish? I need to know that in order to point you in the right direction lesson wise."

Again, he considered that and surprised himself by answering, "I guess I'd like to learn enough to be able to get a horse or two of my own and give them proper care."

Monet's placid face took on a skeptical look and she said, "Horses take a lot of work. A lot of consistent work, unless you're going to hire someone to do it for you. Which tends to negate the therapeutic aspect. Do you have that kind of time to dedicate to a horse? With your calendar filled with neurotic blondes? And brunettes. And redheads. And Asians? Thirteen hundred book covers can't have left a great deal of time for other . . . diversions. Especially with the level of octane you must have to burn to keep those fires of passion lit."

She wasn't smiling or flirting with him, but he was sure that she wasn't necessarily complimenting his artful work either. She was just being sarcastic in a thoroughly gracious manner.

In a way, it made him want to say something sarcastic back and get in his car and leave. But in another way, it made him wonder if his life's work hadn't just been measured and found honestly wanting.

Frankly, that was a new concept. Usually women found out what he did and then began this nauseating, gushing, happy puppy routine that tended to polish his ego and irritate him at the same time. Monet's polite professionalism with its hint of disdain was definitely not helping his ego, even if it felt far more real than the gushers. In some twisted way that she certainly wouldn't have intended, and that he could never have logically explained, it almost felt like a subtle challenge to him.

Rather than be offended at what from her perspective must have seemed outrageous, he decided to be real back. Drily, he said, "Actually, that's why I do need a good, honest hobby. I'm far enough past my prime that those fires of passion have guttered to a struggle to actually ignite a pilot light. It's a business. I'm basically an actor. It's just not the big screen." He gave her a humorless smile and shrugged. "It beats bussing tables."

She subtly looked him up and down again and then said, "Past your prime? Sure. What? Twenty-eight? Thirty? I'm just going to venture a guess that a therapist would give you some line about how pilot lights have to be lit by at least some minimal emotional ownership. Although, in reality, I'm not sure I necessarily believe that. But it sounds good. It must be true in some cases. It should be."

That made him finally crack a grin. "What, am I prematurely graying? I'm twenty-six. Are you saying that the old adage about how women need to be in love, but men just need to be in the room, isn't true? Or that it is?"

She gave him the first hint of true humor he'd seen from her. "Who knows? Certainly not me. Human intimacy is far, far from my specialty. All I'm saying is

23

that horses take time. If you think you can fit a moment or two in for a horse, come into the office next door and we'll schedule you."

In the small building annexed onto the indoor arena, Nick followed her in a door and was surprised to see what appeared to be a state-of-the-art office, its walls filled with photos and posters about the stables and events the stable had done, along with trophies, ribbons, and even race win pictures.

Nick looked around in surprise. The breadth of what they did here was impressive. He'd originally thought it simply a boarding stable, but it appeared to be more of almost a medical facility to help children using what they called therapy horses.

Sitting behind the somewhat cluttered desk, Monet opened an old fashioned day book and asked, "What do you have in mind Mr. DeGrassi? A scheduled lesson once a week? Or do you want to try to work around your calendar?"

"No. I'm my own boss. I can work around your calendar. Is once a week all you can fit in?"

"No. I could probably fit in more than that. Twice per week? Every other day? And do you have a preference for instructor? I teach, or I've got a cowboy if you prefer a man, or a more mature and far more expert woman who I charge a fortune for. She's a hundred and sixty bucks an hour. But she's an international champion. It's my mother, actually. And she's mostly retired."

Nick considered his options and said, "Twice a week would be great. As late in the afternoon as possible. And I don't need an expert yet, and don't care if my instructor is male or female."

Turning a page or two and back, she asked, "Tuesday and Thursday? Four p.m.? Schedule at least two hours. It'll probably be with me unless something comes up unexpectedly. Will that work for you?"

He nodded, thinking. He was surprised at how much he was looking forward to this and told her, "That will work. What do I need to bring?"

"Only yourself. Wear suitable clothing and heeled boots or shoes. We'll supply everything else."

She stood up from behind the desk and he couldn't help but notice that her riding clothes showed off her pretty figure in a completely respectable and tasteful way. Feeling almost guilty for thinking such a classy woman was attractive, he asked, "Can I look around again? Or will I be in your road?"

She shook her head. "You won't be in the road. On the contrary. That is in large part how you learn. Look around. Just don't get in any stalls and close any gates you open." A horse chose that moment to neigh ringingly and then there was a crash.

Monet frowned, but simply said, "And stay completely away from the huge brown beast that is neighing and trying to kick my barn apart. He's dangerous. If you want to visit with one of the horses, there's an angelic old white one who wanders around here loose, usually carrying a brush in his teeth, hoping to beg some attention. His name is Dan and you can begin learning on him. He's wonderfully bulletproof. I'm usually around somewhere, as well as two other men here if you have questions." She put out a hand. "Welcome to Healing Creek."

As he returned her handshake, he said, "Thanks. I'm looking forward to this."

Pulling on a small pair of thoroughly worn leather work gloves, she gave him a polite smile as she walked out the door, saying, "Perfect. I'm sure it will be rewarding.

25

Good luck clearing your calendar. Excuse me."

Nick found Dan, who did indeed have a brush nearby, and spent an enjoyable half hour brushing the ancient campaigner, who seemed to relish the attention. As Nick combed, he watched the goings on around the Healing Creek Stables. Monet kept constantly busy and seemed to be as nice as she appeared as she worked with the two men who came occasionally to speak to her.

Just before Nick was going to leave, a little brown haired girl arrived with what must have been her mother. The mother stopped to talk to Monet for a moment, but the little girl headed immediately to where Nick was combing Dan. As she approached, she caught sight of Nick and stopped short, then turned instantly to almost cower behind a corner of the nearby barn, peeking surreptitiously towards Nick and the old white steed.

Realizing that she must have been afraid to approach the old horse with Nick there, Nick reluctantly laid aside the brush he'd been using, petted the calm ancient beast one more time and said, "Goodbye, Old Dan. It was good to meet you, sir." With that, Nick went and got into his car and the little girl did, indeed, come out from behind the corner and to the white horse. She glanced toward where Nick still sat in his car watching, then picked up the brush and went around to the other side of Dan and began to groom him.

Nick smiled at the two of them as he started up his car. He was a stranger, after all, and most kids these days had been taught to fear strangers. But the little girl had seemed unduly frightened.

It almost made him sad. He liked kids. There just wasn't much opportunity to be around kids in the romance novel image business. He had always hoped to someday have kids of his own, but so far, he hadn't even figured out if there were truly any marriageable women left in the world. If he thought about it too much, it tended to make him a little depressed, frankly.

Checking to make sure that the little girl was safely near the horse, he put his car in reverse and looked one more time toward Monet. The girl's mother was openly watching him pull away, while Monet was focused on the mother and then the daughter. Without realizing he was doing it, Nick noticed that Monet was a profoundly poised young woman. Either that, or it bugged him that she was so markedly not staring at him in his Ferrari. Maybe both responses were the same thing.

Jaclyn M. Hawkes

Chapter 3

Tuesday morning, Monet went through her schedule for the day and paused as she came to Nick DeGrassi's name. *This ought to be interesting.* Even after having three days to plan for his lesson, she still wasn't sure of what to expect from Mr. snake charmer when he wasn't in front of a camera. When he had been making arrangements with her, he had been nothing short of professional and impersonal, but when she remembered back to how he had been with the blonde model who'd been nervous, Monet began to wonder again.

He was insanely attractive, that was for sure. Even to a woman who was a world class cynic about men like herself, he was gorgeous. But his occupation made her feel even more distrustful towards him than she typically felt—which, before him, she hadn't even thought was possible.

She thought back to her ex-husband. Man, could you even imagine how much of a player 'Frank the perpetually unfaithful Johnson' could have been with a mentor like Nick the Italian Romeo? At least Nick didn't try to pass himself off as respectable faithful, Christian husband material like Frank had. Even with a master's degree in clinical psychology, Monet hadn't seen Frank's deceit coming until it was too late and she was married to the man.

She caught herself thinking about Frank and checked her train of thought. It had been more than eighteen months since their divorce had been made final and she refused to waste any more energy on him. And just because Nick had a strange occupation and was the beefcake especiale was no reason to assume he was as devious as Frank had been. He probably was, but it wasn't fair to assume it. He might actually turn out to be a salt-of-the-earth kind of guy.

Monet shook her head and smiled as she walked out her door to head over to the stables. Who was she trying to kid? He was nothing more than a soft-porn star in front of a still camera instead of a moving one. There was no sense sugar coating it simply to try to be objective. And knowing just how handsome but lethal he was, she was perfectly wise to pep talk herself into beefing up her emotional guard.

He was income to help her finish buying this place from her parents and pay off the house she'd built. That was all. She did try to truly serve her clientele and give them more than they asked for. But the bottom line was, he was just another paid horseback riding lesson, despite the fact that he was the stuff of dreams, literally. She'd woken up twice this week after dreaming of Adonis Nick in one romantic setting or another, and frankly, it had been embarrassing. Entirely dreamy, but embarrassing. She was far too mature and schooled by reality to ever be taken in by a professional seduction wizard like Nick.

When he showed up at a little before four that afternoon, she had to pep talk herself again, because he looked hotter than ever in plain dark gray boots, faded jeans that fit him marvelously, and a soft looking gray-blue button down that couldn't hide the muscles beneath its understated color. The stupid looking fashion cowboy hat was gone and his hair hung just over the collar of his touchable looking shirt in a casual tousle. The powerful sense of confidence wasn't nearly as overt as it had been the first day and strangely, it made him more attractive than ever.

She had him sign some paperwork in the office, wondering as he did so, how it was possible for the simple act of picking up a pen to somehow make his shirt stretch over his shoulder muscles, and then the two of them headed over to the main barn to pick up their horses. They walked side by side and she could just smell his aftershave. She took him to a stall containing a large creamy buckskin gelding, and as she took the halter off the hook and opened the stall door, she said, "This is Buttermilk. He's sweet and reliable and even more patient than Strawberry Gold. I'll think you'll love him. He's taught many a new rider."

Nick followed her into the stall and patted Buttermilk on the head. "Even more patient? That's comforting. That horse was named Strawberry Gold? I thought that was just the color."

"It was the color and her name. Well, nickname. Just like his." She nodded at the creamy buckskin. "Buckskins this light are sometimes referred to as buttermilk buckskins. Probably not very creative, but it works when you have a lot of horses whose registered names are long and impossibly boring. I typically let an autistic child nickname them anyway. We get some pretty interesting named horses here. The last one was dubbed Lickeo."

Nick grinned, "Is that a horse color, too?"

"No." Monet shook her head with a small smile of her own. "That's three seven year olds with the giggles from excitement at seeing a new baby horse. I haven't a clue where they got it, but it stuck, poor horse."

"Well." Nick reached a strong brown hand up to

rub Buttermilk's face again. "She won't accidentally come when someone is calling a different horse. I've never heard Lickeo before. Although, wasn't there a name like that in one of Shakespeare's works? Petruchio or something?"

Holy Copernicus, a smoking hot male model who knows Shakespeare? Monet had to mentally nudge herself to answer him lucidly. "You're right. There was. Even so, Lickeo is still a little strange. And uh, horses don't usually come when they're called, except in the movies, or if you're carrying a bucket of grain. If you are carrying grain, you could call them all Shep and they'd still come. Sometimes much faster than you'd prefer. Watch yourself if you're ever in the middle of a herd. Even the little ones feel like a draft horse when you get stepped on."

He nodded. "I'll keep that in mind."

As she finished introducing him to his horse, and then to her slender sorrel, he occasionally commented, but mostly he simply listened to her instruction and seemed to be honestly respectful of her expertise and focused on learning. It surprised her, but it was pleasantly refreshing not to have to deal with any macho bravado or flirting.

At the hitch rail outside the outdoor arena, she helped him saddle his horse, and then unsaddled it and started again to familiarize him with it. Then she had him saddle Buttermilk a third time himself and she instructed him on how to tie a horse safely. Next, they went into the arena and she showed him the proper way to get on and off. Then she had him get on again and showed him how to get the horse to move, turn, and stop.

Mounting her own horse, she turned to him and said, "Okay, Mr. DeGrassi, the main thing you need to know is Buttermilk is going to reflect what you do. If you're calm, he'll be calm. If you're rough, he's going to want to fight. If you're nervous, he's going to get nervous. If you want to enjoy this, and have him like seeing you show up at his stall, you need to stay relaxed and happy. If you cooperate with him, he'll be more than willing for you. If you catch yourself getting nervous or uptight, just mentally step back for a minute. Take a big, deep breath." She demonstrated a deep breath. "Drop your shoulders. Sit for a minute. And relax. It's all joy. No worries. He's one of my best beginner horses. Not that you're that much of a beginner, but he's big enough to handle a rider as large as you."

Nick nodded. "A big, deep breath. Okay. In case of an emergency, a big deep breath." Monet smiled at his earnestness and then he asked, "Do I have to be Mr. DeGrassi? Is that a teacher pupil requirement? Or can I just be Nick and you be Monet?"

Monet laughed softly. "Would you prefer Nick?"

"Yes."

"Then Nick it is. Come along, Nick. Buttermilk. Walk him beside me and we'll go through his paces."

Inside the arena she said, "Everyone trains their horses differently. My horses are trained that whoa means stop. Not slow down, not pause for a sec, but stop. Easy is slow down. Or just calm down. If you want to take it down a notch, say easy. And click your mouth and gently kick to start or speed up. Just don't get too enthusiastic. It doesn't take much encouragement."

Nick was a natural with horses. Monet resisted the urge to shake her head at her naiveté. She should have realized that he'd be every bit as soothing to Buttermilk as he had been to the neurotic blonde model. His people skills were his gift, after all, and that sense of reassurance would be as comforting to an animal as to a woman.

He was absolutely competent and a natural athlete,

33

picking up even things as advanced as balance and leg cues within a very short time comparatively. After only a half hour in the arena, Monet opened the gate to take him out onto the nearby bridle path. There was no point in having him riding around and around in the arena when both he and Buttermilk knew he'd figured out what he was doing.

As they rode, Nick asked questions and listened attentively as Monet attempted to condense all that he would need to know to truly be able to handle a horse of his own. It would take awhile, no matter how good a student he was, but it appeared he would be the quickest study she'd ever had.

At a long flat part of the trail, she had them take their horses up to a lope and watched, satisfied that he could stay atop the creamy buckskin without struggling for balance. She then slowed again as they approached a gentle climb to a ridge top. Nick probably weighed two-hundred and thirty pounds. Buttermilk certainly wasn't used to carrying a rider that big.

When Nick's time was almost up, Monet turned back toward the stable. It had been the easiest, and most worry-free first lesson she could ever remember giving. It had been more like a pleasure ride and she felt almost guilty for charging him the full fee, except that she knew her overhead included a lot more than just the actual time spent on the ride. Still, Nick was proving to be an easy charming student. She needed to remember that Nick DeGrassi wasn't just a harmless, great looking, nice guy.

Back at the hitch rack, she hardly even had her horse tied up before Nick had her saddle loosened and asked, "Are you going to be putting this right onto another horse? Or are you through with it for the evening?"

"I'm through with it." Nick automatically picked it

up in one hand and his horse's saddle in the other and took them both into the tack room as if they weighed nothing while Monet followed with the rest of her horse's tack. Then while she put everything away, he went back out to retrieve his horse's remaining tack.

In only moments, they had both horses sprayed off with the hose and returned to their stalls, where Nick gently petted Buttermilk's nose and took his halter off, then gave him the slice of apple Monet had handed him earlier. It had taken a mere fraction of the time it typically took with her younger students, and the instructor in Monet had to compliment him with a sincere big smile. "You're a prodigy, Nick. I don't think I've ever had such a fast learner. At this rate, you'll be an expert in no time."

Nick just gave her the now familiar half-smile that crinkled his eyes, but didn't reveal much of his teeth and said, "Thanks."

As they emerged from the main barn and were walking toward Nick's car and her office, a big, shiny, silver pick up truck pulled into the parking and a tall man got out. *What is TG Alder doing here?* She hadn't expected him tonight, but then she never expected TG. At least she never invited him. He was nice, but she wasn't interested in whatever it was that he was interested in with her.

TG hesitated just for a split second when he saw her with Nick and she concentrated on having a perfectly placid face to greet him, even though she wanted to grin at his instant attitude toward Nick, which Nick appeared to be sending right back at him with change. She had never given TG the slightest hint that he had any ownership where she was concerned, and there wasn't a bit of a reason for the wary sizing up of each other that was going on here. But it might come in handy.

When the three of them paused near Nick's sleek

car, she smoothly said, "Tege, I didn't expect to see you here this evening. What are you up to? This is Nick DeGrassi. Nick, this is TG Alder. He's one of our neighbors down the valley."

Nick put out a friendly hand that TG was just a hair slow shaking and Nick said, "It's good to meet you."

Nodding, all TG said was, "Nick."

For a moment there was a strained silence as they looked squarely at each other and then Monet said, "Were you heading right out, Nick? Or are you going to stay for awhile again?"

Nick looked back and forth from her to TG and then shook his head. "I'm heading out."

"I'll see you next time then. Be sure to watch for deer on the road down the canyon. They come out more in the evening. If you hit one, it would land in your lap in this car."

Nick looked at TG one more time, then grinned at Monet. "I'll keep that in mind. Take care." He got in the car, fired it up and pulled slowly out, with TG watching it all the way.

When Nick had finally purred away, TG turned back to her and she asked, "What brings you out on a Tuesday?"

"Oh, not much. I was just up this way. I wondered if you've had any issues with flooding. My lower pond is over its banks."

Shaking her head, she said, "No. The creek is high, but it always comes up a little this time of year. And the bottoms are damp, but that's April for you. Do you need some help mopping up? I could send Miguel and Cal over."

"No. It's probably just a head gate problem. Who's the guy?" He nodded toward the lane where the

36

red Ferrari had just disappeared.

She followed his gaze and was tempted for a moment to hint that Nick was a friend, but instead simply said, "He's taking riding lessons. Seems nice." She left it at that, and turned aside to pick up a shovel to clean up the hitch rail area. When TG didn't say anything, she glanced up to see him still looking off down the road and she had to stifle a grin.

TG stayed for several more minutes, but Monet continued to do chores as he visited and he eventually got back in his truck and followed the Ferrari down the lane. At length, Monet locked up the office and she and Sherlock walked back across the stable compound to her house.

On Thursday when Nick arrived looking as attractive as ever in well broken in jeans that fit him to perfection, and then flashed her a full blown smile that made it just a smidgen hard to get air for a minute, she felt herself mentally backing away from his magnetism. In an absolutely professional way, she said, "Good afternoon, Nick. Give me just a moment to grab my riding gloves and I'll be right with you."

To which Nick replied just as professionally, "No problem."

When she came out, she was surprised to find that he had both her saddle and his hanging on the hitch rack, and was back in the tack room, getting their other equipment. As they went to collect their horses she walked slightly behind him wondering if he was stiff and saddle sore from their Tuesday lesson. She didn't really want to ask him such a personal question, but typically she had to take it easier on the second day. He seemed to be walking fine—more than fine, and she decided not to ask.

Holy Copernicus, but he could wear a pair of jeans.

She shook her head to clear her thoughts and detoured into her own horse's stall, where she could hear him in the next stall, speaking quietly to Buttermilk as he put his halter on him to lead him out. As he exited the stall, she glanced up to check that he had haltered the horse right and when everything checked out, she said, "Buttermilk seems glad to see you."

Nick put a gentle hand to the horse's neck. "We're buddies now. Aren't we Buttermilk?" The buckskin put his nose into Nick's chest and gave a gentle snuffle that made Nick give that half grin that made the oxygen scarce.

Monet nodded and softly said, "Apparently so." Nick seemed to have a way of getting through any skepticism and Buttermilk was no different. For that matter, neither was she, and she had to consciously remind herself to keep her guard up against his very persuasive and attractive powers, because his abilities were bone deep and smooth as silk. She needed to watch herself. Nick was eminently easy to get comfortable with.

Switching into riding instructor mode, she went back over the same fundamentals she had shown him the first day, touched more on grooming and essential equine healthcare, and then she took him and Buttermilk back out into the arena to work more on balance, leg cues, and posture.

Watching him on the big mellow buckskin was incredible. The horse was beautiful and Nick was magnificent. She shook her head and mentally shook herself as she sat her own horse and called out to him as he rode in circles around her. Focused on Buttermilk and what he was doing, Nick's responses were minimal, but always up-beat and positive, albeit soft-spoken. This was not what she would have expected from the hot-shot model who had climbed out of that racy little car that first day. A brash, loud, egomaniac, Nick was not.

He was an amazingly quick study, and as they headed to the bridle path she made a mental note to get the cowboy who sometimes taught for her to come and work with Nick as well, to round out his horse education. A different instructor, and a taste of the working, western side of horsemanship, would open up Nick's perspective.

Nick got the rudiments down remarkably fast, and while he had an innate sense of how to work quietly *with* his horse, the very speed that he was able to grasp concepts, worked against him in understanding that to his horse, some things took time. Buttermilk was wonderfully easy going, but for most creatures, humans included, it usually took awhile to build up a rock solid foundation of trust. Monet wasn't sure he understood that. She wished he had been taking lessons longer so she could move him on to other horses.

Any horse he rode would need time to learn what to expect from him, and especially as Nick began to ride different, and more green horses, he would need to be able to gauge his mount as well. She would need to substitute horses for him often because much of what he needed to grasp was simply a matter of saddle time--spending enough time with a lot of horses to learn their behavior.

On thinking back to how he had been able to show such faux emotion with the drama queen blonde model, it was no wonder she worried that Nick didn't quite grasp earning a foundation of trust. Still, he had a remarkable work ethic, a brilliant mind, an athlete's coordination and balance, and was singularly dynamic without seeming to try. Then he was almost old-fashionedly chivalrous as he always offered to help her carry her horse's tack when they were unsaddling.

Although Monet considered herself a world class cynic, interacting with him during the lesson was energizing enough that she still found herself making more mental notes to keep her distance from him emotionally. He was sharp, articulate, and far too attractive for either of their good; even when she had such first hand knowledge of his distasteful and less than trust-inspiring occupation.

She watched him get back in his sleek racy car and gave a sigh that could easily have been relief that she could let her guard down. Sometimes, when she was riding beside him, she was hard pressed to remember that she was beyond being affected by attractive men. It was something to work on.

Chapter 4

TG again. He got out of his truck and all but swaggered over to where Monet was working near the hitch rack and then he and Nick went into their strange threatening look and pause before shaking each others' hand stand-off that tended to make Monet ache to crack a smile. This was the third week in a row TG had shown up on a Tuesday evening, incidentally just about the time her lessons with Nick were ending, and it was beginning to be suspect. Monet squelched her grin and watched the two men go through their ridiculous masculine posturing ritual. Apparently TG had figured out Nick's Tuesday lesson time and had decided Nick was a threat to some nonexistent claim he had on Monet, and now TG felt a need to defend his turf.

It was ludicrous. She was so not TG's turf. He hadn't so much as even asked her out, hopefully because he knew that she would turn him down flat. It was also ludicrous that TG didn't realize Nick was scheduled Thursdays in addition to Tuesdays. She wondered if TG would start showing up on Thursdays too, if he found out.

That Nick acted territorial at all back tempted her to smile again. This had gotten all but silly. There was absolutely nothing going on between her and Nick. They were strictly professional with each other. It wasn't like she and Nick did anything but have a riding lesson. Well, and do an excellent job of pretending that there wasn't any physical attraction frissioning across the stable yard around them.

At least she did an excellent job of pretending. Surely Nick, with his considerable experience in handling a myriad of women, literally, wasn't troubled with the frissioning, but it had become an issue with Monet. He was beyond handsome and was far beyond sensual. All the logical reasoning of her head struggled to overcome her illogical physical reaction to Nick. He was a remarkably frissioning man.

After that first moment of male attitude, Nick extended a hand and a seemingly genuine smile and said, "TG. Good to see you again."

Monet wondered if it was another moment of acting for him. He always seemed personable and out going, but the weird guy moment was a bit stronger this time and she had to wonder. *What was up with these two?* She rolled her eyes as TG once again hesitated just a nano second before taking Nick's hand with his signature unenthusiastic, "Nick."

Nick turned back to her, grinned like he knew exactly what she was thinking, and said, "I'll see you later, Monet."

Monet watched him get into his car and drive away as she picked up the scoop shovel and went to work near the hitch rack, feeling suddenly tired. Her energy left with Nick and she didn't have any left over to deal with TG this evening. She'd slept fitfully again last night. It seemed like she never slept well the night before Nick's lesson lately. For three weeks in a row she had been plagued with dreams of that dang website of his. That was probably the reason for all the frissioning anyway because she still was so not interested in being interested in a guy yet. She wasn't sure she ever would be. Especially not a professional seduction wizard.

TG seemed to sense her mood and was quiet for a moment, watching her shovel, but then he asked, "Just here for a lesson again?"

Nodding, she went on with her shoveling and in a skeptical voice, he said, "I've seen him ride. He's not here for lessons."

Wondering if TG was going to suddenly get more overtly territorial, Monet looked at her watch, then put the shovel aside and said, "I'm sorry to shovel and run, TG, but I'm supposed to be somewhere in ten minutes. Excuse me, will you?" At his nod of assent, she turned and headed towards her house. She didn't mean to be rude, but she wasn't going to lead him on either. And she had no intention of becoming his territory. Not even marginally.

Ten minutes later, her parents were just firing up the grill in the picnic area between her house and theirs and the outdoor arena. Her little sister and her family would be here shortly for one of the casual outdoor dinners they would enjoy all spring, summer, and fall.

She gave her dad a one armed hug as he went past with a plate of hamburger patties, then she went inside to where her mother was mixing cranberry juice and Sprite in a pitcher in the kitchen and gave her a hug as well.

Her mom gave her a cheerful smile and then spoke as she went back to pouring the Sprite, "Hi, sweetie. How was your day? Was that TG's truck?"

Monet began to fill the boiled eggs that sat on the counter with the deviled egg filling waiting next to them. "Yeah, it was TG. My day was good. And yours? Did you paint today?"

"No. But I got some good photos to work off later. I took some of you and the man on Buttermilk. And that luscious red Ferrari. Is he a new student of yours? I'm going to drive a red Ferrari before I die."

Monet looked up at her mother smiling back at her and was glad her mother had called the car luscious and not the man. You could never tell with her mother. She was the epitome of graciousness, but she was also known to call it like she saw it. Monet shook her head and grinned. "He wants to learn enough to get a horse of his own. You want to paint a man on Buttermilk? Is that a subject? We were only in the arena. That can't be very paintable."

Her mother only raised her eyebrows and grinned back, and Monet rolled her eyes. "Mother."

"What?"

Monet hesitated, wondering whether to tell her mom about Nick's chosen profession and then shrugged. "He seems nice. He'll be back on Thursday. I'll bet you could talk him into letting you drive his car." She smiled. "Just don't crash. Daddy would not be impressed if you wrecked that spendy of a car. What else can I help with?"

"Stuff the celery. Leave a couple of small ones so Mia can stuff them and then lick the Cheese Wiz right back out as neatly as possible. She eats them just like you did at two years old. She'll probably grow up to be just as awesome as her Aunt Monet. And your father would still adore me, even if I wrecked a Ferrari."

Monet grinned at her mother. She was right. Her parents did adore each other.

On Thursday it rained, and all morning Monet expected a phone call from Nick saying he was canceling, but it never came. She was ridiculously glad. As much as she tried not to, she'd begun to look forward to Nick's lessons. They were now the highlight of her week.

He showed up in black jeans, black boots, a snug dark moss green cashmere sweater that made his eyes all but glow, a long charcoal gray duster, and a flat brimmed black cowboy hat that kept the rain off. His chest muscles rippled under the cashmere sweater and Monet couldn't help thinking that if there was ever a real life Kilkenny from the Louis L'Amour books, he would have looked just like Nick. She couldn't remember for sure, but it seemed like Kilkenny even rode a buckskin horse. She shook the fanciful thought out of her head, put on her own duster and hat, and they saddled their horses.

They started in the indoor arena, and for some reason the low light of the storm, the absence of any other activity around the stable yard, and the low growl of the rain hitting the metal roof seemed somehow intimate. It was as if the low storm ceiling was insulation from the normal pressures of the outside world. After warming their horses up, Monet paused her horse next to Nick's with their knees all but touching, glanced at his rain protection and wondered aloud, "Should we stay in here out of the rain, or should we go out and enjoy the storm. There's no lightning, and we're dressed for it. What do you think?"

"Will the horses be miserable?"

"Unless it's a wild storm, they hardly even seem to notice the rain."

Nick hesitated and then said, "That would be great. Do you mind?"

"No. I love the rain."

Nick gave her a smile that glowed white in the dimness. "Then let's go. By way of my car so I can grab my camera. This misty light is phenomenal."

They took the bridle path, and then for the first time, when they hit the end of the Healing Creek property, Monet pulled up and asked, "What else have you got planned for tonight? Have you got anything pressing on your calendar?"

He shook his head, dribbling rain water off his Kilkenny hat, his green eyes deep emerald under its brim. "Not a thing but a fire by myself at my condo, and paperwork. Why?"

Nodding her own hat towards the gate in front of them, she said, "There's a trail to a small waterfall and pool up the canyon. It's always beautiful, but in this it would be incredible. The only thing is, it's another half hour ahead."

He met her gaze steadily. "I have time if you do."

Monet had things to do, but in all honesty, if she hadn't been out here riding with Nick, she would probably be at home in front of her own fireplace in such weather. There was something so evocative about riding in the rain with him. She nodded to Nick and rode forward, then leaned to open the gate and take her horse through. When Nick and Buttermilk were through as well, she backed her horse around and shut the gate, then motioned toward the trail. "You lead out this time. Just follow the trail, and go slow. Buttermilk is as sure footed as they come."

She rode behind him, completely comfortable to be following, knowing that he was the most competent man she'd ever met. The rain pattered on her hat and the creek bottom smelled of wild blossoms and wet cottonwoods. The light was getting even lower which made the storm seem all the more intimate somehow.

At the waterfall, there was a place on the leeward side of the rock face where the water cascaded off that was protected. Free of both the rain and the spray from the fifteen or twenty foot fall and protected from the slight wind, Nick edged Buttermilk over to stand out of the weather and Monet followed them. The rain had picked up to a downpour, and while it was exhilarating, the shelter was welcome. Once under the overhang, Nick turned Buttermilk's rump to the wall and rested both hands on his saddle horn, looking out at the storm with Monet beside him.

He dug inside his duster at his chest and pulled his camera case out, unzipped it to reveal the camera and then polished the lens with some kind of a soft cloth. For a few minutes, he snapped photos, making adjustments on the settings from time to time. His brown hands were fascinating to her as he worked the camera. He had excellent hands. It was weird that even just watching his hands could bring on the breathless feeling that was contagious only from him. Finally, he zipped the camera back away and sat his horse in silence again. Here in between the rocks in the wildness of the canyon, it felt as if they were the only two people in the world.

At length, he nodded out at the storm from the protection of the overhang and said quietly, "This is exactly how it is for me sometimes, coming to your stables from the rat race of the city. It's like a place sheltered from the storm of business as usual. I needed this today. Thanks for bringing me."

Monet nodded, unsure of whether to ask him the obvious questions, or continue to try to ignore his vocation the way they had for these weeks. After a moment's hesitation, she said, "You're welcome. Rough day?"

He glanced at her, shrugged, shook his head and gave a nondescript, "Mmm. It was okay."

She considered that for a second, and then asked, "Okay as in fine? Or okay as in, it was awful, but I'm not going to share the day's garbage and muck up your day too."

He gave his half smile. "So, you've actually had *okay* days, even here in paradise?"

Nodding, she said, "Occasionally." There was no reason to disclose that she'd had a lot of those days before divorcing 'Frank the perpetually unfaithful Johnson' and coming back home to buy Healing Creek Stables from her parents. Instead, she continued, "So some days your gig doesn't really beat bussing tables?"

At that, he gave a short, soft laugh, "No. It always beats bussing tables. I learned that early on." He paused, seeming to ponder being a bus boy, then said stoically, "I was seventeen, my grandfather, the only family I had, was dying, and I still had five months of high school to get through. I was bussing, trying to keep up with the rent and his medical bills, not quit the football team because I had given them my word, and still find time to study occasionally. And the child protection people kept trying to force me into foster care. It was tough.

"Then a girl from my photo class took some pictures of me for an assignment. She sent them to a modeling agency. Surprisingly, they bought them. She gave me half the money, and it saved me financially. Much more so than bussing."

Calmly, he went on, "It still didn't pay everything. Or heal my grandfather, but without modeling, I doubt I would have finished high school." He ended his little heart-wrenching tale with his half smile and Monet didn't know what to say. She now felt completely foolish for being critical of his profession, even if he had ended up an accomplished snake charmer.

Softly, she asked, "What happened to your parents?"

Still stoic, he said, "My mother died when I was twelve. And I, mmm, I'm just going to guess that my mom never knew who my father was."

Confused, Monet asked, "Why would you guess that?"

"Because I think she would have told me who he was if she knew. And she never did." Monet thought about her own life at seventeen — how close her family had been and how supportive her parents were. About her two parents, who were still so much in love. She couldn't even wrap her brain around what he was describing and didn't know what to say. Finally, she settled on, "I'm sorry, Nick. That must have been so hard."

He shrugged again. "What doesn't kill you, makes you stronger."

After a moment he continued, "I was devastated over losing my grandfather, but I couldn't dwell on it. I had to survive." He shrugged one more time. "I learned fast. I had to. It was like being a nice fat piece of bait tossed into a shark feeding frenzy. There were a couple of older women who I started out thinking were going to help me. It didn't take long to realize that they were the queen sharks."

Monet considered a seventeen year old kid who looked like Nick, in the clutches of hardened women in the modeling business, and all but shuddered. She'd had far too many psychology classes not to have an inkling of the kind of danger he had been in. He was lucky he did survive.

She was just trying to figure out how to ease Nick's discomfort and lighten the conversation, when Nick said matter-of-factly, "Now you know why I love your peace here."

She nodded, wondering if she should admit that she'd had a nearly fairytale upbringing, or if that would be rude. At length, all she said was, "I'm glad it helps you. I love the peace too."

It wasn't much, but it fit the moment and didn't make his tale worse, nor belittle it. And what could you say about a casually dropped tidbit that alluded to such a hard time? He'd been making simple conversation, but it had to have been a bitterly tough life at the moment. All of the moments. From a single mom dying young, to never knowing his father, to losing his only family and struggling with funds. Even without her degree, she would have read between the lines to know it had been a refiner's fire.

As they sat there in the quiet of the storm, she thought about his savoring the peace. He was right. There was something truly strengthening about Healing Creek Stables. It had helped her to pick up the pieces of her life and begin moving forward again after Frank. She wasn't sure she would ever stop feeling like a failure over the wreck of her marriage and career, but other than that, she had succeeded in building a thriving therapy horse practice. At least she was able to help people with what she was doing. And apparently not just the children. She glanced up and met Nick's green eyes in the shadows under the flat brim of his hat. He was so definitely not a child.

Pulling his car smoothly out of the rain and into the garage attached to his condo in the city, Nick got out, slammed the door a tad too hard and stabbed a finger into the key pad to let himself inside. Tossing his car keys, he ignored the mail on the floor inside the front door and the blinking light on his answering machine as he headed for a shower.

As chilly as the ride in the rain had been, his shower was definitely still going to be a cool one. Maybe not ice cold, but hopefully cool enough to ease the irritation that he could have labeled as romantic frustration, except that he wasn't going there. Monet was far too classy a woman to use trivial slang with, but whatever he was feeling toward his private riding instructor was starting to make him nuts!

He'd been trying to ignore it for weeks now, but that incredibly evocative ride in the rain had been too much. He could finally admit to himself without hesitation that he had a robust heart case on the classy woman in the oh so attractive riding breeches.

He'd wanted more of the ambience he'd felt that first day at Healing Creek Stables and he had definitely gotten it. But what he hadn't fully realized that first day was that it was only partly the horses. Most of it was that innate incredible femininity and class or grace or whatever it was that Monet McLaughlin exuded. The more he was around her, the more refined she appeared, the more attracted he became, and the more he felt like he lived on a different planet than she did. Even when she was only doing chores around the stables, she seemed regal.

It had something to do with the way she acted and dressed, but it was more than that. It was hard to explain, but he could almost swear it was the way she thought. The way she seemed to perceive herself. She had this innate sense of self that made him feel as if he was in the presence of royalty. For some reason that bothered him.

Reaching into the shower, he pulled on the handle so hard that the valve made a chunking sound and he was grateful that the whole thing hadn't come off in his hand. Although maybe it would have been good to have cold water spraying out of control all over his bathroom. It would have taken his mind off this insane situation where he was nervous about a girl. That was crazy! Girls were his vocation. They never, ever, ever made him nervous. He hadn't been nervous about a girl in years.

Chapter 5

Tuesday the sun was brilliant enough that it seemed to be trying to make up for the clouds of Thursday. Nick arrived at Healing Creek determined not let the attraction to Monet get to him like it had, or else find a way to do something about it. What that would be, he had no idea, because he'd known from the very first day he'd met Monet that she was disdainful of his modeling. Not only that, but he'd been absolutely careful not to do one thing that could be construed as hustling her. He had done it on purpose to put her at ease in spite of her obvious distaste at his profession, which was good and seemed to have worked. But now after four weeks of lessons with her, he was at a loss as to how to take that pure professionalism in a different direction. Which wasn't so good.

He realized now that his interaction with Monet needed to be able to be channeled in a direction that would eventually lead to something more than just friendship or he was going to end up a nutcase. She was far and away the most intriguing girl he'd ever known.

She was riding the white horse over the fences again as he came around the curve and Nick stopped the Ferrari right in the middle of the road to get out and dig his camera out of the trunk. The lovely rider in the form fitting breeches and the dark saddle and bridle on the white horse made for striking images and he leaned against the car and unabashedly snapped photos. He was just going to guess that Monet wouldn't be thrilled, but the artist in him couldn't resist anyway. There were times she was so beautiful she took his breath away.

When Monet cleared the last fence, slowed her horse on the bridle path, and finally disappeared up the trail toward the barns, he put his camera away and headed that way himself. He wasn't even sure what he would do with the photos, but if any turned out, he was going to frame one and put it in his condo. Who knew? Maybe it would make Monet in person less intriguing. Or maybe it would make him more frustrated than ever.

At the hitch rack he tossed a small wave at the shy little brown haired girl who was combing old Dan across the way, as he approached Monet. He was surprised when instead of leaving her saddle out to put on another horse to ride with him, she picked it up and headed into the tack room. He strode to her side to take it from her saying, "I'll get that for you."

She relinquished the saddle, but said, "You know, I really can carry my own tack. I've been doing it my whole life before you showed up. You do realize that, don't you?"

"Of course. The key words being, before I showed up. I know it's not politically correct, but my grandfather would come back and haunt me if I just let you take it. I'd feel like an idiot. So don't go all feminist on me. Do you not need it to ride with me?"

Monet shook her head as they entered the tack room. "No, we're going to be working with some foals today. Don't call me a feminist. But then, don't tell me I'm incapable either."

Nick swung the saddle up onto the saddle rack and put the pads on the bar to air dry. "I'm not telling you you're incapable at all. I'm telling you the saddle is heavy.

54

What are we going to be doing with foals?"

"Halter breaking. It's not that heavy."

At that, Nick turned squarely towards her and said, "Is this a big deal, Monet? Really? Can you not just let me serve you because I think you're a lady and should be treated like one?"

Monet turned to look at him with what could almost be considered a look of surprise on her usually perfectly poised face. For a long, long moment, she seemed to be studying him speechlessly, and then she gave him the tiniest sweet smile, put a hand softly on his arm and said sincerely, "Then thank you. I would love your help. Thank you."

"You're welcome." He glanced down at her hand, stoked that she was the one who touched him first. This was progress.

She followed his glance to her hand and seemed to realize what she had done, looked confused for moment, and then hesitantly removed it. So maybe it wasn't that much progress, but it was a start. Touching him had been very natural for her and he knew she was always petting the horses and hugging her other students. She was affectionate at heart. He just needed to help her get to the point that she was affectionate with him. It was probably going to be a project after her remarks about him handling women models. He wasn't too dense to know that. But he was up for any project that involved Monet. He turned to go back out to the hitch rack and get her bridle, smiling as he walked.

When Nick turned and went back out of the tack room Monet stood for just the briefest moment in a turmoil of surprise and delight, and a little panic. His comment had caught her completely off guard and was at the same time unbelievably sweet. And those eyes . . .

He thought she was a lady! And wanted to treat her like one. That was adorable! It was about the last thing she had expected from Mr. Italian Adonis romance model. And she probably should totally not trust him, but it was still a delightful thought. It had been a long time since anyone but her family had even hinted that she should be treated specially. She felt herself sigh like a school girl. Chivalry felt wonderful, even if it was supposedly outdated.

Nick walked back in with her bridle and she couldn't help noticing the muscles stretching the sleeves of his golf shirt as he reached to hang the bridle on its hook. It was a wake up call that shook her out of her reverie. This was Nick DeGrassi—the man who could charm the clothes off of women, literally, with nothing more than a whispered comment. For a second there, Monet had almost forgotten that he had influencing women almost hypnotically down to an art. That was something that would be incredibly naïve and even dangerous to forget.

She tore her eyes away from his bicep. What was it that they were supposed to be doing right now? Halter breaking foals. That's right. They were going to be working with the foals this afternoon. She reached for a soft cotton foal halter. *Focus, Monet. Focus. The foals. Not the muscles. Not the sweet chivalry. You know he has the ability to tell you just what you want to hear. Don't be an idiot. Get a grip here.*

Snagging a halter for the broodmares as well, Monet picked up a small bucket of sweet feed and led her muscle-bound student out to the round pen where she had corralled three of the mares and their foals. Nick could put his hypnotic skills to good use learning to teach the new babies to lead and be handled. His gentle, soft spoken voice and manner was exactly what the babies needed.

She approached the mare with the youngest baby, put the mare's halter on and then looped the end of the lead up over her back. The broodmare was seasoned and when she realized that Monet wasn't going to let her get her nose into the bucket of sweet feed, the mare simply went back to eating the flake of alfalfa Monet had thrown to her earlier. Monet stood beside her, waiting for her foal to become curious enough to approach her as she petted the mare.

To Nick, Monet said, "We'll just stand here quietly until he comes over, and then watch how I catch him. This one has never been handled much. I'll try to move quietly and gently and catch his neck with the lead. Then at first, I'll try to move with him rather than fighting him. When we first work with them, we try to keep it short and pleasant. That way, they'll want to do it again. They're just like us humans. They don't like to be controlled, but they love the attention and the treats."

Nick nodded silently and it wasn't but a few more moments before the foal did indeed wander around to where Monet stood with the little bucket. She let the baby put his nose in and lick the grain that was still relatively strange to him. Monet calmly slipped the lead around the foal's slim neck and then took up the slack.

At first, he didn't even realize that he'd been caught, but then he wised up fast and went to spin away from Monet on his hind legs. She moved with him, maneuvering so that she could avoid having a tug of war with the baby hanging back. In just a moment or two, the foal calmed and once again tried to put its muzzle into the sweet feed and she slipped the tiny halter on his head and buckled it.

Monet glanced up at Nick with a small smile and said, "Work with them, not against them. Come on over.

Just go slow and talk softly to him."

For several minutes the two of them petted the baby and let him gum the feed as they got him used to being controlled by a human. He occasionally tried to rear, or bolt, or hang back, but the two of them held him and kept him calm for the most part.

As the foal moved around, the two of them moved as well and Monet found herself bumping into Nick repeatedly as they worked. There was no way around it. That's just how handling babies for the first time was, and Nick didn't appear to mind any of it. He was focused, but there was a look of mellow satisfaction on his face as he slowly helped the foal to become comfortable with them.

At length, Monet showed Nick how to weave the end of the lead rope diagonally across the foal's back, around its rump and back up into her hand that gripped its halter just below its hairy little chin. She clicked her mouth and at the same time pulled on the leads and the foal was tugged forward as she said to Nick, "Where the head goes, the body will follow. Especially when the rump is roped in as well."

Nick gave her a heart stopping smile where he stood immediately beside her, trying to keep the strong little horse under control with her and he said, "That is slick! I've always wondered how horses learned to lead like that."

The foal chose that moment to rear and jerked Monet straight into Nick's solid chest as it continued to fuss. Monet gave Nick a smile of her own as she admitted. "The key for me is to do it when they're teeny, tiny. They're far easier to handle at a day or two old like this, than at a month or two, or a year or two."

The foal tried to rear one more time and Nick pulled it back down with sheer muscle power and said, "I can only imagine."

Monet smiled again, "But you'll be amazed how fast they learn. In another two minutes, he'll figure out he has no choice and be tentatively walking along beside us. As long as he learns that we are always in control, it works. If we accidentally train him that *he's* in control, we're sunk." Nick hauled the little horse gently forward and Monet added drily, "Having a brawny assistant is always a plus."

Nick gave her his mellow half smile, clicked his mouth just the way she had earlier, and Monet stepped back a half step to let him have room to move. "That's the way. Gently, but firmly. When he gives and moves on his own, let off on the pressure to the lead rope. Then when you stop, reward him. Pet him, or give him a treat, and use a happy voice. He'll figure it out quickly. Horses are a lot like people. They respond much better to being asked than being forced."

For a couple of minutes, Nick alternated between hauling the baby forward when he clicked, and walking beside it calmly when it moved forward voluntarily, with Monet standing nearby coaching him along. Then, unexpectedly, the foal reared again and then tried to hang back. When Nick was too strong, it jumped forward instead. Nick lost control of its rump rope and it barreled into Monet. Just as it hit her, it raised its head, smacking her full in the face before Nick managed to muscle it under control again.

Stifling a groan of pain, Monet put a hand to her nose and wasn't surprised to see blood. With nothing to mop it with, she leaned over slightly, cupped her hand to catch the blood and put pressure as she took a step away from Nick and the skittish foal. Nick did groan under his breath, and she glanced up at him to see him looking at her in concern and say, "Oh, Monet, I'm so sorry. I thought he was going to settle down. Are you okay."

With a distinct nasal twang because of her grip with her bloody hand, Monet said, "I'm fide. I just did't move fast enough."

Holding the foal's lead with one hand, Nick reached into his jeans pocket with his other and produced a soft white handkerchief that he offered to Monet. "Here. Use this. I'm so sorry."

Monet gratefully accepted the proffered cloth, put it to her nose and then attempted to wipe her bloody hand on the thigh of her riding breeches as Nick continued to apologize. This happened sometimes. It was the nature of working with horses. It wasn't a big deal. She backed further away from the mare and foal and Nick, then leaned back against the round pen fence and tipped her head back. Her bloody nose was a gusher and still hurt enough that it was making her eyes water.

She closed them and then tried to speak past the pressure she was applying. "Give that one another couple of minutes, Nick. And then we'll turn him loose and go to one of the others."

With her eyes still closed, she stayed still against the fence and listened to Nick talking quietly to the little horse. Even through the pain it was soothing to hear his soft voice. A few moments later, he came close to her and said, "Come on, Monet. It's soaking through everything. Let's get you in and find some tissue. We need to get the bleeding stopped. We'll come back to the foals."

Monet opened her eyes and nodded, knowing he was right. "Okay." He put a hand under her elbow and together they headed out the gate of the round pen where she turned toward her house that was closer than the office restroom and said, "This way. It's closer."

Before they made it even into her yard, the handkerchief soaked through and she felt blood drip down her hand. Nick still held her elbow, helping to guide her because it was hard to see. On her porch, she dropped into a patio chair and said, "Will you grab me a hand towel? I don't want to trail blood everywhere. Inside, straight through into the kitchen, in the top drawer between the sink and the stove. And maybe a wet cloth as well. Thanks."

A moment later, Nick reappeared with the requested cloths and he crouched down to help her swap out the bloody handkerchief. Gently, he pulled the handkerchief back, tossed it onto her lawn, and while holding the towel under her nose, he gently put a finger against the side of her nose to apply pressure as he asked, "Can you feel where it's bleeding?"

Looking up into his face, she gave a miniscule shake of her head. "Doh. Somewhere higher than I can press, I think."

He slid his finger higher. She winced and he said, "Sorry." He looked incredibly guilty as he said sadly, "Monet, honey, I hate to tell you this, but this is swelling. We may have just broken your nose. I'm so sorry."

She blinked slowly. "I think you may be right. It really hurts. And it's still gushing." Pushing the dish towel tighter against her nose, she struggled to reach for her phone but she couldn't reach it in the front pocket of her riding breeches.

After her digging for a moment, Nick asked, "What do you need?"

"My phone."

As she started to get up, he pulled his from his pocket and held it out to her. "Can you use mine?"

She glanced at it and then relaxed back into the chair. "Sure. Can you put the number in for me? 403-721-4984." He punched in the number and then handed it to her and she leaned her head back against the chair again and put the phone to her ear. It rang for several seconds and finally, she pulled the phone away and handed it back to him, saying, "She's not answering her phone. Could I ask you a favor? Could we postpone the rest of your lesson today?"

"Of course."

Monet got slowly to her feet. "Good. Thanks. If I can get this to stop, I may run in and see if it needs set before it swells anymore." She finally got her phone out of her pocket and called Cal to ask him to move the mares and foals out of the round pen, only he couldn't understand her with the hand towel in the way. Finally, she handed Nick her phone. "Could you tell him."

Nick explained to Cal, hung up and then put a hand to the small of Monet's back and asked, "Do you have to stop the bleeding here? Or can we try to stop it on the way?"

She narrowed her eyes as she looked at him, questioning, and tried to say, "I can't drive and hold the towel."

He shook his head. "It's okay, I'll drive. Just the sooner we go the better. It's swelling pretty fast."

As much as she would have loved to be driven, Monet tried to shake her own head. "No. I'll be fine. I don't need to bother you to drive me."

"It won't be a bother, and it was my fault anyway." He turned toward her door before she could argue. "I'll grab another hand towel. Is there anything else you need?"

Suddenly without the energy to resist, Monet sighed and said, "Just my purse. It's in my coat closet. If you can get me there, my mom can come and pick me up."

Nick put his hand to her back again to nudge her

toward the chair. "Sit back down. I'll get your towels and purse, then run down and grab my car and come get you."

Sinking gratefully to the chair, Monet leaned back again and Nick squatted down next to her with concern in his eyes. "It's still really bleeding. Is it going down your throat, too? Is it making you sick?"

"No. I'm fine. But would you grab me a bottle of juice out of the fridge just in case? Any kind is fine. Grab one for you as well."

He nodded and stood to enter her house. When he came back out, he set the juice, purse and towels on the table next to her and strode away towards his car. Monet closed her eyes again. She really didn't need him to baby her so much for just a nose bleed, even if it did hurt like the dickens and refuse to stop bleeding. Maybe she would drink that juice in a minute. She was getting a whopper of a headache.

Three minutes later, Nick loaded her carefully into his racy little car, and then drove much too fast across the stable yard and out the main gate. Actually, she was incredibly grateful for his fast car when she never was able to get her nose to stop bleeding on the whole drive into town. If she hadn't hurt so badly, she'd have been completely worried about getting blood on his cushy leathery seats. Both of the towels she'd brought with them were all but soaked through by the time the office girl at the medical clinic took them straight back into an exam room.

By that time, Monet felt lousy enough that she appreciated Nick's arm around her steering her and even catching sight of herself in a mirror in the hallway didn't register too deeply. About all she could muster was mild surprise that it looked like both of her eyes were bruising. Her nose was still buried in the bloody towels, so she didn't have an inkling about how bad it looked. What she saw was bad enough.

In the exam room, Nick helped her up onto the paper covered exam bed, then pulled several tissues out of a box. He brought them to her and leaned in to carefully pull the towels away and replace them with the tissues. The towels he tossed into the garbage receptacle before dampening a paper towel at the little sink to try to help her to wash some of the blood away.

She looked up at him as he worked and he shook his head and said sadly, "Monet, I am so sorry about all of this. Your pretty dainty nose is hammered. I never dreamed that little horse could go in so many different directions so fast. Or that he'd be that strong. Please forgive me. I'm so sorry."

Tiredly, Monet said, "It happens, Nick. It wasn't your fault. I'm fine. I knew how strong they can be. I should have moved faster. This wasn't your fault."

"Well, it happened on my watch."

She tried to joke. "At least it was me it happened to, and not you. We could have ruined your career for a while."

He grinned. "Naw. Chicks dig scars and black eyes and stuff. Don't they?"

She looked up at him to make sure he was joking. "Uhm. No. Not any *chicks* that I know. And certainly not when it ruins such perfection. Your entourage of fans wouldn't be impressed."

Nick chuckled. "Such perfection? Right. So, I'm just supposed to be able to swordfight, or ride horses through a gun battle, or beat the crud out of someone defending some fair maiden's honor and always come out unscathed?"

"Always."

"I see. Well, so far, so good. I still wish he had gotten me instead of you. My nose is a much bigger target."

Monet studied his nose, trying to think more clearly, which was hard because looking up into his handsome face scrambled her brain even more. She said, "But mine isn't my livelihood." Then she carefully shook her head and glanced down at his chest and arms. "But then again, it's probably not your nose that garners you those covers, though it is an excellent nose."

Nick shook his head and gave a short laugh. "I'm going to ask your doctor to check you for a brain concussion. You're being weird."

She sighed. "I feel worse than weird. I hate not being able to breathe." She glanced behind her at the pillow. "Do you suppose it would go down my throat if I laid down?"

"Probably."

The doctor and a nurse came in just then, and Nick moved to stand across from the doctor near Monet's shoulder. The nurse paid more attention to checking out Nick than Monet's nose, while the doctor pulled the tissues back long enough to see how badly it was bleeding, then glanced down at her bloody blouse, riding breeches, and boots and asked, "Hmmm. Riding accident?"

Nick looked into Monet's eyes and answered for her. "Sort of. A young horse head butted her. My fault. It won't quit bleeding and we're worried it's broken. Can you help her out?"

"Yes, but I'm afraid it won't be all that fun. And yes, it's broken. How long ago did this happen?"

Monet glanced at her watch as Nick said, "Forty five minutes."

65

The doctor took out a light and began shining it in Monet's eyes. "The good news is I can deaden your nose before I cauterize it and set it. The bad news is the anesthetic shots hurt worse than both. What do you prefer?"

Nick put a reassuring hand on her shoulder and Monet sighed softly and said, "Just do it."

The doctor nodded and the nurse quit ogling Nick long enough to begin pulling things out of cupboards. When they were ready, Nick moved his hand from Monet's shoulder to put his arm around both shoulders. For a second, Monet was irritated that he thought she was just another girl he could handle. Then, when the doctor closed in with his instruments and pulled the tissues away, Monet leaned right into Nick's solid strength. It may be some form of using him, but just at this moment, Monet was incredibly grateful that he had insisted he bring her. When he took her hand with his free one, she gripped it even as she looked up at him.

He simply met her eyes and quietly said, "I've done this before. Someone holding my hand would have helped."

Forty minutes later, she was sick to her stomach, light headed, sore, and positively whiney. The bleeding had stopped, her nose was packed and splinted, and Nick was loading her back into his Ferrari when his phone rang. From his end of the conversation, Monet could tell it was her mother calling to find out who had called her from his number. Monet almost got up the gumption to grin as she tried to figure out what her mother was saying. She was concerned about what had happened to Monet, but she had also apparently figured out that Nick was the man on Buttermilk. Monet could almost hear her mother's speculation about her and Nick through the phone.

If she had felt better, she would have enjoyed that call. As it was, she really just wanted to get home, have some dinner, swallow one of the pain pills the doctor had sent and fall into bed. Man she felt like a wimp over one silly little bop in the face. She folded down the make-up mirror on the sun visor and then regretted it immediately. *Holy Copernicus.* She was a complete wreck. She pushed the visor back up with a sigh and closed her eyes. She really was going to have two black eyes, not to mention a nose that could double as an air craft carrier.

Mere minutes later, Nick touched her gently on the arm. When she opened her eyes, he said, "If we feed you now, you can take the pain pills that much sooner. Would you like something?" He nodded out the window at the handful of fast food restaurants he'd pulled into the midst of. "Anything sound good?"

"No, but it makes sense. You pick."

"How about a milkshake? Would that go down easy?"

"Mmm. Maybe. As easy as anything."

He bought her a milkshake and shook out a pill for her to take, then helped her recline his exotic, luxury seat. It was amazing how nice it was to be babied just a little. For so long, she had been the one trying to heal everyone. It was nice to pass the torch for an evening.

At her house, she was glad to see her mother hurry out of her parents' house as soon as Nick's car pulled in, but then she definitely wasn't glad to see TG's truck pull in and park right beside Nick's car. Had her mother called TG? No, her mother wouldn't have done that. It was just that time on a Tuesday. Crud, but she was too hammered to deal with TG and Nick's posturing tonight. Especially with this lovely nose splint and the black eyes. She didn't want anyone seeing her like this.

She was incredibly grateful when her mother fussed over her for a few minutes as she sat in the car with the door open and then her mom graciously dragged TG away. Monet had no idea where they were headed, but it made climbing out of that sporty little car seem easier.

This time, Nick was practically carrying her as he helped her into her house. He probably would have if she would have let him, knowing Nick. It wasn't like he was short on muscles. He got her inside, then she could see the hesitation in his eyes as he glanced down her hallway. *Oh no. She may be whiney, but not that whiney.* As out of it as she was, she still sidestepped the issue of him helping her to her room by turning instead to her living room and all but collapsing onto the couch.

There was a throw draped over the back of it and she reached for it, but Nick beat her to it and gently draped it over her and then tucked it around her. With a tired sigh, she closed her eyes and said, "Thank you, Nick. For everything. Sorry I was so fragile today. I'll do better tomorrow."

She was drugged enough, and sore and tired enough, that she wasn't really sure what Nick did next. At some point her brain registered her mother's voice, and Nick's soft spoken reply. They talked for a while. At least she thought they did. Or maybe she just dreamed it. She dreamed that Nick helped her lie down and then sat beside her while she slept off the codeine. Nick had a really nice voice.

Chapter 6

The birds started way earlier than usual the next morning. They usually started singing awhile before it started getting light, but this morning they were ridiculously early, bless their hearts. Monet struggled to wake up and was surprised that she was in her bed. She couldn't remember getting there. Or maybe she could. Yeah, her mother had helped her change clothes and get into bed.

She forced her eyes open and found her mother sitting in the recliner beside her bed, sound asleep. That was so like her mom to watch over her like that. Slowly, Monet turned her head. It still ached, and her throat was sore from having to breathe through her mouth because her nose was so stuffed up with the packing. She had to stay like this clear until this afternoon. Aah, it was miserable.

Struggling up, she shuffled into her bathroom and then wished she hadn't. She looked like she'd been hit in the face with that proverbial truckload of ugly her brother Barry had always teased her about on bad mornings.

Still, she felt much better than she had last night. Her head ached, but it didn't pound, and she looked bad, but other than trying to breathe, her nose was much better. Resolving to get back to her life whether she looked trashed or not, she picked up her bloody blouse and breeches and put them to soak in a sink full of cold water and then turned on the shower. A warm shower could fix anything.

All morning long, she had to keep re-explaining what had happened to her. Caroline came for her clinic and hesitantly asked, "Did someone hit you?"

Monet gingerly shook her head. "No. One of the baby colts accidentally smacked me with its head. It looks pretty bad, but I'm okay, really."

"Does it hurt?"

Knowing that it had taken weeks before Caroline would even speak to her, Monet didn't want to frighten her, but she wanted to be honest with her too. She casually said, "A little, but I'll be fine."

Monet's heart nearly broke as the little girl, who was in therapy because of physical abuse from her father said, "My face used to hurt when it looked like that. I didn't like how I looked when it was purple like yours, but it's fine now. Don't worry. It will get better."

She was so matter-of-fact about it that it was pathetic and Monet was at once glad she could move on, yet horrified at what the sweet seven year old had had to deal with in her young life. At least her mother had been able to get Caroline away from her ex-husband with a court ordered restraining order in place to protect her from her violent father.

Now they just had to find a way to help Caroline learn to trust in the human race again. Horses she was fine with, but Monet had yet to see her even speak to anyone other than her mother and Monet, and on a good day, Monet's parents. It was going to be a journey still, and as Monet waved goodbye to the little girl, she hoped she hadn't put Caroline back by showing up for her clinic with the bruises and the nose splint.

She gave a tiny sigh and went back into her office. Even though it was only her face that was thrashed, she was ridiculously tired today.

Finally, when Nick's car pulled in in the early afternoon and he climbed out and looked at her without saying much, she decided to have some fun with it and said, "I was doing the stunts for the new Angelina Jolie movie and it went south, okay? But don't worry. The Screen Actor's Guild is going to pay for plastic surgery, so it will all work out."

Nick laughed and she smiled back at him, even though it pulled at her nose splint. He reached and pulled a piece of grass hay out of her hair and asked, "You ready to go have that packing removed? Are you sick of it yet?"

"Like before they had even put it in. I can take myself to have the packing removed. I didn't expect to see you here today."

"Well, I was under the impression that you would be under the influence of codeine. And your mom said she had an appointment so I said I would take you. She's very dynamic, by the way. I can't even imagine being raised by a mother that entertaining. You weren't going to drive drunk, were you?"

"She sometimes too entertaining. Of course I wasn't going to drive drunk. I haven't taken any pain pills since this morning. They say I can drive after four hours."

He studied her with concern in his eyes. "Are you okay without the medicine?"

"Yes. It's not comfortable, but I'm fine."

"Well, is it still in your system then? Are you still drugged?"

She considered that for a second and had to honestly wonder if she was completely out from under the codeine. Looking up at him, she admitted, "I thought so, but who knows? Maybe not completely."

After hesitating for a moment, Nick asked, "So does that mean you're going to cooperate with me taking you? Or not? What can I expect here? And make it fast, because we need to leave right away."

The fact that his questions made Monet laugh only made his concerns valid. She was definitely still a bit loopy. Why else would she laugh instead of sticking to her guns about not needing him? Still smiling, she gave in. "I'll cooperate. To a point."

With his signature half smile, he said, "I'm glad to hear that, Monet."

"But people are going to pity you for being seen with me." He rolled his eyes and she laughed again. "Or they'll think you did it."

He only shook his head and said, "Go get your purse."

TG showed up at her house that night at dusk with a bouquet of flowers. She wished it had been completely dark, because she looked so rough, but then decided it didn't matter. It was what it was. Big and bruised with a lovely small white splint plopped on top of it all. At any rate, Monet stood on the porch with him for the few minutes until he left. When he was gone, she put the flowers in a vase and took them over to her parents'. Her mother had more than earned flowers for sleeping in a chair last night.

When she walked into their house, her mom looked up and smiled. "Well, hi there, honey. How are you feeling?"

Her brother Barry was there visiting and said brightly, "Better than you look, I hope, Momo. You look like heck. Or is that a clown nose? Come on over here and let me give it a squeeze and see if it squeaks."

Monet walked over and gave him a hug. He pulled back and looked her face over, and then shook his head. "You'd make a great gargoyle. In case anyone needs a gargoyle anytime soon."

Monet laughed, "Thanks, bro. That's exactly how I felt last night." She turned to her mom. "These are for you. TG brought them to me, but you earned them watching over me last night. Did you get a nap today?"

"Yes, I was napping when Nicholas took you back to the doctor. He is a very nice young man, by the way."

Monet stopped and narrowed her eyes. "I thought you had an appointment."

Her mother didn't even bother to look penitent. "I did. With my pillow. I knew I'd be too tired to drive and why deprive you of getting to ride in that adorable little Ferrari again?"

Monet put her hands on her hips. "Mother. I was once told by a wise woman named Marni McLaughlin that liars go to hell."

Barry broke in. "You're dating a guy who drives a Ferrari? Since when? I didn't even know you were dating anyone."

"I'm not dating anyone who drives a Ferrari. I'm not dating anyone. Including TG Alder. Just in case you want to hint that to him if you see him."

Barry looked confused. "TG drives a Ferrari? How the heck does he afford that? His spread isn't that big."

Their mother laughed and Monet repeated, "Mother." She turned to Barry. "Nick drives the Ferrari. TG drives the big Dodge. And no, I'm not dating either of them."

Smiling placidly, their mother said, "Well, you do spend time with Nick twice a week for a couple of hours. That has to count for something. And he's such a nice man. It's obvious that he cares for you."

Monet shook her head. "Our time spent counts for riding lessons, Mother. Nothing more. Trust me. He doesn't care for me beyond my teaching him."

"Oh, come now, Monet. He practically carried you in last night and was devastated enough to stand guard over you until one o'clock in the morning."

"One o'clock in the morning! Mother, do you mean to tell me that you didn't send him home! What in the world did you talk about . . . Oh, no. Please tell me that you and Nick didn't sit over there and gossip about me 'til the wee hours. He said you were very entertaining. Do I need to be panicking here?"

"Of course not, honey. You know I don't gossip. And Daddy was there with us. He and Nicholas hit it right off. We talked about all kinds of things. He's an artist as well, you know. He's a photographer."

Under her breath, Monet said, "Yes, among other things." Louder she said, "Dad was there 'til one, too? Oh, man. And he had to work today. You should have just insisted Nick go home. You shouldn't have had a stranger in my house 'til all hours."

Barry broke in again. "Wait a minute. You're dating a strange artist? And teaching him to ride? How old is this guy? I thought you got turned into a gargoyle halter breaking a newborn foal."

Monet looked at him and rolled her eyes as their mom said, "Oh, don't be silly, Monet. Nicholas DeGrassi isn't a stranger. You've been working with him for months. He's a very respectable, caring man who felt completely responsible for your nose. Well, for your face. How are you feeling, by the way?" She studied Monet's face. "It's looking so much better already."

Barry made a tsk tsk sound with his mouth and asked, "It was worse than this? Man, you must have been a sight." Then he became more serious and a hint of the tough lawyer that he was came through as he asked, "This guy didn't hit you, did he? Why did he feel responsible?"

Monet shrugged, "Well, he was the one holding the leads, but it wasn't his fault. He certainly didn't hit me. Nick is definitely a lover, not a fighter. The cussed little foal was just plunging around and then reared into me."

"So this guy is a puny artist. Not even strong enough to hang on to a two day old foal. Monet, you can do better than that. I know Frank toasted your confidence, but . . . And you think a ninety pound weakling artist is a lover?"

Monet thought back to that first morning with the neurotic blonde model. Yeah, Nick was definitely a lover. Her mother brought her back to the present when she laughed at Barry and said, "He is most definitely *not* a ninety pound weakling, honey. More like two hundred forty pound Adonis. He's a totally beefy male model, actually. Definitely not a weakling."

Barry swiveled to Monet. "You're dating a male model? Really?"

But Monet turned to her mother and asked, "You know he's a male model and you still persist in thinking we're going to get together?"

"Well. Yes. Is there something wrong with being a male model? Other than that he rocks your equilibrium?"

"Rocks my equilibrium? Mother. Yes, there's something wrong with being a male model! What he does is a problem."

"Oh, honey. Don't be self-righteous. There's nothing wrong with being gorgeous. And he can't help the way he looks. How he treats you is the issue. And has he ever treated you less than respectfully and kindly?"

Barry was looking from one woman to the other

and had stopped interjecting while Monet took a moment to consider her mother's question. Finally, Monet had to admit, "No. He's always treated me respectfully and kindly, but still. There's no way, Mother." There was no way she would ever consider dating Nick, even if he was interested—which he wasn't. But she couldn't tell her mother just exactly what kind of male modeling Nick did, either. So she simply said, "I'm not looking to date anyway."

Her mother only gave her a knowing smile and said, "All right, sweetie. Whatever you say. But I think he's very charming."

Drily, Monet said, "Oh, he is. He definitely is." In a King Cobra kind of way. But she wasn't going to be the one to tell her mother about how Nick literally handled women. Instead, she hugged her mother and her brother and then went into the other room to kiss her dad goodnight and went home to bed. It had been a long day and she still definitely wasn't a hundred percent yet.

Nick showed up on time for his lesson, but he wasn't wearing his boots. Monet noticed it right off and asked, "Where are your riding boots?"

He looked at her calmly for a second before saying, "They're home."

Raising her eyebrows, she asked, "And why are they home? It's much safer to ride in boots."

"They're home so that we don't feel obligated to ride. I wasn't sure you'd be up to it."

"Thank you, but I would have canceled if I hadn't been up to it."

Again, Nick looked at her calmly before replying, "I know. And I'm sure you're up to it. You're bulletproof.

But there's no reason to be tonight. Isn't there something pertinent you can teach me that doesn't demand doing it hands-on? I'll feel a lot less guilty knowing you are completely out of harm's way. Humor me." Monet considered his request, wondering whether giving in would constitute wimping out. He must have known it because he added, "Please. Just this once."

She decided she could acquiesce—unless it was him who needed to come to grips with her getting banged up by the horse. To make sure, she asked, "Are you asking this to protect my nose? Or did what happened freak you out a little? Not to be rude."

He grinned. "I'm not freaked out. At least not about the horses. You getting hurt troubles me, but I don't want you to get bumped again. I'm just going to assume that it's tender. Huh?"

"It is definitely tender. Okay. You win. Come into the office and let me get a book and we'll go into the tack room and I'll teach you what to watch for in common horse medical issues. And I'll explain about registration papers. You're right. There are some things you'll need to know that can be learned without a horse."

So, for the next two and a half hours, they either stood side by side discussing medicines or equipment, or studied next to each other, his short all but black hair nearly touching her long dark brown hair as they sat at her desk going over paperwork. He was such a focused and fascinating student that she didn't even notice they'd gone over his lesson time for nearly a half hour. Either that, or his aftershave had intoxicated her.

And it wasn't until she dreamed about him again that night that she realized she'd gotten far too comfortable with him being close. It wasn't wise. After all, he was still Nick DeGrassi, the steamy hypnosis king.

Jaclyn M. Hawkes

Chapter 7

On Friday afternoon, Monet was finishing up her last outside chores as the sun hung low in the western sky. It had been a long week. She took the last horse off the walker, put it away, and stopped to lean her head against old Dan where he dozed in the slanting sun near the corner of the indoor arena. She had been talking to the sweet, old, white horse and didn't hear the Ferrari until it crunched in the gravel. She turned around to look into the glare, wondering who was arriving at this hour on Friday. Miguel and Cal were long gone, and her parents were out to dinner. Even Cade probably wouldn't show up here on a Friday until late in the evening.

When she saw it was Nick, her gut reaction was to be glad to see him. Really glad to see him. Then, when she recognized that she felt that way, she had to stop and do the self-lecture thing as she walked over to speak to him—although, watching him unfold his model's body from the sleek car did nothing to squelch her enthusiasm for seeing him. He was an unbelievably attractive man and there was no denying the fact.

He stretched his back and smiled at her. It made him even more lethal and she couldn't help feeling self-conscious about her funny nose splint. He came up to her and studied her face for a second, then gave his half smile and said, "Slowly but surely. Your pretty little nose is returning to us. How does it feel?"

He touched her chin gently to look at it from an angle and for some reason that small gesture made Monet uncomfortable. They'd hardly ever touched except for when she was hurt on Tuesday, but the conversation with her mother about what he did for a living, had brought all the feelings of distrust about his prowess in charming women, right back front and center in her mind.

She casually took a step back as she replied, "It's getting there. Still a little tender. Still a little green and yellow from the healing bruises, but I'll live. What are you up to tonight?"

When she had stepped back, he'd noticed and she felt the slight tension as he said, "Not up to much. I have the evening and thought I would come spend some time with old Dan. Do you mind?"

She felt guilty for seeming rude about his touch and tried to compensate by smiling and teasing him. "Of course I don't mind, but why are you not out doing something exciting on a Friday night?"

He smiled back, but it didn't reach his eyes. "Who's to say that combing Dan isn't exciting?"

"Oh, sure." She nodded positively. "He's the epitome of exciting. Although, surely he can't compare with all your girls. And horses are great, but they tank as a spouse."

"Oh, I don't know. They don't tank as spouse material nearly as much as my girls, as you call them."

He sounded bitter, which was so unlike him. Monet looked at him more closely to notice that for the first time he looked exhausted. She tried again to joke. "They can't all be unsuitable. Can they? Weren't there like twelve million? Surely there's one who's marriage proof. No?"

Without even bothering to grin and deny that there

were twelve million, he shook his head and said simply, "No."

The healer in her couldn't help her gut honest response as she said without a hint of teasing, "Uhm, Nick. To be brutally honest with you, that's because everything there is backwards. Those models could never be wife material, no matter how beautiful they are. They wouldn't be doing what they're doing if becoming a wife and mother was a priority. I mean, I know you landed there by chance, but surely, you of all people can recognize that."

He looked at her and asked just as seriously, "Why would being a model preclude being happily married?"

Wow. How to answer that as a friend instead of as a has-been marriage counselor? He was obviously honestly asking, and she should honestly answer, but how? Finally, she just asked, "Nick, does this scenario really work? One of your girls is leaving her house in the morning on the way to work and she says to her husband, 'Bye, hon. I'm going to go dress slutty and have another guy touch me in intimate places while we pretend to be nasty with each other. I hope the kids don't ever see the pictures. Have a nice day at your work. See you tonight.'"

She paused, and then shook her head and added, "I'm sorry, but it doesn't. It couldn't work. Good marriages are based on trust. Trust that you'll be faithful. All around faithful. Physically faithful. And while monogamous intimacy is the marital glue, the opposite is like acid in relationships."

Nick looked at her for a moment, then let his breath out in a long sigh and turned to look at the sun setting in a haze of pink and apricot in the west. At length, he said, "It was good of you to sugar coat that."

"Sorry."

After another long pause, he asked, "It works both ways, doesn't it?"

"What do you mean?"

"For both men and women."

Monet hesitated and then asked, "Should I sugar coat this?"

Nick gave another ragged sigh. "No. I, of all people, know the answer." There was a long sad silence, and then he said, "I thought it was just that I wasn't patient enough. That I just hadn't found the one scantily clad, surgically augmented woman whose life's dream was to be a stay-at-home mom. For a long time, I really thought that." He gave one of those sad laughs.

"Then I thought I just needed to find someone far away from the modeling or acting business. I even tried some on-line dating services. Geez. That was a mess. But for a while now, I've been wondering if I'm looking at everything from a skewed perspective. If there was some secret rule that I was missing that was vital." He looked over at her. "I guess there was. The secret rule of being all around faithful. How did you figure out the secret rule? You're not even married."

This time she was the one to turn and look at the sunset. "Uh. I've always known the secret rule. My parents taught it by example all my life. It's pretty simple to figure out, once you know who you are. If you know deep in your heart that you're an intrinsically valuable child of God, with a measure of divinity, you can't help but act it. And expect it in return. But there's a problem with the secret rule. Both spouses have to obey it."

She didn't really want to admit her big ugly, but she thought it only fair at this point. "I, uh, I was married once." She knew he turned to look at her, but she couldn't face him as she eventually added, "I was also a licensed marriage therapist once. A long time ago. When I was younger and thought I was more capable than I am."

There was another long weird silence. Finally, he said, "No kidding?"

She shook her head sadly. "No kidding."

The sun finished setting during the next long silence. At length, Nick asked, "How do you know you're a child of God?"

She finally looked over at him, surprised that that was his question. After a moment, she answered, "Initially, my parents taught me. As I grew up, I had to learn for sure for myself from personal study and from all the times in my life that He's helped me and blessed me."

Nick silently raised his chin in a nod to her.

They stood there, each busy with their own thoughts, until eventually Nick said too cheerfully, "Well, I'll visit Dan awhile before it gets dark. Drown my sorrow at knowing that I'm doomed to eternal singleness." He gave her a half-hearted smile. "Thanks for revealing the secret rule anyway."

"Sure. Anytime." Monet stifled a groan until he had walked off. *Nothing like burying yourself in a casual hopelessly deep conversation.*

Jaclyn M. Hawkes

Chapter 8

At her house, Monet puttered with picking some lettuce for a salad for her dinner, feeding the cats and filling the bird feeders before she finally quit fussing and took a note over to leave under Nick's windshield wiper that read, "Nick, since we already know each other's big hairy issues, can you come have dinner with me? Monet

It was probably stupid. Just this evening she was telling herself she needed to keep her distance from him. Still, after their gut deep conversation, it felt like something had changed. Who knew what that something was, but at least Nick knew how her thoughts went and asking him to eat with her felt like the right thing to do.

She put away the frozen dinner she was going to have with her salad and got out some chicken. She had no idea what Nick liked, but most people liked chicken. On thinking about what a large man he was, she went back to the fridge and got out more. The last thing she wanted to do was starve him just after he thought she had consigned him to eternal singleness.

When he knocked on her door, for the first time since she'd met him, he almost seemed unsure of himself. Not quite, but almost. She gave him the best encouraging smile she could give him behind a nose splint and said, "Thanks for not turning me down flat after all that baloney."

As he came in, he said, "Please don't tell me it was all baloney. For the last hour I've been thinking I've finally found the secret rule. Don't ruin it already." He walked into the kitchen and glanced around and said, "I know you're tired too. What can I help with? You have a great house. It's beautiful."

"Thanks. In all honesty, I was going to have a TV dinner, salad and yogurt. So we're starting from scratch. Does grilled chicken sound okay?"

"Wonderful. Do you want me to grill it?"

"Sure. Do you have a favorite recipe?"

"Of course. But I like it all. We can make your favorite."

"And I like to try new things. What ingredients do you need?"

"Can I just dig in your spice cupboard and your fridge?"

"Sure. And is a salad and au gratin potatoes with it okay?"

"Great. Do you want me to make them as well? You can rest."

Monet did a double take as she was peeling potatoes. "Really? Are you a gourmet cook or something?"

"No. I just don't want you to over do. You should relax."

"I'm relaxed. But I'll certainly let you cook. I'll just peel these and chop vegetables and you can do the stuff that takes talent."

Nick laughed. "Deal. Now, do you have any balsamic vinegar?"

Ten minutes later, when there was a lull in the conversation, Monet said, "I've got a solution."

Nick looked up from the rub he was putting on the chicken. "To what?"

"To being eternally single."

He grinned. "I refuse to marry you until you get the nose thing off."

She laughed and shook her head. "No. I'm serious."

"Well, let's have it."

"You just need to retire."

He looked up again, obviously confused. "Monet, I'm twenty six."

She shrugged. "Retirement isn't a function of age. It's a function of money. You can retire when you can afford to retire."

Shaking his head, he laughed. "Well, I can't afford to retire either."

"I'm sure you've got an exit strategy somewhere. Even Adonis himself probably got old. Unless you're planning on doing a lot of book covers for *The Little Mermaid* and you're portraying King Triton, you can't do book covers forever. Just head for the exit now, and ta da. You can settle down to holding only one woman's uhm… Uh, holding only one woman and live happily ever after."

"That simple huh?"

"That simple."

"You're nuts. What would I do?"

He kept on cooking and she got the impression he was stringing her along. So she asked, "Who owns your website, Nick?"

"Me. Why?"

"And who owns all the copyrights?"

"Me. Until I sell them. When I sell an image, I usually give limited copyrights."

"And who does the design work?"

"Me. What are you getting at?"

She put one hand on her hip. "Are you just giving

me flack for the fun of it? Don't play dumb with me, Nick. If you've done all that, then you aren't just another piece of meat hunky body."

He grinned. "I'm not?"

She rolled her eyes. "You've just admitted you have a brain. If you didn't, one of those queen sharks you were talking about would own you."

"They very nearly did. You know, you're the first person who has ever intimated that I do indeed have a brain. Thanks. But I still can't just quit. I like groceries. Shelter. Frivolous things like that."

"Then cut back to modeling fully clothed. Keep the buttons of your jeans done up. Frivolous things like that. It's no wonder no one intimates you have a brain. You trained them. Your brain isn't what they're thinking about when your abs are unleashed. Sell the car and get a Jeep like other twenty-six-year-olds."

He shook his head and gave a real honest-to-goodness laugh that sounded adorable to her as he went back to working on his chicken. At least he wasn't completely disgusted with her for all the naggy motherly things she had just said.

For several minutes they worked side by side in silence. Finally, without looking up he said, "I have an MBA."

She wasn't sure she'd heard him correctly. "What?"

"I have an MBA."

"That's what I thought you said." She stopped peeling potatoes to stare at him. "And you're giving me this bit about the secret rule and not retiring?"

He looked up and shrugged and it made her mad. She didn't reply, but the little voice in her head went into frenzy mode. *Holy Copernicus! Why not just admit that he loved what he did? Why bother whining about not finding a suitable spouse? Why even drop the MBA bomb? He was miles ahead letting her think he was just some poor orphan who couldn't help that he was filthy stinking gorgeous!*

She went back to peeling potatoes almost with a vengeance, her mind working overtime as she struggled to balance his seeming lack of moral character with her Christian obligation to leave judgment to God. All of it was tangled with the frissioning he dragged around with him, and topped off with a healthy dollop of her professional cynicism. It was like having a small nuclear missile ricocheting around in her brain, made more obnoxious because, for a woman who knew better, she enjoyed him and she looked forward to time spent with Nick a little too much. He was an eminently intriguing man, bless his heart.

Glancing over to where he was finishing seasoning his chicken, she saw that he was watching her and seemed to pick up on her inner conflict, because he asked, "Didn't your mother ever tell you not to frown? It will give you wrinkles."

Monet picked up a French chef knife and began slicing the potatoes just as militantly as she had peeled the last one and retorted, "Yes, but my mother didn't mention wrinkles, she just told me it would get stuck in a frown. Didn't your mother ever tell you that your body was a temple? Not a commodity?" She put out a hand for the chicken. "Is that ready for the grill?"

He nodded and handed it to her and replied, "Actually, my mother didn't usually say those kinds of things. She uh, she didn't do mothering kinds of things that much. She was busy a lot."

Monet paused at the door to her patio. "What do you mean? Busy with what? Just with work?"

"Yeah. I guess you could call it that." Monet frowned at his answer and he gave that half smile and said, "Your face is going to get stuck like that."

"What did your mother do? Professionally?"

"Mmm. I'm not sure, exactly. I was pretty young when she died, but when she was there, she never woke up before I left for school and then in the late afternoon, she'd dress up in elegant clothing and go to work and didn't come home until after I was in bed."

Monet could feel her eyes widen and her grip tighten on the plate of chicken. "Are you . . . Are you trying to tell me your mother was a prostitute?"

Nick went to the sink and began to wash his hands as he said, "Well, no. Not exactly. I think she was more of a call girl, actually."

He looked up at Monet with a completely straight face and she couldn't tell if he was teasing her, or if he was serious. She raised her eyebrows in utter disbelief and Nick added, "I mean, I don't know for sure. At the time, I was too young to understand much, but . . . Maybe she was a hostess for a restaurant or whatnot. Although she never mentioned a restaurant. Something was definitely strange there."

Monet blinked. *Holy Aristotle! He was serious!* She mentally shuddered and thought of her own gracious, refined, former PTA president mother. *A call girl for a mother?* Knowing that Nick was watching her, she pasted on a stoic face and said in an impressively placid voice, "Yes, that would be a little strange." *A little strange? Bizarre!*

She glanced down at the plate of chicken and took it out to put on the grill, suddenly feeling asinine for being critical of his screwy value system. No wonder he was so out of touch with what appropriate intimate behavior would be. Look at his role models. A call girl mom. And no clue who fathered him. But then, that probably happened occasionally in certain professions. Like prostitution. Or call girls. Good heavens! And she'd thought his big, hairy issue was being a snake charming model. The more she thought about it, the more off the wall it seemed.

Walking back in the door, she schooled her face into the stoic mask and took a deep breath, feeling like she was back in her counseling practice. *Chill Monet. Just chill. Don't make this a big deal.*

Nick was still watching her as she came in and she couldn't help herself. She had to ask, "So where was your grandfather before your mother passed away?"

"At sea, mostly. He was a fisherman from the old country and when he came to America, he bought a little boat and fished here as well. I hung with him a lot. And in the summers we practically lived on his boat. It was probably not ideal when I was small, but it was better than being home alone in Seattle. Nights frightened me when I was a child."

She nodded. "I'm sure. Did he know what your mother did for a living?"

"I assume so, although obviously nothing was said in front of me. They didn't get along so well."

"But you got along with him?"

"Oh, yeah. I thought he was the bomb and he adored me."

"How did you and your mom get along?"

"Fine. It's not hard to get along when you're not together much."

That made sense. It didn't work so well for married people. One of them tended to be angry or hurt over being neglected, but a child couldn't drag a parent off to a counselor the way some spouses did. Which was too bad for Nick. Someone should have dragged his mother into counseling.

Okay, so even if he did have an MBA and was still a trashy romance novel cover model, with his upbringing it was no wonder. The anger Monet had felt a moment ago dissipated magically. What he did was still a problem. The secret rule of being faithful was still universal-- circumstances wouldn't change it. It was just a lot easier to see why he was the way he was when you understood the back story. But then all of life was that way, wasn't it?

Monet picked up her knife again, much more calmly this time, and asked nonchalantly, "So, Nick, you got any more earth shaking tidbits in your closet? Uncles who are spies? Brothers into growing pot? Sisters into witchcraft? Or is this your best stuff? 'Cause there are any number of people with weirder stories. That's technically not true, but . . . Your grandfather wasn't a mafia kingpin or something? Was he?"

Nick smiled and picked up the cheese grater. "No. He wasn't. Just an easy going fisherman. But once this guy who looked very much like me, only thirty or thirty-five years older came into the Italian restaurant where I worked. I saw him and was staring at him through the little windows in the kitchen doors and my boss, who was one of my grandfather's friends, came to see what I was looking at. He grabbed me by both shoulders and literally shoved me back into the kitchen and said "You don't want to know anything about him. Ever. Don't even think about going out there." He sent me home right then, even though I was supposed to work for the rest of the night. When I asked my grandfather why his friend did that, my grandfather explained that the man who looked like me was, in fact, affiliated with the mob. But he looked *a lot* like me. For a while, I toyed with the idea of meeting the guy anyway. But then he was killed in a shooting on the waterfront."

Monet laughed. "You made that up just to tease me. Did you make all of this up? That's a good one. Killed in a shooting on the waterfront."

"You liked it?"

"No. It was pathetic. Totally Maury Povich."

Nick chuckled and stole a shred of cheese and said, "Actually, I wasn't kidding. But I hadn't thought about Maury Povich. He could probably actually do a paternity test. Dig up the remains or something. I could probably get on the show. I wonder if contestants make enough money to retire. Or maybe the guy *was* my father and was rich and had no other heirs. At least none that his attorney is aware of. Then I could retire for sure."

Monet was trying to keep her face bland, but it must not have worked, because Nick looked over at her and laughed again and said, "Aah, but with my luck, I'd get involuntarily drafted into the mafia. That's probably worse than having a call girl for a mother, *or* undoing the top button of your jeans in photographs."

Monet was almost sure he was joking, but he looked kind of serious in a joking sort of way. Finally, she asked, "Are you teasing me again? So, you were kidding? Or you weren't?"

"Yes, I'm teasing you." He paused just long enough for her to feel relieved and then continued, "And no, I wasn't kidding that I look very much like a dead mobster. Antone the knife Cartucci. I'm sure it was just a coincidence. So do you like pepper in your scalloped potatoes?"

Monet put a hand to her forehead. All she could think to say was. "Oh my." After a second, she added,

"You're gonna have a New York Times best selling memoir."

Nick finished spreading the cheese on the potatoes and put it in the microwave as he asked jokingly, "So you don't think I should contact Maury Povich?"

"Definitely no."

With a more serious tone, he said, "Good. Because you're the only person in the world who knows what I just told you and I'd like to keep it that way. Point me to dishes and I'll set the table."

She finished the tossed salad as Nick set the table complete with stemware, plaited linen napkin and a salad fork. When she sat down, she thought she was impressed until she tasted his grilled chicken. It was the best thing she'd eaten in years and then she truly was impressed and said, "I thought you said you weren't a gourmet cook."

Finishing his bite, he said, "I'm not, trust me. I just like to eat. It's my second favorite hobby. After horses and you. Working in the restaurant helped." He grinned at her. "Especially after I graduated from bussing."

Monet took a sip of her water and looked at him over the table, wondering how in the world she was going to find a way to mentally file away Nick DeGrassi after this unusual dinner. From her initial glimpse of him that first day as he climbed out of the red Ferrari looking so much larger than life, he'd been like a moving target that she couldn't quite classify. She had pegged him as a prima donna, then a loose and wild player, then, he'd seem like the boy next door. As she got to know him, he'd metamorphosed into an evocative artist with a fascinating mind. Sometimes he seemed a businessman, or a gentle caregiver. Tonight, at times, she had sensed a lost child. And a tease. She couldn't believe he had joked about the things he had.

94

He just kept changing and the impressions in her mind kept evolving until after tonight her brain was in a tailspin. The only constant had been his phenomenal charm, which kept her even more unsettled because it was so darned unsettling. She had no idea how to peg this guy. No idea how to channel the different feelings he bought out in her, from the frission to the frustration, to the need to comfort.

Worst of all was her sense of being unbalanced. Just slightly out of control. She was a woman who was practical, if nothing else. She had been up and down in this life, and the one thing she'd learned for sure was that nothing was as it seemed. Nothing could be trusted at first glance. She was a thoroughly tempered cynic. Nick cranked that up to a whole new level and what was most troubling was that in the end, her gut inclination was to be absolutely intrigued by him anyway.

It made no sense. And it was entirely energizing. She had to be losing it.

He glanced up and his green eyes caught her hazel ones and didn't flinch. He'd obviously learned to deal with his background long ago and had moved on. It was impressive, really. As bad as it had been, he had turned out amazingly successful.

For just a second, she wondered if all of it had been lies. Tales to entertain, or in some way excuse his licentious behavior with the female models. She looked down and then back up into his eyes again. No. As gullible as she'd been with 'Frank the perpetually unfaithful Johnson', then it hadn't taken long before she should have realized the signs of dishonesty. She just hadn't known better. She was too young and naïve. Now she did know better and she didn't think Nick was lying. Smooth as soft butter, and tempting as the forbidden fruit, but he wasn't outright lying.

He was sitting over there, quietly eating his sumptuous chicken and she could almost see the wheels turning in his head, wondering why she was sitting over here so quietly as well. She *was* thoughtful, but mostly she just owed him an apology. At length, she said, "Nick, I didn't mean to insinuate that your mother hadn't taught you that your body wasn't a commodity. I was just being frustrated. That was a horrible thing to for me to say when you have lost her. It came out all wrong. Please forgive me."

He shrugged. "She was what she was. Whatever she was. And I loved her. And I knew she loved me. I'm not the one to judge her. Maybe she was doing the best she knew how. At any rate, I didn't know any better." He gave her the half smile. "When I was little I thought everyone's mother lived like that. When I got older, Grandfather took up the slack. Why were you feeling frustrated?"

Slowly swirling the water in her goblet, she wondered how to answer that without sounding like a busybody. "I guess because it sounded to me like you honestly thought having a strong marriage wasn't worth changing for. That you were 'doomed to eternal singleness' just so you didn't have to give up your models." She shook her head. "I had a terrible marriage. Failed miserably. But I grew up with faithful parents who were near blissfully in love. They still are. They're adorable. So I know there truly is happily ever after. A marriage like theirs would be worth giving anything up for. Even your girls."

"So it's not just a fairytale? A good marriage?"

"No. It's not a fairytale. But honestly, the only reason I can tell you that so surely is because of my parents. And my siblings."

96

Taking his napkin from his lap, he set it beside his plate. "The rest of the world doesn't seem to believe there is such a thing."

She shook her head sadly. "No. But I do. And God does. And He's the one who matters."

Nick got up and helped her pull back her chair to stand and said, smiling, "And you would know. Because you're the one girl I know who knows who she is. Good for you. Come on. I'll help you clean up our mess."

After Monet's door closed behind him, Nick stood on her porch for a moment and listened to the sound of the creek running along the edge of her yard. Even with the aroma of the horses it smelled like paradise here. That smell of the creek, the horses, and her flowers and trees combined to make the fragrance of peace.

He looked up at the stars that were so much more brilliant here than they were in the nearby city and stepped off the porch. Geez, what did he tell her tonight? Only every skeleton he'd ever dreamed of having. For a little while there, he'd fairly unloaded on her.

Still, it was good that she knew about him. The way he was starting to feel about her, he needed to know how she would react to his big hairy issues. He grinned at her use of the term earlier. Of course, she had said it before she really knew of some of them. And yet she'd dealt with it all relatively smoothly. At least he thought she had. Who knew with a woman that poised?

A marriage therapist. A divorced marriage therapist. He'd never really considered that scenario, but that had to stink. She'd said, 'a long time ago when she had thought she was more capable than she was' with that hint of hopelessness coloring her voice. That was infinitely sad to him for a woman as capable and sweet as Monet. It must not have been pretty for her to still be this hurt a long time later.

She didn't look old enough to have done something professional a long time ago. Or old enough to be divorced and sad, although that was another of those things that weren't a function of time.

And that bit about both spouses obeying the secret rule. Knowing her, and after seeing her parents in action, infidelity would have cut deep. Although from what she had been saying tonight, infidelity always cut deep. He wouldn't know. After hugging literally hundreds of girls, he wasn't sure he could honestly say he'd even ever had a real girlfriend. That was pathetic. But then, he had been schooled early and deeply by a couple of truly devious and hard women. That had left a permanent mark.

Until Monet, he'd assumed everyone was that way. Monet had changed that. She was so not devious and hard. More like sweet and gentle and caring and beautiful and . . .

He sighed and got into his car. He had some ground to cover. Monet knew who she was. She had spoken of God twice tonight. And while Nick knew that God was all-knowing and all-powerful and all that, he didn't truly know much else anymore. It had been a long time since he had leaned so heavily on God to get him through in high school and college. Apparently, it was time he remember who he was as well. After all, a wise woman had once told him that both spouses needed to obey the secret rule. And for the first time in a long, long, long time, despite his colorful background, he actually believed he would be a spouse some day. After all, now he knew the secret rule.

Chapter 9

Tuesday Nick wore his boots—which was a good thing, because the first thing Monet did as he got there was say, "Hi, Nick. Buttermilk colicked last night, so I'm not going to have you ride him today. I'm graduating you to a more spirited sorrel mare named Gingersnap. But you'll do fine on her."

Monet had had her warming up on the walker, but it didn't take much of the vinegar out of her. Even just in the arena, Gingersnap kept trying to break into a gallop for the whole first hour of their lesson. 'Easy' became Nick's key word with the spicy mare. For the first time, Nick knew he'd be saddle sore.

Once Gingersnap was safely back in her stall, Nick went to visit Buttermilk. As Nick let himself into his stall, the buckskin gelding swiveled his ears forward, but it was obvious he wasn't a hundred percent and Nick put a hand up to rub his face, saying, "Not feeling so good, buddy? She's right, you don't look so good."

After petting the horse for a minute, and wishing he could give him an apple as was his custom, Nick patted the horse one more time, and went to go out the stall door. On glancing over, he noticed the little girl who loved Dan but seemed afraid of people peeking into the stall between the railings. Expecting her to all but run away the way she had the two times before that Nick had seen her, he was surprised when she said, "Buttermilk is sick today. Miss Monet says we can't ride him."

Nick scrunched his lips to the side and nodded sadly, "No, we can't. She's right. But he still likes it if we stop and say hello. I thought maybe that would make him feel better." Bending down, Nick said, "Monet told me your name was Caroline." He put his hand toward the space between rails. "My name is Nick. It's very nice to meet you."

Surprisingly, she reached a tiny hand through the opening to shake his hand and said, "Hello, Nick."

Monet came up the alleyway just then and said, "There you are. I thought I'd lost you Caroline. I see that you've met my friend, Nick. He's another of my students."

Nick was slightly taken aback when Monet came inside the stall with him and Buttermilk and put a casual arm around Nick's waist as she continued talking to Caroline. "Nick sometimes rides Buttermilk too, Caroline. Nick has been learning to ride him and take care of him, just like you."

The little face on the other side of the stall enclosure nodded. For a second, she was hesitant and then she said, "Buttermilk is the nicest horse in the world except old Dan. Dan is the very nicest. It's 'cause he's old and wise that he loves all of us. I have to go so I can ride Dan now."

Caroline left and Nick turned to see that Monet was beaming at him. She slid the casual arm off of his waist as she asked, "How did you get her to talk?"

Wishing she had left her arm there, Nick shook his head. "I don't know. I'm sure she came over to see Buttermilk, but it seemed like with the stall wall between us, I wasn't frightening to her."

Monet paused as if contemplating that and then nodded and said musingly, "She felt safe with the wall between. Maybe that's the key. Maybe you just lucked into what we've been searching for for months with her. You're a genius! Thanks, Nick. If this works, I'll owe you. I'll see you later."

As she left, Nick visited with Buttermilk for another few minutes, wondering if his accidental act of genius would garner another casual touch from Monet sometime in the future. With anyone but him, she was so sweetly affectionate. But with him she was so frustratingly careful to keep her hands to herself usually. He was sure she had only touched him to send a subtle message to Caroline that Nick was somehow safe, but he didn't care. Whatever the reason, he would take it.

Ten minutes later, he wasn't surprised to see TG Alder's truck pull in again. He should have gotten used to it, but it still irritated the dickens out of him that this guy showed up every week. It was all Nick could do to plaster on his usual amiable face and shake the man's hand again as if he was glad to see him.

Nick had been going to leave and go home and do some design work, but with TG's appearance, he decided against it. It was time Nick stake at least a hint of a claim here, even if it was only to irritate TG right back. With that in mind, he tossed out occasional comments to TG as he made himself useful there in front of the arena that Monet had Caroline working in. And it worked. TG looked none too happy about his being there, to say the least.

Nick had cleaned up around the hitch rack, replaced some tack that was hanging on the rail into the tack room, filled the water trough and was just starting to rake up the scattered hay from around the stall feeders when Monet's mother, Marni came out of her yard gate and wandered over to the arena. Nick could definitely see where Monet got her extraordinary beauty, although

101

Marni appeared to have a larger impish streak than Monet did. Nick had only met her one other time, but then she'd looked as if she was about to pull a prank and she looked it even more now.

She stopped to speak with TG for a moment and then continued on to where Nick was working and held out her hand with a smile. "Nicolas, it's good to see you again. I've wanted to thank you again for taking such good care of Monet when she was hurt the other day. I'm so glad you were there when that happened. And thanks for taking her back into the doctor the next day. She was so relieved to get that packing out."

Nick grinned at the smiling woman, wondering just exactly what she was up to nearly gushing over him in front of TG like this. He wanted to glance up to see how TG was reacting to Marni, but restrained himself as he tried to figure out if she was trying to purposely make TG jealous, or if she was doing it inadvertently. And why.

Deciding that he didn't really care why, as long as it irritated TG, he merely patted Marni's hand where he held it and said, "It was my pleasure, Mrs. McLaughlin. And it was nice to get to visit with you. I can see where she got her beauty and brains."

Marni laughed a musical laugh. "Oh, Nicolas, you needn't resort to flattery. I already liked you right off. And please, call me Marni."

"It isn't flattery at all actually. I was in earnest. Monet looks and acts much like you."

Marni nodded. "She does, poor dear. But she is much sharper than I could ever be. In truth, she gets that from her father. Landon is amazingly brilliant, you know. And Monet is just like him in so many ways. And like me as well. Although she has that darned serious side that she certainly didn't get from me. It takes a near earthquake to get her to loosen up and laugh like she used to. She used to giggle as much as I do. We drove her father crazy. Especially when her little sister Ashley got going with us. And now with Lindsay joining in, Landon is history, even if Monet doesn't pitch in as often. Have you met Lindsay yet? She's Barry's wife. You've met Barry, I'm sure."

Nick glanced up at TG who was leaning on the arena fence watching Monet and Caroline and shook his head. "I'm afraid I haven't met any of them. I'm sorry. Other than you, and Landon, and Monet, I don't know who you're talking about."

Marni looked suddenly concerned. "Oh, my. Well, then you need to stay tonight to dinner to meet them. Everyone will be here except Greg—Ashley's husband. He's interning at the medical center and has insane hours, but Ash will be here and her kids, and Barry and Lindsay. We're just barbecuing. Nothing fancy. But I did hear that you make the most heavenly chicken. Maybe you could even lend a hand. Let us all taste it. Or is it a secret family recipe?"

Nick couldn't help a grin at the thought of a secret family recipe. The closest thing in his family to a secret family recipe was the fact that his grandfather could talk his friend, Vinny, at the restaurant, into putting triple cheese on his take out pizza. Shaking his head at Marni, he said, "It isn't secret, but I couldn't crash your family barbecue. But thank you for the thought."

Waving a hand as if it was nothing, Marni said, "Nonsense. They're not really family barbecues. We have all kinds of people drop in and even if it was, you'd still be welcome. You're here enough that you need to come and meet everyone. Cade, who lives over the tack room will be there, as well as TG if he can. I haven't asked him yet, but please come. We'd all love a chance to sample the grilled chicken."

103

Hearing that TG would possibly be there as well dampened Nick's enthusiasm but made him acquiesce because he still felt inclined to stake a subtle claim here. To Marni, he said, "Well, if you don't think it would be an imposition, I'd love to come. And you can give me whatever prep jobs you feel inclined to. I used to work a lot in a kitchen."

"Perfect. Come with me then. We'll gather up TG and go get started on that chicken and fire up the grill."

When Marni stopped at the arena fence to invite TG, he glanced over at Nick with his typical just slightly less than welcoming demeanor, considered for a moment and then seemed regretful as he declined, saying, "Thanks for the invite, Marni, but I have a water turn in a while. I'll have to decline." He looked up to where Monet was working with Caroline and then glanced back at Nick and added to Marni, "But ask me again. You know how I love your barbecues."

"And you're welcome anytime, Tege. You know that. Well, Nicolas and I are going to go get cookin'. You take care now."

She headed toward her house and Nick gave TG a brief nod, said, "TG," and followed her. For obvious reasons, he was glad TG wasn't going to be there. He seemed like a nice guy, but the look in his eyes as they followed Monet tended to make Nick feel just a touch territorial. At least Monet didn't appear to be encouraging TG as far as Nick could see.

He mentally brushed TG off and instead wondered what meeting Monet's siblings would be like. And honestly, he wondered what Monet would think of her mother inviting him. There was probably a reason that Monet hadn't already asked him to one of these impromptu family get togethers. He had noticed that they had them all the time. And what did he know about family anything?

Twenty minutes later, he was up to his wrists in spicy chicken rub in Marni's kitchen when a small tornado went past him doing ninety and hollering, "Grandma! Grandma! We're here! And we bringed you some fresh tomatoes that we grewed ourselves!" When Marni and Nick looked up, a child of about two with hair just the color of both Monet's and Marni's launched herself into Marni's arms and threw her arms around her grandmother's neck.

In the process, she lost both the tomatoes she had in her little hands. One rolled down between the two of them and then wobbled onto the kitchen counter, but the other one went flying over Marni's shoulder and plopped onto Marni's immaculate tile floor in a small squirt of tomato juice. The little girl leaned over to look down at the flattened tomato, considered it for a second and then burst into tears, saying, "Ohhhh. I grewed that myself just for you, Grandma. And now I squished it all up."

She went on to hide her head in Marni's neck and go on about her tomato woes until she happened to look up and catch sight of Nick standing there beside her. Instantly, the wailing ended and she ducked her head back against her grandmother, leaving just enough room for her to peek out at Nick. He smiled at her and she buried her head further for a moment and then peeked out again as Marni said, "Have you met Nicolas, Mia? He's a friend of Aunt Monet's. He's going to have dinner with us tonight. He's helping me to make the chicken."

Mia hesitantly shook her head and then as if she almost couldn't help herself, she leaned away from Marni and put a finger to her lips as she said, "It's nice to see you, Nicolas."

Marni encouraged the little girl. "Can you shake his hand, sweetie?" Nick wiped his own hand on the hand towel beside him and extended it to the little girl who shook it and he said, "It's nice to meet you too, Mia. Did you really grow those tomatoes yourself?"

She nodded and he said, "Well, do you know what? What I'm making calls exactly for squished tomato. Would it be all right if I used that one, since it's already perfect for what I'm cooking? I'll just cut the part off that hit the floor." After another moment's hesitation, she nodded again and Nick leaned down to pick up the squashed tomato.

Looking up at Marni, he asked, "Is that all right with you if I use your tomato, Marni? It would be perfect for the chicken."

She looked down at the splash of juice on the floor and grinned. "It's fine by me. I'm glad that I mopped it this morning. Do you need the other one as well?"

"Nope. Just one squished tomato." He turned back to Mia. "You got any flattened onions? I also need a squished onion." Mia shook her head silently and Nick added, "Hmmm. Then I'll just have to drop the onion myself. Marni, can I borrow an onion?"

With a huge smile, Marni handed him a large onion. "One Wallawalla sweet. Primed for squishing. Have at it."

Monet walked into the room just as Nick smiled back at Marni and Mia and tossed the onion. As it splatted, Monet looked between the three of them grinning at each other, shook her head and said, "Do I even want to know what's going on here, Mia? What are you three up to?"

The two year old beamed at her aunt and said, "Squishing the onion for your Nicolas's chicken."

Monet nodded. "I see." She turned to her mother and Nick and asked skeptically, "My Nicolas? Hi, Nick. I don't remember you needing a squished onion for your chicken. I must not have been paying attention the other day."

He shrugged. "Guess not. It's the most important part—other than the squished tomato."

Monet grinned. "Ah. Now, I do remember the squished tomato. What can I help you with, Mother? I'm not sure I could squish anything with such technique as *my* Nicholas. But maybe I could do something simple like shuck the corn."

Mia began to wiggle in her grandmother's arms. "Aunt Momo! Aunt Momo! Can I help? I'm a good corn shucker!"

Taking her niece, Monet said, "Yes, you are. The best ever. Of course you can. I couldn't do it without you. Where's the corn, Mom?"

Nick reached to the counter behind him and handed her a large paper grocery bag. "Here you go, Aunt Momo." He kept a straight face as he said it, but Monet glanced up at him with her eyebrows raised.

Taking the bag, she said, "Why thank you, my Nicolas. Come along, Mia. Let's go outside so we don't get silk all over Grandma's kitchen."

They left, and Marni let out her giggle as she and Nick bent to begin cleaning up the floor and she said, "I see your people skills extend to children. That was very impressive. For a minute there I thought we were going to be having hysterics for a while."

Shrugging, Nick grinned back at her. "Well, I don't actually get to be around kids much, but I remember being one. Maybe I still am. Sorry about your clean floor."

Still laughing, she said, "Oh, it was well worth it to

see Monet's face when she came in. Don't you think? And to see it again when Mia called you her Nicolas. She was priceless!"

Nick gave a half laugh and shook his head. "I don't think she was terribly enthralled. But she took it well. And she probably thinks we're nuts."

"Well, aren't we? We've just used the floor to make dinner. That's exactly what I was talking about that Monet doesn't cut up like she used to. There was a time that she would have started a tomato fight. But she's still always a good sport. She may refer to you as 'my Nicolas' for the rest of forever, but what the heck."

That actually sounded pretty good to him. Not that he could tell Marni that. Or admit it to Monet. But at least she hadn't appeared unduly concerned to find him attending their barbecue. He went back to his chicken, adding the tomato. He'd never done that before, but it wouldn't be too bad.

A couple minutes later, a beautiful young woman came into the kitchen holding a baby and accompanied by a little boy a couple of years older than Mia. She kissed Marni's cheek, handed over the baby that Marni automatically reached for and said, "Hi, Mom. It smells wonderful in here." She set down the grocery bag she was carrying and put out a hand, smiling. "I'm Ashley Metcalf. I understand that you belong to Monet and are a gourmet vegetable squisher specializing in floors. I'm Mia's mom. You must be Nicolas. Charming to meet you. How long have you been Monet's?"

Nick shook his head, grinning and worrying at the same time. "Man, I have a feeling I'm in a lot of trouble. I'm just a student of Monet's. She probably won't even let me keep taking lessons after Mia saying that tonight."

Ashley waved a hand much like her mother's tendency. "Ah, no worries. Monet isn't as tough as she seems. But it's not Monet you need to worry about. It's Barry. Does he know that you belong to Monet yet?"

"I haven't met Barry."

"You will. And if you get introduced as Monet's Nicolas, then I pity you. He'll tease both of you forever until Lindsay makes him quit."

"Great. I can't wait."

The back door opened and a man and woman walked in and Ashley and Marni both laughed. They laughed again as Mia came bursting back into the room, much the same way that she had arrived the first time, yelling, "Aunt Lindsay! Aunt Lindsay! Uncle Barry!" She launched herself into Barry's arms, looked right up at him happily and said, "I squished a tomato perfectly for Monet's Nicolas. Then he showed me how to throw onions to squish them too. They're going to make the yummiest chicken. I can already smell it! Can you?"

Barry nodded to the exuberant little girl. "Yes, I can. It smells wonderful. And you helped make it?"

"Yup!" Mia nodded her head enthusiastically. "I squished the tomato. And I even helped Mommy grow it first too."

Barry gave her a high five that she returned with gusto as he said, "Well, good for you, sis. I can't wait to try the chicken." He kissed her temple and then as she leaned towards Lindsay, he handed her off to his wife and extended a hand to Nick. "Barry McLaughlin. You must be Monet's Nicolas. Mother has mentioned you. Good to meet you."

Marni laughed again and put an arm around Nick's waist and said, "God bless the little children. You gotta love 'em. What else can I do to help you get this on the grill, Monet's Nicolas?"

Nick looked at her, wondering how he had gotten into this crazy predicament. "Not you too, Marni. And what did you mention about me?"

Barry laughed and said, "Oh, not much. That you were an artist or something and a little strange." He grinned. "Nothing too outlandish."

Putting her hand on her hip, Marni said, "I did not say he was a little strange, Barry McLaughlin. Wash your hands and mind your manners. You're going to get Monet mad at both of us."

Barry hugged his mother and gave her the same kiss he'd given Mia on the temple as Mia and Monet came back into the room with a huge bowl of husked corn and Barry cheerfully said, "Oh, that's right. It was Monet who said he was a little strange."

Monet got a look of concern. "I said who was a little strange? I never said anyone was strange. What are you guys talking about?"

She turned to Barry who gave her a grin similar to Marni's prankster one and said, "You did too say your Nicolas was a little strange. That day you were a gargoyle. I distinctly remember it."

Monet handed the corn to her mother, smacked her brother on the arm and turned to Nick. "I promise I did not tell this very obnoxious brother of mine that you were strange, Nick. Or that you were *my* Nicolas. I'm so sorry that we've somehow labeled you. Please forgive us all." Then, to change the subject, she said, "Is there anything I can do to help you with the chicken. I know it's like cooking for an army around here sometimes."

Ignoring her apology, Nick sweetly asked, "Gargoyle? You were a gargoyle? What does that mean? You were a gargoyle?"

110

Monet rolled her eyes. "That's what he so generously said I looked liked the morning after the broken nose incident. Please don't encourage it. It will only make him worse."

Nick pretended to consider that for a minute and then said, smiling, "Well, it's not really very kind, but I can see why he thought you were a gargoyle that day. Just for that morning." Barry laughed and put his hand up in a fist and Nick met it playfully with his as Monet raised her eyebrows at the two of them and then Nick went on. "A very pretty dainty gargoyle, of course. The loveliest I've ever seen, even."

Monet put both hands on her hips and tried not to smile as she gave Nick the look. "Very funny, you two. Thanks, Nick, but there's a reason God saw fit to send only one brother to this family. We don't need any cohorts in crime with him. He's bad enough as it is. Don't you think?"

"Actually, I thought he was funny. And you did look a little gargoylish. Which was all my fault. I'm still so sorry."

"Not sorry enough not to hassle me with my brother, I see."

Nick shook his head and grinned. "No. Apparently not. It's a guy thing. We're hopeless. The chicken is ready for the grill. Medium coals."

Monet took the chicken and pretended to grumble, "You're gonna think medium coals, wise guy. Both of you wise guys."

An hour later, Nick carried a loaded tray back into the kitchen to begin cleaning up and Barry walked in behind him with another. They stood side by side at the sink, rinsing dishes when Barry asked, "So, where did you learn to make chicken like that? It was great! Are you a chef or something?"

Nick gave him a sad smile. "Hardly. Nothing remotely so respectable. I'm a model, specializing in romance novel covers. I think Monet considers it the lowest form of life except drug dealing."

Barry paused for a moment and grinned. "Oh." He nodded. "So that explains it. Mom said you were a model, but Monet was kind of weird about it. I thought it was just the medicine she was on because of her nose. Does my mother know about the book cover thing?"

"Not unless Monet told her. Would you volunteer that part if you weren't confessing to a guy? Especially to a woman like your mother?"

Chuckling, Barry shook his head. "No. But then again, I could never pull off a romance cover. My mother would laugh at the idea. I had to get a law degree just to attract a wife. But I'll bet Monet is totally freaked out."

Nick glanced up and then turned back to the dish he was rinsing. "Mmm. Not freaked out so much as totally distrustful. We did a photo shoot here. That's how we met. She was *not* impressed."

Barry nodded and gave another small laugh. "I'm sure." He began loading dishes into the dishwasher and laughed again to himself, then added, "Oh, man. Monet, of all people, wouldn't cope so well. She's a project. That's for sure. She's grown a titanium clad shell over her heart." He turned to look directly up into Nick's eyes and said without flinching, "You treat her like a queen, dude. Or there will be repercussions."

Looking down at this man who was several inches shorter and easily forty pounds lighter, but at the moment had eyes of steel, Nick asked mildly, "Are you threatening me, Barry? 'Cause that sounded like a threat."

Barry smiled just enough to slightly ease the tension, but not retract the threat. "Yeah, I guess I am, Monet's Nicolas, but it's for your own good and you know it. It's not me I'm warning you about. If you haven't figured it out by now, she has her own version of post traumatic trashed trust disorder. You yourself said you sensed it. Skeptical is the understatement of the century. But she's the greatest girl in the world. And nothing short of treating her like a queen for a long, long time will get through the titanium clad shell. I shouldn't have to tell you that being Mr. Romance Novel Cover isn't going to make it easier. Or work, for that matter. If you really just want to learn to ride, then it doesn't matter—and you're an idiot. But if there's more at stake here, that's your only hope."

Nick finally cracked a real smile and shook his head as he scraped a plate. "Geez, you McLaughlins tell it like you see it. It's too bad you're not all politicians. Washington D.C. could use a dose of your candor. Anything else you'd like to tell me while you're playing big brother? I'm all ears."

Barry gave his own sincere grin and as he turned to take the tray back outside for another load, he said, "She always dreamed of a white knight on a charger coming to carry her away. A retired romance novel hunk ought to be able to pull that off someday, I'd think. With a few more riding lessons."

The door closed behind Barry and Nick shook his head again. Retired. There was that blasted word again. And he had met Barry what? An hour ago. How had her steely brother realized just how willing to be invested he was?

Nick involuntarily smiled at the insane slant that conversation had just taken. These people were unreal.

Apparently Barry was thoroughly versed in the secret faithfulness rule.

Retired. At this point, he could admit that that concept had been weighing on him nearly as long as he'd known Monet, although he hadn't wanted to acknowledge it. But toying with the idea, and implementing it were two different things. It wasn't like he was talking about changing his favorite kind of cold cereal. This was going to uproot his whole life. In a good way. It was just going to be a mess going through it.

Mia came racing in the kitchen door just then and skidded to a stop when she saw him. She considered him for a moment, and then turned and went back out the door as fast as she had come in. He smiled at her exuberance in everything she did as he began to wipe down the counters.

Two minutes later, Monet came in the door. Her eyes held just a hint of wariness as she approached him and began helping clean up the prep mess in the kitchen. She glanced over at him, gave him a small smile and asked, "Is something wrong? Mia came out and said your face was going to get stuck in a frown."

He chuckled. "Your mother must have used that phrase with Ashley as well, and she said it to Mia."

"Yes. It's frightening, isn't it? Lunacy is hereditary. Is something wrong? Did someone offend you?"

"No." He shook his head. "No, tonight was actually really great for me. You were probably like Mia when you were two. Even I probably was." He gave her a tired smile. "You have a wonderful family. I'll bet growing up with them was awesome."

She nodded. "It was. Does that trouble you?"

"No. Actually, it gives me hope."

"Then why the frown? What did Barry say to you? He can be so obnoxious sometimes."

114

Nick grinned. "He's a brother. That's his job. He was fine. I really like him. I was just trying to sort something out for a minute."

Monet hesitated. "And should I ask? Or back off?"

Gently, he said, "You can ask me anything you want, anytime you want, Monet. But I'm warning you. My brain doesn't always work exactly logically."

"So, then what are you trying to sort out?"

"Mm. How Jeeps corner. What breaks down titanium. How to tell your mother I do romance novel covers without her being as horrified as you are. Those kinds of things."

Monet only stared at him for a few seconds. Finally, she grinned and softly said, "You're right. Your brain doesn't always work exactly logically."

Chapter 10

Monet had been looking forward to getting the nose splint off for the whole eight days she'd had it on, but when the ear nose and throat specialist's nurse finally took it off, it was like having a Band-Aid ripped off too quickly, and hurt like the dickens. When the nurse left, Monet looked into the mirror on the wall and sighed with relief. Her skin was a little red from the adhesive, but it looked okay. For some reason, she'd been worried that she would have permanent damage from the break, but her dainty nose was indeed back and it was a relief. It had been hard to feel pretty wearing that thing. Not that it mattered.

In the parking lot, she got into her truck, wishing just for a moment that she was climbing back into the racy little Ferrari that she'd ridden in the last two times she had been into town for this nose hassle. It had been nice to be babied for those couple of days when Nick had brought her.

She thought about Nick, still perplexed about what he had been talking about in the kitchen last night. The Jeep thing she could kind of assimilate, maybe. And she understood his hesitation to admit things to her mother. But what the heck was he talking about concerning titanium? She had even asked Barry after Nick left if he knew what Nick had meant, but all her brother had done was laugh and say, "I think I like your Nicholas, Momo," before hugging her goodbye and taking his wife and leaving. Monet was more confused than ever.

Why would Barry say he liked Nick? He knew Nick was a model, and that their mother had hopes of Monet dating him. Somehow, in Monet's brain, those two things were too juxtaposed to make sense to her. Especially where Barry was concerned.

He had always been hyper-protective of her where guys were concerned. He'd never liked 'Frank the perpetually unfaithful Johnson', and had tried to talk her out of dating him even though Frank had appeared to be a good Christian man. When she had announced that she was marrying him, Barry had been appalled. In retrospect, she had wished a thousand times she had listened to his older brother wisdom. So then why did he laugh and say he liked a guy who was a male model? It made no sense.

Even her dad, a man known for his wisdom, liked Nick. Of course, her father was usually courteous to everyone, but you would think a father would try to shoo an obvious ladies man completely away from his daughter—even a twenty-seven year old daughter.

And her mother was hopeless. Much as Monet had always admired her mother's judgment--where Nick was concerned, her mother had apparently lost all intuition in the face of his obvious charm. Which was entirely understandable. Nick had buckets of charm. Enough charm that after last night, when he had seamlessly fit into her family's gathering, Monet was worried. She had gotten far too comfortable with him. And her immature infatuation for him wasn't waning, even with stepping up her self lectures.

She started up her truck and headed to go get her hair cut and a pedicure. Maybe it was a good thing her mother was going to be taking over his riding lesson for her tomorrow, so she could attend some professional seminars. Nick was starting to haunt her.

Nick could see why Healing Creek Stables charged a fortune for Marni McLaughlin's instruction. She was an equestrienne machine. Where Monet was thoroughly competent, Monet was also more laid back as she taught and more inclined to teach basic all around horsemanship. Marni put him up on a humongous European warmblood dressage gelding and started right in with much more refined riding. She worked on his posture and technique and she had him making his horse do such intricate footing changes and moves that he almost felt as if she had his horse dancing under him. It was amazing, but it was pressing his horsemanship skills to the very limit, and by the time his lesson ended, his brain felt fried. Marni was great, but Monet's lessons and encouragement were far more enjoyable.

Marni must have sensed that she'd stretched him because she insisted he join her and Ashley and the kids for lemonade in the shaded picnic area after the riding lesson. Nick was grateful for the break. He was definitely thirsty and all he was going to do was go home to his condo and work late anyway.

Ashley's two older kids gulped down their lemonade and immediately left to sail leaf boats on the small section of the stream that meandered through the little picnic area, and Ashley excused herself to go feed her baby.

For several minutes, Marni and Nick quietly watched the boating antics until Mia apparently won a race a bit too handily and it made her brother Jack mad enough that he picked up a mud ball and flung it. It splatted against the side of Mia's head.

Expecting Mia to start into the bawling she'd gone into the other day, Nick leaned forward in his chair in concern, but Marni only smiled and motioned him back.

To his surprise, after looking over at Jack in shock for a long second, Mia let out a screech of indignation, reached down and scooped up a gob of mud of her own and let it fly. Jack tried to duck, but wasn't fast enough and it landed on his forehead and began to drip down into one eye. Still expecting theatrics, Nick laughed right out loud as Jack brushed at the mud, smearing it all over the side of his face, and fairly shouted with glee as he and Mia pitched into a full blown mud battle. In seconds, the two were like little chocolate covered children and Nick was even more surprised to look over at Marni and see her smile with contentment as she took a sip of her lemonade.

It made him laugh again as a glob of mud came flying past their table and Marni only ducked. She smiled up at him and said, "Aren't they marvelous? Kids make the world laugh. You don't laugh enough, Nicolas. That's the first time I've heard you truly laugh since I've known you."

Still smiling, Nick shook his head. "Must be because I don't get to be around kids enough. I'm usually around women, and women don't tend to want humorous. They want sultry. At least that's the word I usually get."

Ashley must have heard the commotion, because she stuck her head out of Marni's kitchen door and then walked out to the picnic area carrying the baby. She paused to encourage the children to keep the mud away from their grandmother's table and then came and casually sat in a chair near their table again.

Continuing their conversation, Marni said, "You just need to find women with more substance to hang around with, Nicolas. There's a time and a place for sultry, but in this life, humor comes in a lot more handy than sultry most of the time. Humor and strength. Women are strong, Nicolas. They have to be. And unless

120

the men they associate with are even stronger, the women tend to become hardened and tough, and walk all over them. Then neither the men nor the women are happy. We need men who will protect us. And treasure us. Who will be honorable heads of our homes, and spiritual leaders. We need men who are dependable and trustworthy. In my opinion, what real women want is men who are strong enough to be evenly yoked with them. Strong enough to be gentle and kind. Strong enough for us to lean on when we need it. Then wise enough to pick us up and dust us off occasionally. And happy men. Hug us up, make us laugh and send us back out for another ten thousand miles. Don't you agree, Ashley?"

Placidly, Ashley said, "I have no idea what you're talking about, but you've just described my ultimate male. Strong, gentle and funny. It doesn't get any better than that." Another mud ball flew their direction. Marni ducked again and laughed and Ashley smiled and added, "Although, sultry has its place. But then you tend to get these babies who grow into mud ball champions. So sultry should come with a legal disclaimer. Sorry, Mom. They're getting mud everywhere."

Marni waved her hand again. "That's what hoses are for, Ash. Just like when you and Monet and Barry were mud ball champions in that same stream. It's all joy. You'll be amazed at how much you'll miss this kind of thing someday."

Looking back at the kids, Nick wasn't sure he could picture the poised and gracious Monet ever actually engaging in a mud fight, even as a small child. As if reading his mind, Ashley said, "Those days were fun, weren't they? Although I doubt I ever once won a mud fight with Monet. She was always so darned accurate compared to me."

"Yes, but you won sometimes. You were better at flinging the really wet stuff. And you were patient enough to wait until Monet and Barry had quit fighting and had started building some neato castle and then you'd take them by surprise." Her mother smiled and reached for the baby. "Come here, sweetheart. Grandma will burp you. And look. Here comes Grandpa. He'll want to steal you right away from Grandma."

As Landon approached, quietly greeted everyone, shook Nick's hand, patted Ashley's shoulder, kissed his wife and then did indeed take the baby, Nick looked from one adult to the others to the children, struggling not to feel cheated that he'd never once had a mud fight in a stream in his yard growing up. He'd never even had a yard, let alone a stream. And what would he have given for a sibling? Or a father who casually came in to kiss his mother and touch him.

Nick mentally straightened up and reminded himself he'd had a fishing grandpa. Life on that boat had been awesome, truly. And it was all in the past. He looked back out at the muddy kids and smiled again. The McLaughlins had gifted him some great experiences that had opened a whole new perspective for him. They had changed his views on life and how it was supposed to be forever. His children's lives were definitely going to be different than his own had been.

Marni stood to pour her husband a glass of lemonade and Nick stood with her as Ashley headed for the hose. He glanced at his watch. He needed to get home and get busy. The McLaughlins were probably just about to get started grilling up their dinner again and he didn't want them to feel obligated to include him.

Saying goodbye to everyone, he headed for his car, wishing that he was indeed staying to eat. There was something as comfortable about this family as there was about this place and Monet. A person could really get used to a life like this.

Just as he was relishing the peace, there was a loud crash and a ringing neigh. Nick shook his head. That huge brown stallion was definitely having an attitude this evening. The horse had been kicking his stall and neighing the whole time Nick had been here today. It was probably part of the reason that Nick's first lesson with Marni had been more difficult. It made the rest of the horses nervous as well. He was definitely an animal that would have benefitted from being gelded, regardless of how valuable he was.

Nick looked over to see Caroline's mother standing talking with Cade and he absently glanced around for Caroline. When he didn't see the little girl near old Dan, he got an uncomfortable sense of something not being right. She was probably nervous about Cade, but with that stallion acting up . . . Buttermilk's stall was just across the alley from the big fierce horse.

On an impulse, Nick decided to go visit Buttermilk. Caroline was probably fine, but for some reason Nick was suddenly anxious. Monet was going to have some serious repair to do on her barn if that stallion kept up his kicking onslaught. She had already had to replace his stall panels more than once.

Nick walked down and around the alleyway towards Buttermilk's stall and the ruckus the stallion was kicking up. As he rounded the corner, he was horrified to see Caroline standing outside the brown stallion's stall, staring through the slats in terrified fascination. Inside the stall, the stallion had pounded the panels directly in front of her to shreds with repeated kicks and strikes, rearing around and neighing like a savage.

Swallowing back an impulse to shout at Caroline or run towards her for fear of frightening her even more, Nick strode toward her and spoke her name. When she looked up, he could see the fear in her eyes, at the same time that he could see the hatred in the eyes of the huge brown stallion rearing above her.

Upon seeing the battered shape of the front of the stall, Nick knew it wasn't going to hold the stud back much longer. Even though he knew it would probably frighten the little girl, he picked her right up into his arms and began to run past the stall. It was a long way to the end of the alleyway where he could get her to safety away from the stallion, but maybe there was another open stall that he could duck into somewhere between them and the door to the barn.

He didn't even make it twenty feet before the stallion's stall front gave way with another mighty crash and a dissonant screech of metal that was strangely incongruent with the stallion's screaming neigh that was now coming in their direction. Knowing they would never make it out of the barn, or even to an open stall, Nick looked around frantically, then reached for a pitchfork that stood propped against the side of the alleyway. Shifting Caroline into his left arm, he held the pitchfork like a lance and spun and all but roared "Back!" as he thrust it into the stallion's bared teeth as it lunged toward the two of them.

The points of the fork stabbed into the horse's muzzle, and he screamed again in even more fury and reared to strike viciously with a front hoof. Even as he struck, Nick spun to protect Caroline and knocked the hoof to the side to take a glancing blow that ripped the fabric of his shirt at his shoulder.

Without time to consider the impact of the strike, Nick turned back on the stallion that had spun around to kick out the back at them, and Nick thrust with the pitchfork as he again turned to keep Caroline out of the way of the danger. One hind foot missed them completely, but the other one caught him on the side of the thigh. The force knocked him backwards and he would have fallen except for a stall partition behind him. The impact took most of the air from his lungs and he gasped as he quickly glanced down at Caroline in his arms to make sure that she hadn't been kicked in the process.

She was strangely quiet, her eyes huge and tear filled, as she clung to him in desperate fear. The stallion turned and viciously kicked a hole into the side of another stall, as it neighed once again and turned back on Nick and Caroline. In what felt like slow motion, Nick plunged the fork towards the horse's face again and then swung it as hard as he could at the side of the horse's head, gasping for enough breath to again roar, "No! Back! Back!"

The animal didn't even seem to notice the impact of the pitch fork and put its head low this time in a strange snakelike motion that Nick had seen stallions sometimes do, as it advanced on them once more. He brought the fork down on top of the stud's head and then jabbed at him again. For the first time, the horse flinched, giving Nick just the time he needed to shield Caroline with the side of his own body as another hoof struck.

From somewhere that sounded weirdly far off he heard a woman scream, then running steps, and a part of his brain wondered if he was going to have to try to protect Caroline's mother as well, from this outlaw. Mentally willing her to stay safely back out of harm's way, he swore silently and brandished the pitch fork again, then glanced wildly around to find anywhere that he could get Caroline to safety.

There was nowhere and he tightened his grip on the child and tried to whisper something to comfort her as he returned his whole focus to the crazed horse in front of him. He couldn't keep this up much longer. He wished he could simply put Caroline down and tell her to run, but from her behavior so far, he had no way of knowing if she could do it, or if she would freeze in fear the way she seemed to be. He realized he had to keep holding her. With that in mind, he again faced the stallion, but began to back down the barn alleyway, while still trying to battle the attack.

More running footsteps registered. This time he heard Landon's voice and finally felt a breath of hope that he was going to have help. It certainly wouldn't come too soon. The stallion turned again, kicking as it spun and Nick barely ducked aside in time to avoid having his face kicked in. His and Caroline's.

There was a loud crack from behind him, but it took another crack to realize that what he was hearing was a whip, because the horse in front of him was advancing again with bared teeth and both front feet striking. Geez, he'd never seen anything like this! This horse was crazed!

A front hoof came towards him fast and close enough that he felt he was looking straight into an iron horse shoe. Frantically, he swiveled Caroline to the side, but couldn't avoid the dropping hoof and it caught him coming down, scraping along his belly and groin. Pain exploded in his midsection and he couldn't help the gasp of pain that escaped. It was all he could do to continue to hang on to Caroline as he turned to face the stallion once more.

The loop of a lariat sailed past his head from somewhere to his left, at the same time that the whip cracked again from just behind him, and Caroline hid her face in his neck. The loop seemed to hang in the air and then neatly caught the stud's head. Nick first thought was that now they were in even worse straits because the stallion now had nowhere to go except directly at them.

Struggling to breathe past the pain, he sucked in air and was thoroughly relieved when the horse began to hang back from the rope and did, in fact, retreat away from them. Another loop appeared from a different angle and Nick glanced sideways to see that Landon held one of the ropes and Miguel the other. Monet stood to his right cracking a buggy whip in the horse's face to keep its attention. Between the three of them, they dragged the fiendish beast down the alleyway and put it in another stall where he was sure they would tie it securely.

Cal came and took Monet's whip and she hurried back to Nick and Caroline where he was leaning heavily against the side of a stall. He still couldn't breathe, but he was far more worried about Caroline who still had yet to make a sound. This would probably set her back even further, poor kid. Monet stood beside him with her arms out to take the child, but for some reason, Nick felt he needed to say something to the little girl—even though she was still afraid of him, and he still could hardly draw a breath to talk.

Hesitantly, he lifted the little girl's chin and looked into her fearful eyes. He didn't know what to say, and couldn't seem to get his brain to think of anything brilliant, so finally, he simply said, "I'm so glad you're okay, sweetheart. You did such a great job of being brave. Good girl." With that, he gently kissed her on the forehead and handed her to Monet who hugged her close to her and turned to walk down the way to a bench near the entrance, whispering encouragements to her all the way.

With Caroline finally safe, Nick let out a soft groan and tried to stand up straight but honestly couldn't. The pain in his groin and belly was over the top and there was something wrong with his right leg. It didn't seem to be able to hold his weight. He glanced down to see his jeans waistband ripped in a handful of places in front where the hoof had caught it and scraped down. The side of the right thigh was also torn in a neat half circle, from being kicked there and was beginning to saturate with blood.

Looking up, he saw Monet glance his way with concern and wished he could stand up better in front of her. Marni had come into the barn and stopped to speak to Monet for a second and then rushed on to where Nick still leaned heavily against the stall wall. She took one look at him and said, "I'll call for an ambulance."

He shook his head. "No. No ambulance. It would scare Caroline even more." He gave Marni a tired smile. "I'll be fine in a minute. Just give me a sec to catch my breath. I'm fine."

Hesitantly, she said, "You don't look fine."

He didn't feel fine, but he didn't really want to talk to Marni about it. Instead he tried to smile again and said, "I'll be okay. Go help Monet. Take Caroline in to talk to Dan or Buttermilk. Otherwise, she'll be terrified of horses for the rest of eternity after that stud."

Marni glanced him up and down again and looked hesitant to leave, but he waved her off. Trying again to stand all the way upright, the pain in his belly was still too much, but at least his leg appeared to be working finally. He could put his weight on it now.

Glancing up, he saw that Caroline's mother had finally made an appearance and he tried not to be disgusted with her for not keeping a better watch over her daughter. Seeing that she and Monet were encouraging

Caroline to pet Buttermilk, he turned the other direction, to try to leave through the other end of the barn before Monet noticed him again. He really didn't want to face her like this.

Taking a gingerly step, he headed to where Landon and the men were still dealing with the stallion, and tried to inhale a big breath to bear the pain in his belly and leg as he tried to move. He'd taken bad hits like this before, even if not quite like this. He'd been an athlete. He knew the routine. He would be sore for a couple of days, but he'd be fine.

He felt blood drip down his right leg below his knee and tried not to groan. It would be interesting to see what his thigh looked like when he was finally able to get his jeans off. His Jacuzzi was sounding really good right now--if he could bend enough to sit down in it. This might turn out to be a long night.

When he finally made it to his car, he stood beside it, looking at it. He really liked this car, but honestly had no idea how he was going to get his body to fold into it right now. He'd hobbled here okay, but the thought of bending or stooping made him wince. He opened the door. *Okay, tough guy. Suck it up, and get in, and quit being such a wimp.*

Just as he was going to grit his teeth and raise his leg, he heard footsteps and looked up to see Monet and Barry coming toward him from the barn. They approached him but neither of them said anything. They just looked at him and then at each other until finally, Barry asked, "You sure you don't want that ambulance? 'Cause you don't look sure."

He nodded. "I'm sure. It might take me a minute to get in, but I'll be fine."

Monet and Barry looked at each other and seemed to be communicating silently and then Monet said, "I'll get my truck. You go get Dad's foam camping mattresses to take him to the hospital."

Barry nodded. He and Monet hurriedly left and Nick sighed. He hated to admit it, but he was going to take them up on a ride. But he wasn't going to the hospital. He turned around and leaned against his car, and glanced down at his ripped and bloody jeans. He might have to postpone the photo shoot he was supposed to be doing tomorrow at the beach. He didn't feel up to pretending to be amorous right now.

When Monet and Barry got back to him, she was surprisingly subordinate when Barry announced that he was going to be the one to drive Nick. It didn't seem like her, but Nick was relieved. Much as he was beginning to adore Monet, having a guy help was somehow less embarrassing as sore as he was right now. But she wasn't nearly so subordinate about Nick insisting he wasn't going to the hospital. For just a second there, he actually thought she was going to win the battle.

Eventually, she gave in, but even with the foam padding, his guts ached with every bump and the drive to his house seemed ridiculously longer than usual. Everything he owned was stiffening up on him.

Once there, he thanked Barry, waved away his offer of helping him in, hobbled to his front door and pushed in the code to unlock it. The first thing he did was cancel his appointments for the next day. There was no way. He wasn't going to bother with the Jacuzzi tub either, or even dinner. He was only going to swallow some Ibuprofen with a glass of milk and lie down. Once he got these jeans off anyway. He was still sore enough that that was going to be a project.

It took him a full five minutes to get the jeans and the blood that had gotten stuck to the wound to finally slip off. He looked at the bruised horseshoe shaped cut on his thigh and thought that if he had felt better, he would have gone and gotten a couple of stitches in it. As it was, he dragged himself into the shower and then pulled it together with three butterfly bandages, slid on a pair of soft basketball shorts and hobbled into the kitchen. He should have taken the Ibuprofen before showering. He was really starting to stiffen. Until he'd seen it in the mirror, he hadn't even realized that he had another cut and big bruise on his shoulder too. At least nothing seemed to be broken.

The sound of his garage door going up took him by surprise and he opened the door to look out and see Monet pull his car inside. He glanced down at his bare chest and bare feet, and then shrugged, too tired and sore to worry about changing.

She looked really good in that car. Really good. Not that she wouldn't look just as good in a Jeep. She'd look good in an old Geo for that matter.

She got out and glanced around his garage as she came towards him and he hoped he hadn't left any socks in his living room or something. She even looked really good out of his car. It was the first time he'd seen her in business dress instead of her riding clothes, and it made it easier to picture her as a professional. She was a beautiful poised divorced ex-marriage counselor.

Jaclyn M. Hawkes

Chapter 11

When Monet had realized that Nick had been hurt by that stupid vicious stallion, she had been crushed. Then, when she'd realized that part of what had been hurt had been in a rather delicate place, she'd been a bit hesitant to try to do what she could to help him. Now, as she stood looking at Nick's battered and bruised and unbelievably gorgeous physique in nothing but a pair of knit shorts, she was frankly star struck. Star struck enough that she was actually a little hesitant as she came toward him in his garage.

She had needed to bring him his car, and now, seeing him, she knew she was right in her assumption that he would need some of the same babying and watching over that he'd done for her those days earlier when her nose had been injured. But, for once, her in-controlness was in hesitation gear. He hadn't invited her here, and all she had to do was look at him to know that he didn't feel good. Moreover, it wasn't like she could put a bag of frozen peas on his injury and hold his hand. So what the world was she doing here in the very lair of the beefcake especiale? Holy Copernicus but he looked amazing with all that skin and muscle exposed.

Actually, checking out his meaty shoulders brought her back to some semblance of confidence. Even his brawny shoulder was injured and she switched into health care professional mode as she approached him.

He was a hero. Nothing less. Tonight he'd saved Caroline's life. There was no doubt of that and Monet wasn't going to let her normal reservations about his prowess with women keep her from both caring for him and thanking him for his willingness to risk his own life to save another. In light of what he'd done, that would be far more than petty.

Climbing the two steps out of his garage, she stopped to put a hand on his arm and study his shoulder. She looked up into his sweet green eyes and said, "Nick, I'm so sorry. And so incredibly grateful for what you did. I have liability insurance to cover anything you need. Use it all you feel necessary. Are you okay? Really?"

He stood back from the door to let her inside and nodded. "I'm fine." He gave her a minimal smile and accepted his keys to toss them on the counter. "Movin' a little slow. But I'll live. Thanks for bringing my car. Did you have trouble finding me?"

"No. I just asked your GPS to go home. It told me the way. Barry just lives a couple miles away and will bring me my truck to go home in. I hope you don't mind me driving your car. I have a perfect driving record."

"I don't mind. Thanks for bringing it. Sorry I didn't drive it myself."

They moved into a remarkably neat luxury kitchen and Monet glanced around and then bravely approached him and said, "Can I see your thigh? Not to be pushy, but your jeans were pretty bloody. Do you need stitches? Or surgery?"

Without offering his thigh, he said, "Stitches maybe. But I'm going to make do with butterfly bandages. Surgery definitely no. He didn't connect directly, obviously. I think you should get rid of that horse."

Sadly she nodded. "The second its owner gets back into the country. He brought him and then had to leave for a few months. In the meantime, I've had Cal beef up his stall significantly. If I'd known what he was like, I would never have let him come. I'm so sorry for everything. I didn't even know Caroline was going to be there tonight. I had canceled her lessons, but her mother brought her anyway just to see the horses. Apparently her mother got sidetracked outside the barn."

"Apparently."

Moving to stand in front of him, Monet said, "You were going to show me your thigh."

He gave her the slightest hint of a mischievous smile. "No, I wasn't. It's fine."

Monet put her hands on her hips. "Don't even start, Nick. You have to know I'm not leaving until first off, I know you're okay, and secondly, you're repaid for how you took care of me the other day. Not that I'm going to hang out until the wee hours and listen to you snore like you and my parents did, but . . . I do want to make sure you're as comfortable as possible. It's the least I can do after what you did."

He only went to a cupboard and got out a glass. Holding it up, he offered, "I'm going to have a glass of milk. Would you like one?"

Shaking her head, she said, "No, I wouldn't care for any, thanks." Going to stand directly in front of him, she added, "I would like to see your thigh, however."

He got out a bottle of Ibuprofen and opened it, then blew out a breath when he dumped it and only a single pill fell out.

Picking up his keys from the counter, she said, "I've got some in my purse in your car. Hang on."

When she came back in with the small bottle, she said, "I'll make you a deal."

He finally cracked a minimal smile, but said, "No deals tonight, Monet. Just give me the pills."

With a small frown, she said, "What gives, Nick? It's not like you don't show people your thighs. Knock it off and let me see. How bad is it?"

Almost sounding a little disgusted, he returned, "Forget it. I'll go without the pills."

Confused now, Monet handed over the bottle. "Okay. Okay. Why is this a big deal?"

He turned to her. "You know, Monet. I've been coming to your stable for months now. I've tried to be a perfect gentleman. I've never come onto you. Never flirted. Never once done anything the slightest bit suggestive. So what is up with your snarky little insinuation about what I do and do not show people?"

She studied him for a moment and then said, gently, "My question first, my Nicolas. Why is this a big deal?"

He sighed and tossed back the pills. "Because, frankly, I don't feel good enough to fight with you about going for stitches right now. And knowing you, you'll toss in another pointed little comment about my thighs, or some other of my parts being my livelihood and try to make me. So lay off, huh?"

She nodded, watching him quietly, taking in the slight grimace between his brows and strain around his eyes. She still felt responsible, and she knew she ought to be taking better care of him, but he was a big boy. Well, actually, definitely all man, and he could decide what he wanted. At length, she merely grinned at him and said, "Chicks do dig scars. Can I at least talk you into ordering a pizza? I haven't had dinner yet either. I'll stay and eat it with you if you like and then I will quit fussing."

"Promise?"

"Promise."

"Deal. But you still owe me my question."

"All right. But can I be thinking about my answer while I order? What kind of pizza do you like?"

"I like it all, unless it's that frozen stuff at the grocery store. Although they do have the funniest commercials. I love that one where the pizza falls through the floor into the apartment below." He gingerly edged down onto the nearby sofa. "There's a flyer for Tony's Pizza Pie in the drawer below the phone. Order what you want."

She made the call from Nick's land line and asked the man who answered the phone, "Can I get a large of whatever is your best selling pizza?"

When he'd taken her order and she thanked him, he said, "It'll be there in 35 minutes. Tell Nicky, Joe said hello."

Going to where Nick was sitting, she picked up a throw pillow from the end of the couch and handed it to him and asked, "You want to stretch out? Joe said to tell you hello."

"Have a seat. I'll stretch out after you're gone. You owe me an answer to why you always insinuate that I'm promiscuous."

"Promiscuous? I've never insinuated anything like that."

He closed his eyes. "Don't play dumb, Monet. Every once in a while you let a gracious little barb fly and you know it. Be honorable. We had a deal."

She considered for a moment and didn't have a clue how to answer him. Finally, she softly said, "I don't know."

He opened his eyes and then rolled them in disgust. "You call that honorable?"

"I call it the truth."

"No. You know the reason. You just don't want to spill it. This isn't a counseling session. Just tell me."

She hesitated. "Does saying that what you do professionally kind of weirds me out sound any better?"

"Weirds me out." He closed his eyes again and chuckled. "Please tell me you didn't say that to your clients in your practice."

"You wanted honest, and you said this wasn't a counseling session."

"Well, I already knew what I do weirds you out. That's no revelation. I knew that the first day. The question was why do you say snarky comments about it?"

"I don't know. I guess I didn't even realize I do it. I'll try not to in the future."

He opened his eyes. "Good. Because I'm not promiscuous. At all. Not in the slightest."

"Well, then you have to cut me some slack because you certainly had me going there that very first day."

"I'm a romance novel cover model, Monet. That doesn't make me promiscuous. I'd never seen her before or since."

"You're burying yourself, Nick. And you don't feel good enough to have this discussion. Remember."

"How am I burying myself?"

"How did your behavior that day not seem promiscuous? Not knowing her makes it worse, not better."

"Seeming and being are two separate things."

Monet shook her head. Did the differentiation change much? Really? This was hopeless. They were definitely not sharing a perspective here. Even with a masters degree in psychology she didn't have the smarts to make sense of this conversation and it was almost painful to dredge up that initial day after how much she had learned to truly like Nick. Painful and dangerous.

She looked over to where he was watching her. She'd gotten too comfortable with him and far too trusting of him. His rescuing Caroline tonight only intensified that. He'd edged right up there into hero status. Make that wounded hero status. And she wanted to give in to the urge to comfort him. Not remember that he was a snake charmer. It would be wise to remember what he was capable of. But she would worry about that later. Tonight she was going to comfort him and be as good to him as he was to her.

At length, she only said, "I'm sorry I offended you, Nick. I'll try not to make snarky comments ever again." She gave him a penitent smile. "Would you like some frozen peas?"

He grinned. "Italians don't eat frozen peas on their pizza."

"I meant, uhm, . . . I, uh . . . Peas on pizza might be all right."

"Maybe another time, thanks."

The pizza when it came was marvelous. Which was a good thing because the atmosphere was definitely weirded out for a second there. It made Monet feel guilty.

She watched Nick occasionally grimace in pain and when the fabric of his shorts happened to slip above the wound on his thigh, she was horrified and regretted promising not to fuss. He really did need stitches and was lucky that leg wasn't broken. And she didn't think that his thigh, or even the cuts and bruises on his shoulder were the worst of it. But she definitely wasn't going there. He may have been a snake charmer, but he was still every bit a hero. He'd been so sweet tonight when he'd spoken to Caroline to try to reassure her. She probably would have been killed if he hadn't been there.

At least he wasn't going to bed hungry. Monet refilled his milk and after a third piece of pizza he finally did stretch out with another grimace. She pulled a nearby throw over him and tucked a pillow under his head, then smoothed his hair back off his brow. Just for a moment, she left her hand on his head and watched him. Then, going to his entertainment system, she fiddled with it until she found some soft music and turned it on low, and put the left over pizza in his fridge.

Dimming the lights, she wandered over to his front window and looked out at the city. His world was so different from the one she lived in now. Although she'd once been comfortable here, when she was in the professional world, now it seemed far in the past. Far from Healing Creek Stables. It was good to be able to go home when life came crashing down.

Sometimes she was amazed at how well Nick had melded into her world for his lessons when his background was so opposite of hers.

Going back to look down at him lying there, for a moment, she wished that they weren't so far apart. He was really easy to be around. Even when they were having a pointed discussion. She wasn't sure why he'd wanted to know why she picked at him. Or why it made him testy either. Why did he care what she thought of his profession? He was the most confident man she knew. It must have just been that he was so hammered. But he'd communicated his thoughts well, in spite of being testy. She had to hand it to him.

With Nick sleeping soundly, she texted Barry to come and get her, and then wandered around Nick's living

140

room for another few minutes. He had a nice house. And it was neat for a bachelor who hadn't known anyone was coming over. She wondered if he had taken all of the many photos that were arranged around the room. If he had, he was definitely a gifted photographer.

Her phone buzzed and she knew Barry was there. With a last glance at Nick's magnificent sleeping form, she took her purse and slipped out his front door. She needed to be a lot more careful about falling for lethally attractive heroes. She of all people ought to know that. Even if she couldn't articulate the difference between seeming promiscuous and being it.

Jaclyn M. Hawkes

Chapter 12

He'd been awake a good portion of the night which was why he wasn't truly up and around when someone rang his doorbell. Still in the knit basketball shorts, he stifled a groan as he went to answer it. Barry stood grinning on his porch and Nick motioned him inside saying, "What are you doing here at the crack of dawn?"

Barry glanced at his watch. "It's the crack of eleven-fifteen. I'm on my lunch, you slacker. A slightly irritable but beautiful woman I'm related to insisted I come check on you. How is your skanky-novel gracing body feeling today?"

Nick blew out a breath before admitting, "Less than skanky. And you?"

Barry flashed a smile. "I'm a guy. I'm always open to suggestion. But then I didn't take a horse hoof to the uh, skanky operational apparati last night, either. I caught a line drive once in Little League baseball right there. It was the worst. I feel for you. Did you ever make it in to a doctor? Monet said your leg and shoulder needed seen, too."

"What's a doctor going to say? You should be more careful? Sorry, you just kissed off your future family? Bet you felt stupid in front of everyone groaning like that."

"You've got a point. So, what do you want me to tell Monet? I'm surprised she didn't come herself except that she didn't want to fuss about your parts."

Nick wandered in to the kitchen to open his fridge. "Thank goodness. Have you eaten? Why is she irritable, anyway?"

"Not a clue, unless it's because she's worried about you. Which probably means that she's got a thing for you. I'll take a piece of that leftover pizza."

Putting the pizza box on the counter, Nick opened a cupboard to hand him a plate. "Women who have a thing for a guy, don't send their brothers to check on their injured apparati. At least not any women I've ever known. But then I guess Monet isn't like any women I've ever known."

"No. She's refined if she's anything. Do you want me to run you to the clinic? I can take the afternoon."

Nick shook his head. "I'll live." They got their pizza and then Nick slowly and carefully sat down at his table. He gave Barry a half smile. "You know. After watching Ashley's kids mud fight yesterday, I'd finally decided that someday I was going to have kids. About half an hour later that stupid horse clocked me."

"Man, you watched 'em and wanted kids? Sometimes I watch 'em and decide we'll be childless forever. But then Lindsay will just get Mia to smile and hug me and I want ten. I'll bet your future family is still intact. No worries. If not—you can always adopt. God has a plan for you, Nick. Monet believes you saved Caroline's life. She bawls just talking about it. You'll be epically heroic forever after, at least to her. That's worth getting clocked for, huh?"

"When I try to move, I'm not sure. Who bawls? Monet? Or Caroline?"

Barry shook his head as he finished a bite. "Monet. Caroline doesn't talk. Not more than a word or two. At least not that I can tell. Although she won't really come

144

near me, so I don't know. It's Monet who cries. Something about you protecting Caroline makes her very emotional. Of course, that could be partly because of whatever it was that made Caroline like she is. Which of course Monet never can talk about. Sometimes Monet internalizes things. She should never have become a counselor. It'll be good when she finally settles down to be a mom and quits. But no. I think it's your heroism that makes her bawl."

"I can't picture Monet getting emotional. She's always too poised. And refined. I wouldn't have thought a little heroism could get to her."

"Oh, Monet is the biggest softie of all time, although 'Frank the perpetually unfaithful Johnson' definitely schooled her."

"He's the ex?" Barry nodded and it made Nick grin. "And that's what you call him?"

"Hey, he was unbelievable. It fits, trust me. Thus the titanium clad shell. Which is really a façade. Deep down she's a marshmallow. She just doesn't dare to trust you. I'll bet it's the skanky book thing."

Nick thought about that and frowned. The skanky book thing. Wasn't that just another smart alecky way of saying that he continually broke the secret rule of being completely faithful? Completely trustworthy? How did you fix a problem like this?

Barry wiped his mouth and got up to put his plate in the sink. "If you don't want me to run you in to a doctor, then I gotta go. Your face is going to get stuck like that. Don't worry. Monet'll be fine once you retire from the book thing."

🐎

Monet herself showed up at his house at four-thirty that afternoon with a glass baking dish full of something with chicken in it that smelled delicious. For some reason, he'd been half expecting her, and had finally gotten fully dressed in order to pull off looking like he felt better than he did. He was glad he had because she was in business slacks again and looked like a million bucks.

As he went to let her in, she said, "No. I won't stay long in case you have plans. I just wanted to make sure you were okay."

"My plans are to lounge around here tonight. I'm fine, but thank you for checking."

She glanced at his thigh and he could tell that she dearly wanted to ask, but she didn't. It was almost disappointing, although he was sure it had something to do with her promising not to fuss last night. Instead, she asked, "Is there anything I can do to help you?"

He shook his head and smiled at the fact that she actually seemed nervous. "Nope. Just drop by and bring me something homemade and make me feel watched over. That's all I need. How is Caroline?"

"I think she's going to be okay. I had her come back today just to have an extra day to help her be comfortable around Dan. And we'll do it again Monday. Hopefully, she'll be able to learn to listen to the Spirit to be able to know when she's safe and when she's not. I'm sure she already does that and doesn't realize it, but she needs to learn to recognize the Spirit so she can be confident that she's safe, or doing the right thing."

He nodded, considering that thought. Monet was so matter-of-fact about things like this, it sometimes amazed him. Caroline was seven and Monet thought she could learn such a concept. So maybe he could, too. Maybe he could even learn how to understand Monet. Or help her understand him. Maybe what he needed was to enlist God's help in getting Monet to trust him. If he could be trusted. He felt trustworthy, but then again, sometimes he didn't understand all the rules.

At length, he said, "I hope she's okay. And that I didn't set back everything you're trying to do there."

Monet shook her head. "Who knows with a child that troubled? The best thing for her was just what you did after everything was over, when you spoke to her so genuinely. The Spirit will whisper to her at times like that, that she can trust you. If she can just hear."

He didn't know how to answer that, and after hesitating for a long moment, Monet said, "Well, okay then. I'll let you get back to whatever you were doing."

He couldn't admit to her that he was just lying around, trying to do some artwork, feeling lousy, and mostly thinking about her. Or that he was honestly too thrashed to want to visit, so instead he just said, "Thanks, Monet. I appreciate you coming. I'll see you later."

"Take care." She gave him a sweet smile before she turned to go, and he watched her walk back to her truck. She was a truly kind, lovely woman. Barry was wrong. Even if it was hard on her, Monet was an excellent counselor. He wondered if she had any idea that she'd just deemed him able to be trusted. He wanted to call her back and draw her attention to it, but then decided that instead, he was just going to savor it as he hung out here alone tonight. He should have asked her to stay.

Sunday dinner was over and cleaned up and Monet was sitting in a lawn chair in the shade holding baby Bethany, watching Greg and Ashley play croquet with their older two kids when Nick's car pulled up near the arena. She watched him get out and approach Dan, who was standing beside the gate. Monet was glad that he seemed to be moving much better than he'd been the last two times she'd seen him. Glancing over at her parents who were sitting nearby, it was almost as if her mother could read her mind as Marni got up to go and talk to Nick.

A few minutes later, her mother and Nick ambled over, and in no time at all, her mother had Nick sitting in a lawn chair beside Monet. It almost made her laugh. Monet just wanted to know that he was all right, but her mother still obviously had other designs on the poor hapless Italian heartthrob. Then, seemingly moments later, her mother got up and pulled her dad up with her, to supposedly show him something on the other side of the yard, and Monet did laugh at her mother's transparency.

Her laugh disturbed the sleeping baby and Monet put her up to her shoulder to gently pat her, kiss her soft cheek, and shush her back to sleep as she grinned over at Nick who had to know just what her mother was up to. Shaking her head, she said, "I'm so sorry, Nick. She's hopeless. Just try to ignore her. Hope springs eternal in mothers."

He only chuckled back. "I think it's kind of endearing. Don't you?"

Monet laughed quietly again. "No. I think it's manipulative, but her heart is good. Even if it is misguided." She put a casual hand on his arm. "How are you feeling?"

"Perfect. Bored with being lazy. I'm terrible with sitting around. I had to come and visit Dan and Buttermilk."

Realizing that she'd touched him without thinking, she removed her hand and said, "I'm sure they're glad to see you." She glanced over at him and decided that the word perfect about suited how good he looked this afternoon. But she had to wonder if he really felt okay or just how much he was acting. He'd been pretty hammered only three days ago. And she knew exactly what a good actor he was.

They sat in comfortable silence for several minutes, then Nick gestured out toward where Greg and Ashley were laughing with Mia and Jack. "That's the husband? Greg was it?"

"Greg, yes."

"And he's an MD?"

"Working on an osteo surgery specialty. He's interning right now."

"And with three small children. They're busy. And brave."

"Yes. Very. But they're also very happy. They're working together toward a common goal. For their family eternally, and for the betterment of society. I think that's when couples are happiest when they have the same goal in mind and are pulling side by side for it. Especially when the goal is perfectly in line with God's will. They're trying so hard, but they know who they are and where they're going. It's awesome to watch. But yeah, they're busy and brave."

She looked down at the baby. "So sometimes we have to help. It's a tough job, but somebody's got to do it." Leaning, she tenderly kissed Bethany's head. "For a few years they were gone to St. Louis to med school and we really missed them. Luckily, for them and us, they got transferred back here."

Her parents came wandering hand in hand back through the yard and beside her, Nick nodded at them and said, "Your family is so affectionate. I don't think I've ever seen a family so comfortable hugging and touching."

Wondering what he was getting at, she asked, "Do you think that's a good thing? Or a bad thing?"

"Good. You don't need to analyze me. I know affection is good."

She nodded. "It is."

"So can I analyze you and ask you why you're so affectionate with your family and your students, even your horses. Even with me when you don't think about it. But when you do think about it with me, you weird out. Why is that?"

She looked over at him, wishing he hadn't asked this. Maybe she should just tell him that no, he couldn't analyze her. It was so not a subject she wanted to go anywhere near. Not with Nick.

He simply looked back, expectantly and she realized she had to discuss it. She wondered if she should ask him about sugar coating it, but then he made her laugh when, just then, he said, "Be honest. And not clinical. And don't sugar coat it. I can take it."

Nodding hesitantly, she said, "Hmm. Well, uh. Do I really do that? Weird out about touching you?"

"Be honest, Monet. You know darn well you do it."

She sighed, already feeling defeated. "Okay. I do do it. But is this something we should discuss? Or just ignore?"

"I wouldn't have asked if I hadn't wanted to know the answer."

"But it might not be very fun to hear."

"I'm sure it won't, Monet. But how can I ever fix it if I don't understand it? And you're the perfect person to be able to explain it best. We've talked about big uglies before and we did fine. I know you'll tell me the truth."

She shook her head and sighed again, still hesitating. Finally, she admitted, "I don't know, Nick. You touch people commercially. A lot. Sometimes intimately. It makes me weird. Touch is supposed to mean something. It's important. It releases endorphins. Builds trust. Usually it builds trust. It didn't take me ten minutes upon meeting you to realize I couldn't trust you. Emotionally, I mean. To you, touch means nothing.

"You're an incredibly gifted actor. You are. I was amazed that first day. But it was almost frightening. You can portray whatever you want and it doesn't have to be even remotely genuine. But you seem genuine. Honestly, that would scare someone who is emotionally invested. Actually, how could anyone who knew how talented you are even dare to become emotionally invested?"

She gave him a sad smile. "So touching you seems somehow foolish. Or fake. Dangerous. I don't know. Something. I'm not sure how to explain it, honestly. Like I could never be sure of what's really going on in your head, so I can't ever be completely emotionally honest myself. Like I should keep my guard up on the real me." She looked down, away from his seemingly frank green eyes. "I'm sorry. But you did ask."

"I did. But I needed to ask. You're always kind. But I can tell when you're distant. Sometimes I feel like a leper. I just wondered why. Now I guess I know."

"I guess so. Sorry I didn't sugar coat it."

"No." He returned her sad smile. "One of us needs to be genuine."

"Yeah, but this time genuine felt mean. I'm sorry. I wasn't trying to be mean."

He leaned back in his chair. "You don't have a mean heart, Monet. I know that. It's okay. I just need to understand it all at some point, don't I?"

She nodded. "You do. Because someday, you're going to find a girl who will make you want a more permanent relationship that will require someone being able to truly trust you, so they can dare to be emotionally or physically intimate. You'll have to work it all out."

"What do you mean? You were just saying that being intimate was the problem."

"No. I was saying that you're such a talented actor that trust was the problem. But in any relationship that has substance, you can't have true emotional intimacy, or meaningful physical intimacy without trust."

"So tell me what you mean by emotional and physical intimacy. Apparently they aren't the same thing."

"Well, sometimes they are. In theory, they need to be at least connected. But in reality they're often not. The word intimacy just basically means close. So, of course you can understand being close emotionally or physically. But what we mortals sometimes don't understand is that intimacy is tender and fragile. Close means vulnerable. The closer, the more vulnerable. It's a risk to expose your heart or your body either one, unless the person you trust with your most easily wounded underbelly is deserving of that trust. It's all part of God's plan to make marriages stronger. Emotional and physical intimacy is often the glue—the mortar in a marriage. Outside of it, or in a situation where someone trusts someone else when they shouldn't, being intimate, emotionally or physically can leave a person open to a lot of heartache. Does any of this make sense?"

"I think so. But then sometimes lately, I'm beginning to realize my brain doesn't grasp some of this stuff like most people's. Every once in a while a whole new concept pops up. So who knows?"

She rubbed Bethany's little back for a moment as she watched him, and then asked, "Nick, do you remember when I was talking about Caroline learning to hear the Spirit whispering to her so she can know when she's safe?" He nodded and she went on, "Well, do *you* ever use the Spirit to know when something is true and right? If you truly wonder about something, just listen. The Spirit will testify of truth. Oh, you won't hear voices. You'll get that warm peace of heart that's so reassuring. Or he'll warn you of lies. You'll feel anxious. Definitely not peaceful. Just listen. Just like Caroline, you've probably been getting promptings and even responding—maybe without even realizing you've been doing it. But if your heart is good, then you've been doing it. Just learn to recognize it and listen."

His green eyes held hers and then he silently gave her one slight nod. She took her hand off Bethany's back and put it on his arm and for just a second she gave him a gentle squeeze and then put her hand back to Bethany. "You'll figure it all out, Nick. Maybe someday so will I. That's what this whole middle mortal muddle is all about. We'll figure it out."

She smiled and patted his arm again. "Whew! Betcha wished you had stayed home on your couch watching ESPN now, huh?"

He returned her smile. "Heck no. I'm just wondering how much I owe you for your professional wisdom."

With a sad smile, she said, "Oh, hey, professional nothing. Those morsels were learned in the trenches of failure. Not grad school."

"That only makes them more valuable, doesn't it?"

Bethany started to wake up and fuss and Monet snuggled her close again. "Who knows, my Nicholas? I'm really not an expert. I realize now I never was. I'm actually only Aunt Momo."

153

Nick spent more than an hour with Dan and then Buttermilk. The whole time he was thinking about what Monet had said—and done--trying to pick it apart and make sense of it and figure out how it all applied to his particular situation. Left intact, it was too much to wrap his brain around. Even when he dissected it, it felt a little bewildering. All he really understood was that every day his universe centered more and more around a beautiful, gracious, Godly woman who, he was finally coming to realize, considered herself a failure. And tried not to touch him.

It was funny that Monet said that bit about someday meeting a girl who would make him want a permanent relationship. Well, he had met the girl, and she was the very one trying to help him understand why she wouldn't be involved with him in a permanent relationship. It was like showing the starving man a steak dinner—letting him see it, and smell it, but then keeping it just out of his reach.

Great. Just great. He'd been coasting along in his life thinking he had everything relatively under control. From the average person's perspective, he had it made. Then he'd get a glimpse from the perspective of a lovely girl who knew she was a child of God, that she had divine parenting and that there was a purpose to this life. It toasted his comfort zone.

If he was honest, what he wanted to do was rubberstamp the whole conversation as the knee-jerk diatribe of a woman bitter from a marriage gone bad, but he couldn't. Even as she'd lowered her voice to speak about the Spirit testifying of truth, his heart had begun to pound, and he felt that rush of warmth and instantly understood exactly what she was speaking of. Truth. She'd been speaking truth and he'd heard the Spirit loud and clear.

With her insight, he could see that if he wanted the bigger perspective—the real perspective—the one where he too knew who he was, he was ripe for an extreme life makeover. A makeover that he didn't want to face. It would thrash his whole life. And with his background, he still wouldn't get a decent shot at a relationship with Monet. She'd made that clear. He swore right out loud as he brushed Buttermilk's mane.

Maybe it was time to stop taking riding lessons.

And wanting the girl he could never have.

Jaclyn M. Hawkes

Chapter 13

Monday morning there was a message on the machine in Monet's office from Nick saying that he needed to cancel his lessons for the time being. The wording was ambiguous and made Monet wonder if it was a temporary interruption, like he'd tried to make it sound, or if it was simply a way of saying he never wanted anything to do with her again, after their awkward talk about touch the day before. Something made her think it was the latter and as much as she tried to lecture herself into believing it would be wise, her heart wanted to shrivel in her chest.

Tuesday dragged on for weeks and when TG showed up again that evening and seemed pleased at Nick's absence, Monet was hurt enough that she half snapped at TG and then begged off on having dinner with her family. She called an old friend instead and they decided to go to a movie. But then when the only movies at the theater all threatened to simply make her think about Nick, she switched gears and they went out to dinner.

Even that didn't really help. She ordered the grilled chicken special and then was disappointed that it wasn't nearly as good as Nick's, and she missed him miserably anyway.

Wednesday she struggled to choose happy all day and by Thursday evening, when she skipped dinner again, even her mother knew that her emotional slump and Nick's disappearance were correlated.

Friday afternoon, when her mom asked, "So, is

Nick out of town this week?" For just a second, Monet didn't know what to say.

After a moment's thought, she answered with, "He didn't really say where he was headed. Just that he couldn't make his lessons." Trying to change the subject, she asked, "What are you and Daddy up to this evening?"

"He's taking me to an opening at an upscale gallery downtown—even though he hates them, dear man that he is. What are your plans?"

Airily, Monet answered, "Dinner and a long Jacuzzi tub."

She could tell her mother wanted to say something to her—probably one of those discreet motherly hints that danced around the fact that she was twenty-seven and single. Or at the very least, pry about what had happened with Nick, but her mother only smiled instead and said, "That sounds very relaxing. I hope it makes you feel better, sweetie."

As her mother walked back into her own yard, Monet chastised herself in a sugary voice, "As in, I hope it will make you stop being so stinking blah, sweetie." She knew darn well what her mother wasn't saying. Walking into her own house, she switched gears and opted for the tub first. As it filled with water, she dumped in some freesia scented bath salts and wondered for the millionth time if she should have done something different with Nick, or not. She also wondered why this weird hole in her life was getting bigger by the day instead of smaller.

It was just a song on the radio of his car. Sure, it was a love song. About a beautiful girl. Who still haunted his thoughts in the daylight and his dreams at night. Who was out of his life.

So what if just the thought made him tired and the colors in his brain fade? So what if it was the song that had been playing that first day he'd seen her jumping the white horse? So what if it made him think about her, and how lovely and graceful she was, every single blasted time it came on the radio? It was just a song. Any day now, he would be able to hear it and not smell her shampoo and hear her sweet laugh. He only needed a little time. It was just a song.

By the second Tuesday, even TG asked where Nick was when he showed up at his typical time. When Monet said that Nick had canceled his lessons for a while, TG said in a satisfied voice, "Wasn't like that fancy boy needed to learn to ride anyway. That's not why he was here. You couldn't trust him as far as you could throw him." It was not a moment that endeared TG to her, to say the least. His criticism made her furious and although she didn't tear into him, she wanted to.

Instead, she simply walked away. But all the way from the arena to her house, she recited comebacks to TG in her head about just who could be trusted. TG was jealous. That was all. It was just that he realized Monet had much preferred Nick's company over his. That was the only reason he was impugning a guy who had heroically rescued a defenseless little girl just a couple of weeks ago. It had to be a jealous guy thing, because Nick had never been anything but polite to TG.

Monet was in her house, had checked through her mail and was about to step into the shower before she realized just how outraged she felt over TG questioning Nick's trustworthiness. The realization made her stop dead still and look at herself in the mirror. Her reaction to TG had been from her gut, and she hadn't even caught the irony of being disgusted with TG for doing the exact same thing she had done concerning Nick a hundred times. What's more, the outrage toward TG felt founded. It did feel right to want to defend Nick just now. In this light, believing him worthy of trust was a given.

She felt her forehead crease as she finished stepping into the shower. How could she be so sure right now that Nick was trustworthy, and yet question it when he was around? It made no sense, but still, TG's insinuations offended her most basic instincts. Her intuition. Her gut.

So, where in the heck was this intuition when Nick had been there tempting her in the flesh? And which one was she supposed to believe? Even as she asked herself that, she knew what she felt now was right. In spite of that first day, for some reason, she knew he she could trust Nick. Man, she wished she could have been so sure he was an honorable, trustworthy man before he'd left for good.

As she lathered her hair, she sighed. What did it matter? Nick was gone. It had been ten days since he'd been anywhere but in her dreams. She still dreamed of him almost nightly, bless his very attractive heart.

They were scalloped potatoes for heaven's sake. That's all. Just a simple side dish that his photographer, Marco, chose to have with his steak at the diner. They didn't even look the same as the dish he and Monet had made that night they'd made dinner together, so why did even Marco's dinner make him think about Monet? He looked away from Marco's plate and out the window and let out a long breath.

160

It made him want to swear when even the most random things wouldn't let him forget. Grumpily, he reminded himself, *Shake it off, big boy. She's there—you're here. Different worlds. Get over it. Over her. Just grow up and move on.*

Nick blinked himself back to the present and then looked over to see Marco watching him. He picked up his fork. It had been weeks. Just give it more time. It would get better. It had to get better.

Monet stepped into Buttermilk's stall to halter the big horse for her clinic and paused to pet his patient, all-knowing face. His kind, deep brown eyes seemed to see right into her heart as she sighed and he nuzzled her hair. He let out a gentle breath and Monet patted his nose. "You miss him too, don't you, buddy?"

Buttermilk seemed to almost nod as he slightly raised his head. With another sigh, Monet whispered to the horse what she could hardly even admit to herself, "Me too, Buttermilk. Me too."

"Nick, what's your problem today? You never get like this. The light's almost gone. Get your head together." Nick looked at the man who had been his photographer for the last four years, but was just now completely disgusted with him. Then he looked back at the bikini clad girl he was supposed to be cuddling with, and then into the last rays of a perfect mauve and tangerine sunset. It wasn't happening. He just didn't have it in him today.

Turning back to his photographer, he said tiredly, "Pack it in, Marco. I'm sorry. We'll try it again on Friday."

Marco began to back peddle. "No, man. We've got a couple more minutes. Just focus here and we'll get the shots." Nick shook his head and looked back into the sunset, the breeze off the water tugging at the open tails of his thin white cotton button down.

From where he stood, he saw Marco glance at the bikini model and their assistant and silently motioned with his head for them to move off a ways while he came to stand beside Nick. After a long moment of just looking off into the sunset with him, Marco finally asked in a low voice, "Nick, what's going on?"

Again Nick shook his head. "Nothing's going on. You're right. I just don't have my head together tonight. I'll be fine Friday."

"You haven't been *fine* for weeks, Nick. Something is going on. You used to be a machine. Enough that I worried that there wasn't a heart in your chest. For the guy who used to be able to churn through an intense shoot for hours like it was nothing, you've gotten positively frigid. You've hardly touched that girl over there. And look at her, man. She's hotter than a nuclear reactor. You wanna talk about it?"

"She's a young woman, Marco. Not an object. Watch your mouth. And no, I don't want to talk about it. Just tell her I'm temperamental and send her home. We'll try again Friday."

"It's supposed to storm Friday and I'm not lying to her for you. You're the least temperamental person I know. Or you used to be."

"I will be again. Keep your shirt on."

"My shirt's not the issue here. You haven't even taken yours off today. Those muscles are your secret weapon, man. You can't hide 'em. They're what sell books. I'll send 'em home, but consider checking into a therapist, would you? You're a head case right now."

Nick finally grinned. A therapist was the problem, but Marco wouldn't understand that. He gave him a single nod. "I'll consider a therapist. Just for you, Co. Now leave me alone. Go ask for her number. She seemed half-way intelligent."

"What? Now you're interested in a girl's brain? In that suit?"

"No. I'm not. I thought maybe you were."

"The last thing I need in my life right now is a girl with a figure like that and a brain. Take it easy, man. And get your head on straight. If it's not raining cats and dogs and elephants, we'll come back Friday."

"I'll be here."

Marco headed towards the others and Nick kicked off his deck shoes, left them lying in the sand and walked out to where the water rolled up onto the beach. A therapist. He knew a therapist with a beautiful figure and a brain. And a kind heart. And a strong will. And a knowledge of who she was.

He faced into the breeze and took a deep breath filled with the tang of the sea and loneliness. He'd been mad at her for weeks for messing with his head and his life. Honestly, he still was. Only now he was mad and heart broken.

When he'd left there that Sunday, he'd decided he would quit going to Healing Creek and try to forget all about Monet. Thought it would be so much simpler than trying to uproot his whole career and lifestyle. He'd canceled his lessons and thought he'd moved on. But the damage was done.

He would think he was fine, but then over time it had gone from uncomfortable to near impossible to play at being amorous in front of a camera. No matter how hard he tried to simply be self disciplined, he just couldn't fake any emotion for the girls. He felt like a complete amateur all of the sudden.

It was troubling enough that he'd finally called a broker to find out how much his business was worth. It was a lot more than he'd thought, but still not nearly enough to consider walking away from. So he'd had a long talk with himself and rescheduled another photo shoot. The shoot had ended up successful, but only because they'd been able to capture some great solo images of him that had a wistful feel. He thought they could make good book covers even without a girl in the picture. It had made him wonder if there truly was a way to make modeling work without hinting at the erotic.

And he'd gone and test driven Jeeps, and trucks. They didn't corner all that badly, actually.

Then he went through a stage where he tried to back off from thinking about her because it was going to mean changing too much. But somehow, he'd found himself sitting on a church pew on Sunday morning, wondering how to remember exactly who he was in relationship to his Father in Heaven. Just the act of wondering brought a rush of warmth to his heart that he recognized instantly as the Holy Spirit. It was heavenly — but made him miserable again because he knew he couldn't just ignore it.

How was he ever to get all the different aspects of his life back into some semblance of order again? And even if he ever was able to get his life in line with the secret rule, would it matter? It wasn't like Monet was ever going to honestly want a relationship with someone who had his baggage, no matter how he made his life over — because she had too much baggage of her own to dare to trust. What a mess!

Even as he had that discouraging thought, there was this little voice at the back of his brain saying, 'She's worth fighting for.' It was seriously jerking his common sense around.

Moving toward a huge dark rock that rested in the slick, he leaned back against it and watched a gull playing in the salt breeze, its wings an iridescent lavender from the sunset's reflection. Finally taking his shirt off, he tossed it onto the boulder behind him and ran a hand through his hair. The final rays of the sun cast a trail of tangerine fire across the sea in front of him. He glanced down to the last scabs from the cut on his shoulder that had caught on his shirt as he'd taken it off and noticed that the sunset even colored the contours of his skin into sharp relief.

Walking back out and into the surf, he let the cool pastel painted water wash on and off of his bare feet, the foam hissing quietly as the waves receded. He faced the tangerine fire. It would have been phenomenal light for photos, but he simply bent down and skipped a rock as he watched the sun sink past the edge of the world and the last of the riotous dye fade from the sky. The damage was done. And he still wanted the girl.

Chapter 14

It had been a month. The longest month of her life, and honestly, as Monet dragged her discouraged body out of bed and got dressed, she was disgusted with herself as she admitted how much she missed Nick DeGrassi. How in the world had she let herself get this attached to him? She was much sadder now than she'd been after finally leaving Frank. If she'd known she would miss him this much, she might have changed her mind and tried to actually encourage a relationship with him, as crazy as that sounded.

All morning as she worked, she thought about him. It had been four weeks ago yesterday afternoon when they'd had that fateful talk about touching him and trust and intimacy. Monet had dreaded talking about it at all, but after they had talked, at first felt it had gone okay. Nick hadn't seemed angry or sad. But then again, he *was* an actor extraordinaire. Apparently it hadn't gone well at all. He'd left that evening, left a message the next day to cancel his riding lessons "for awhile", and she hadn't seen or heard from him since.

It was for the best, considering how much she still thought about him, even after this long. She knew it, but she was still miserable. She hadn't realized that she'd let her attraction get so far out of control. And now, in retrospect, if she could take it back, she probably wouldn't have agreed to have the talk, but that didn't change the fact that what she'd said had been the truth. She *was* a little weird about touching him, and trust *did* have everything to do with intimacy. That hadn't changed.

Crud, here she was again, daydreaming about him instead of going out and getting the gear ready for her clinic with Caroline. She shook herself out of her reverie and got to work. It was important that Caroline have a good experience again today. That day with the stallion when Nick had rescued her had really set her back in her progress.

Monet brought out her soft cotton foal halters, trying not to think about how sweet Nick had been to her the day she'd broken her nose. Her dad was going to be helping with Caroline today and working with the baby colts. Caroline was beginning to truly trust him and he had such a way with the young horses. Monet was hoping that his soft spoken demeanor would help Caroline to come more out of her shell.

When Caroline arrived, Monet got them started working in the small arena, and then discreetly went out of the arena fence to let her dad work, making sure to remain visible to Caroline.

They were fifteen minutes into a clinic when Monet imagined she heard the familiar purr of a high end engine. *Now I'm even hallucinating about him.* She turned to see if she was truly hearing Nick's Ferrari like she thought she was and was ridiculously thrilled to see the actual Ferarri.

The racy, little, red car pulled up beside her and she tried to keep her heart rate under control and her demeanor casual as Nick rolled down his window. For a long moment, they only seemed to search each other's eyes, then finally, she calmly said, "Hello, Nick. How have you been? We've missed you around here."

He gave a smile that didn't quite reach his eyes. "I've been fine. Busy. I missed you all too."

"How's your thigh?"

"Fine. All healed up."

They were still studying each other and at length, she admitted softly, "I thought you had decided you were through here. I didn't think you'd be back."

He looked out toward her dad and Caroline. "I had decided that, actually." Looking back toward her, he added, "But then staying away from you . . . all . . . made me miserable."

She nodded in understanding. "I see." She hesitated, wondering if it was wise, and then decided she honestly didn't care to be wise if it made her this unhappy and said, "I'm glad you changed your mind. Please forgive me for driving you away in the first place. I'll try not to do that again."

Shaking his head, he said in a more relaxed tone, "It wasn't you, Monet. You didn't drive me away. I made the decision."

Still meeting his eyes, after a pause, she said mildly, "I don't believe you." At that, he didn't look away, but he didn't answer either.

A second later, she glanced over to where Caroline and her father were and Nick got out of the car and asked, "How's she doing?"

Monet shrugged. "All right. As all right as we know how to make her. Some things mere humans can't overcome. Some things take God's help."

They turned, walking to the arena, and side by side, leaned their arms over the top rail of the arena fence and focused on what Landon was saying to Caroline as he crouched down between her and a foal he had on a halter. Petting the little horse's head, he said, "Sometimes if you make yourself smaller, you don't scare these little guys so much, honey. You see, they have to learn whether to be afraid of us or not. It's kind of natural for them to fear humans, but then if they always have a good experience with people, pretty soon, they learn that it's going to be okay. We just have to build up their trust in us."

The little girl nodded wordlessly, but she reached out a hesitant hand to pet the foal and Nick and Monet looked at each other. Softly, Landon went on, also petting the little foal as he said, "But sometimes, every once in a while, one of these little guys has a bad experience that really scares them deep inside and they forget all the good experiences. That can be bad for the little guy's training, especially if that foal is somewhat skittish or fearful in the first place. When that happens, we have to work extra hard to overcome the negative experience with lots and lots more positive experiences. Do you understand what I mean?"

Again, Caroline nodded without saying anything and Landon put out a flat hand with a little grain to let the foal have a taste as he went on again. "You see, the key is to make sure that they consistently have a good, happy experience. Consistent means regularly and always and often. They have to learn to feel safe again. A good day, over and over and over, and sometimes over again, will eventually help the baby horse to trust you again. Here. Do you want to give him a taste of the grain this time? Horses love grain so that helps him to enjoy being handled. But too much can make them sick, so only give it to them if one of us says you can, okay? Here, hold out your hand."

Caroline put out a little palm and Landon placed some grain on it, and then he continued, "Sometimes, if the young horse, or even an older horse had a really bad experience in their past, it will seem to take far more positive reinforcement or happy experiences than you'd ever imagine to make up for it until they learn that you're safe. Sometimes, you have to work for months and months, or even years to help them trust again. But do you know what I've learned, Caroline?"

She shook her head, but held out her palm again as he went on, "I've learned that if you just keep trying, and never do anything to harm him, pretty soon, even the most frightened horse will finally learn that they can trust you. They may never learn to trust everyone, but if you treat them gently, over and over and over, eventually they'll come around. See how he's gotten so comfortable with us and will touch us with his muzzle? Horses like to be touched, just like us humans. They love it. He finally feels safe with us. Pet him a little more and give him just one more little snort of grain and we'll take him back to his momma and bring out another one. Doing this is what I like to call gentling the foals. Are you ready to go get the next one with me?"

When Caroline nodded, they took that foal to its mother at the side of the arena and brought back another one that was obviously a bit more hesitant. Monet looked up and caught Nick's eye and gave him a small smile as Landon started right in with the same type of dialogue all over again. To herself, she thought, *People are like that too. Just like that.*

Fifteen or twenty minutes later, Landon walked the foal and Caroline over to where Monet and Nick were watching on the rail and Landon asked, "Is there anything you want to add, Monet?"

Monet ducked through the rails and bent down on one knee to talk to Caroline on her level and asked, "Caroline, do you remember when I talked to you about listening to the Spirit to know when it's safe to trust?" At Caroline's minimal nod, Monet asked, "And have you been trying to listen?"

Caroline only nodded again and Monet went on, "Can you see that what my dad has been telling you about the baby horses, is the same with people? That sometimes people have to have a lot of good experiences with good people to overcome the bad experiences?"

This time, Caroline looked up at Landon and then at Nick, but she answered out loud, "Yes. And it might even take lots and lots of good 'speriences."

"It might." Monet smiled and put a gentle hand on Caroline's shoulder. "Well, can you see how we'll put both ideas together to overcome bad experiences with people, and know when you're safe with them?" Caroline hesitated with a look of confusion on her face and Monet went on. "When you were here with my dad, did you feel safe?"

Another nod and Monet asked, "And did you happen to notice that you were listening, or have you just had enough good experiences with my dad to know that he's safe? Did you feel that warm, peaceful feeling?"

"Yes."

"And I don't want to frighten you again, but do you remember the night that that big mean horse broke out of his stall? Do you remember the feeling you had then that was so scary that you didn't dare to even move?"

Caroline gave a little shudder with her nod and Monet asked, "So can you tell the difference in those two feelings? The peace and the fear?" A tentative nod this time, but Monet could see that she was getting it, and it felt like a huge victory as she said, "Good girl. That's exactly what we're hoping for you. That you can begin to listen with your heart. That way, you can be more at ease when you know you're safe, and it will make you feel less afraid. Keep trying, okay?"

She stood up and gently ruffled Caroline's hair, saying a prayer in her heart for the little girl that she could indeed get it. As Monet took a deep breath and was headed to go help her dad put away the mares and foals, Caroline tugged on her arm. Glancing down, Monet asked, "What do you need, sweetie?"

With a tentative look at Nick, who had come into the arena as well, Caroline said, "That night. With the mean horse. I was so scared."

She hesitated and Monet encouraged her, "Yes. I know. I am so sorry."

"Well, then when Nick picked me up." Monet nodded and Caroline went on. "And I was still scared, but then I knew I was safe. Did I do it right?"

This was the most that Caroline had ever spoken by far, but Monet was confused about what she was asking. "I'm sorry. What do you mean, honey? Did you do what right?"

"Did I listen right? I felt like I was safe with Nick. Did I listen right? Can I trust Nick?"

"Oh. Okay." Monet looked up from Caroline's small face into Nick's eyes and she could see the tension as he waited for her to reply. Surprisingly, there was no question. The answer was simple and without taking her eyes from Nick's, she said softly, without hesitation, "Yes, honey. You did it right. You can trust Nick. He won't ever hurt you."

Caroline squeezed her hand and gave a big smile. "Aw, I did it right!"

She let go of Monet's hand and looked up at Nick, who smiled down at her and put out his hand for a high five and said, "Good job, sis!"

Unbelievably, Caroline gave him an enthusiastic high five, and then turned and ran toward Monet's dad, hollering, "I did it right, Mr. McLaughlin! I did it right!"

As she rushed up to Landon, the foal he had on the lead next to its mother spooked away from the dashing little girl. For a moment there Landon had to hang on to the foal and Monet worried that he would get rope burned, but then Caroline realized her mistake and immediately began to softly say, "Easy. Easy little baby. Easy. Easy now."

The foal calmed down at her soft voice, and Monet turned to give Nick a huge smile, even though she knew there were tears in her eyes and she whispered, "She did it right. Oh, Nick, look at her!"

The tears welled over to spill down her cheeks and she was embarrassed, but the feelings were too tender to help. Caroline was almost acting like a happy, healthy seven-year-old. It was practically a miracle.

As Caroline and Landon headed toward the paddock with a mare and foal, Monet turned away from Nick and put up a hand to wipe away the tears that became a veritable flood. She sniffed as she struggled to deal with the whirlwind of emotions from both Nick's sudden appearance, and Caroline's breakthrough, but it was too much and she couldn't stem the tears.

She felt one of Nick's hands warm on her shoulder. His gentle voice was only her further undoing as he said, "Here," and handed her a handkerchief. She put the cloth to her eyes, and when Nick hesitantly put his arm along her shoulder, it was the most natural thing in the world to turn into him and let him pull her into the strength of his chest where he wrapped his other arm around her as well, and just let her cry.

She couldn't help it. She'd worked with Caroline for almost a year, praying for her like she was her own child—hoping desperately for something—anything that would help her overcome her problems.

But if Monet was honest, that was only part of it. What was an even bigger deal was this man standing beside her, holding her. She put her arms around him too and held on. It was ridiculous, but she'd missed him so much. So very much. And as much as she'd tried not to, she had dreamed of him holding her like this. It had been a couple of years since she'd had an honest hug from someone other than her family. She shouldn't want it. Not from Nick. She knew that. But she did. She always had. And finally being close to him was heaven.

All this time, she had hesitated to touch him. But hugging him now was like a soothing balm to her tired heart. Talk about your warm and sweet. Your peace. His solid body felt so reassuring and safe to her right now. It made no sense, but in seconds he had not only plugged the energy leak in her spirit, but felt like he was helium for it as well.

His hug brought healing. Healing she hadn't even dared to acknowledge she needed. Warm, strong, incredibly masculine, comforting healing. It was unbelievably nice to be able to let her guard down and lean on him, just for a minute. A minute when she could admit weakness, and revel in letting him be the strength while she rested.

She turned her face into his neck and he gathered her more tightly into his arms and she literally felt him sigh. Her own heart echoed it.

She could smell the faint scent of his aftershave and took a deep shuddering breath and tried to get a handle on her tears. She could finally admit, to herself at least, that she was thrilled that he'd come back here today, but she didn't want him to find her such a baby when he did. He gently rubbed the flat of his hand across her back for a few seconds in a touch that she could swear gave her strength, and she took another breath and eased her face out of his neck to look up at him.

Almost tenderly, he asked, "You okay?"

It made the tears well again and her lip quivered as she nodded wordlessly and put her forehead back against him to whisper huskily, "Sorry."

He put his chin down against her hair, rubbed slowly across her back again and said, "It's all joy, Monet. Cry if you need to. I've read that it helps."

She nodded against him again. When she could get the words out, she whispered, "It does."

Taking another deep breath, she pushed softly out of his embrace, blew the breath back out and said more clearly, "Sorry, Nick. I don't know why the tears." As she said the word, her eyes filled again and she tried to smile and rolled her eyes. "It's just been so long. With Caroline." She looked down and then had to admit, "And I've missed you."

Mopping at her eyes with his handkerchief, she worked to get control and then stepped back from him a bit, saying, "Sorry." She shook her head and dropped her eyes. "I'll be fine. Thanks. For that."

He still had one arm around her shoulder and put the other hand up to tip her head so he could look into her eyes. He didn't say anything, just looked. Finally, he said, "I've missed you too, Monet." After a long moment, she nodded and looked back down.

She could feel him glance around and then he asked, "What's on your schedule today? How long before you could break away? Do you have clinics?"

Inhaling again to calm down, she said, "Just chores until three o'clock once Caroline leaves. What do you need?"

"Can you get Cal and Miguel to do your chores today? I need you to come with me." He met her eyes and held them for a long moment. "For a date, Monet."

She stared at him, wondering what in the world to think of him just now, and then hesitantly said, "Yeah, I can get them to chore for me. Do I need to cancel my three o'clock?"

He glanced at his watch. "No. I'll bring you back for your clinic. But then can I have you again? Is your family barbecuing?"

She shook her head. And then on second thought, tentatively asked, "Are you sure?"

They were steadily watching each other and after a moment, he asked, "Am I sure what?"

She shook her head again and said a little breathlessly, "I don't know."

At that, he ran a hand through his hair and then kneaded the back of his neck with it and gave a humorless chuckle. "I don't know either, honey."

A few minutes later, with Caroline safely heading home with her mom, on her way to the office to get her purse, Monet called her mom and asked her if she could take her three o'clock anyway. Monet didn't know what was going on, but after working through her own dragons for the last month, she would support him, whatever it was.

Chapter 15

Once he'd helped her into his car, he went around and got in and then looked at her again as if trying to read her mind. Since even she had no idea what was in her mind, she only looked back at him and eventually he pulled out onto the lane without saying anything. At the main road, he turned east, away from the city and for probably more than half an hour they just drove without either one of them saying much. The weird thing was, the silence was comfortable.

Finally, he glanced at his watch and asked, "Did you have lunch?"

"No. No, I haven't. Have you?"

He shook his head and changed lanes. "Is there anywhere around here to eat?"

"Well, actually. There's not much out here in this direction but farms. In another ten miles or so, there's a little country café. It's not fancy, but the food is good."

"Do you mind if we don't go somewhere fancy?"

Monet looked over at him to see if he was serious. His face was more than serious and she said, "Of course not. Just don't order the chicken fried steak. It's a heart attack on a plate. Uhmm, your face is going to get stuck like that."

At that, he looked over at her and let his head tip back in an adorable laugh. When he was through, he said, "I needed that laugh, Monet. Thanks."

"You're welcome. Why are you frowning?"

"I don't know. There are a million things going through my mind."

"Why did you leave for a month and then come back and ask me on a date?"

Shrugging, he said, "I don't know that either. Why did you say yes?"

She shook her head. "I haven't a clue."

He looked in the rear view mirror and then over at her. "That's not a fair answer. You're a psychologist. You know why everyone does everything."

All she could do was smile at that answer and say, "Barry says that people only go into the field of psychology because they doubt their sanity."

"We all doubt our sanity from time to time. They're just the only ones with the initiative to delve."

She considered that and nodded, wondering if he was simply giving her a line or if he truly believed that. Then, because she didn't know what was going on here-- but she needed to, she said, "I came because you asked me to. Now give me a fair answer."

He paused while he glanced across the car at her and said, "That was totally obtuse, and you know it. I left because I thought it was wise. I came back, because wise was miserable. And why does anyone ask someone on a date? Because they want to spend time with them. And I can't keep using lessons as an excuse. I may not be an Olympic equestrian team member, but eventually I'm not going to need lessons anymore. Now give *me* a fair answer."

He made her grin right through her angst and she said, "Obtuse is no different than matter-of-fact."

"Yes, it is. And matter-of-fact is a lot safer than emotional."

180

"True. I'm sorry you need to choose safe with me. I wasn't trying to be obtuse. But I honestly did come because you asked. I was surprised. And I was a little bit afraid. But I trusted you."

Pulling into the parking lot of the café, he parked, turned off the car and looked across at her. "You trusted me." He shook his head. "Are you playing head games, Monet? Or are you just as honestly mixed up as I am? What's up with you all the sudden trusting the eminently untrustable one?"

"You know I wouldn't purposely play head games. And I didn't exactly call you eminently untrustable."

"Close enough."

"Marginally close." She leaned her head back against the head rest. "I don't know, Nick. A month is a long time to consider all the things I did and didn't say. One day TG asked where you were. He intimated that he had known all along that you weren't trustworthy. It ticked me off. Because I knew you were. I don't know how it happened."

"And today?"

"Today what?"

"Why did you tell Caroline she could trust me?"

"Because she can. You would never harm a little girl."

He shook his head. "No. Of course I wouldn't. But I would never intentionally harm a big one either, Monet."

She patted his arm and then took her hand back. "I know that, Nick. I honestly do. Intentionally is a good word and you wouldn't hurt someone intentionally. But Nick, you don't always understand how powerful you are."

"What do you mean, how powerful I am? You mean physically?"

"No. I don't mean physically."

"Well, what are we talking about then?"

"Could we talk about this over lunch?"

"Are you trying to get out of answering the question?"

"Yes."

He looked at her and shook his head and got out to come around and open her door and then resumed their conversation. "Why don't you want to answer that?"

"Because it's too intimate a question."

"That vulnerability thing."

"Exactly." She nodded.

"Well, you were the one to bring it up."

"I know. I'm sorry. I'm slowly learning to be less forthright. You're helping me with that."

"How am I helping with that?"

"Uh, the last time I was completely honest with someone, they didn't speak to me for a month."

He smiled as he opened the café door for her. "That's gotta stink."

"Yes. Definitely."

She picked up two menus from the hostess stand. "We can seat ourselves. There's almost no one in here this late. It definitely stunk. But it was good for introspection. Made me realize that I need to make some changes."

She slid into a back corner booth and he slid in across from her. "You and me both, babe. You and me both. I am starving." He opened the menu. "But no chicken fried steak, huh? What's good?"

She looked up at him, a little surprised that he was being this amiable, but glad about it. And wondering if he was going to drop some emotional bomb on her—other than showing up and asking her out. Pointing to the menu, she said, "What are you in the mood for? The hot roast beef is good if you're hungry. Or the bleu chicken sandwich. It's kind of redneck French. They don't really have anything Italian. Well, spaghetti. But I'm sure it's not authentic."

He gave her his half smile. "Are you telling me the spaghetti would be redneck Italian?"

She looked at him sitting there across from her looking like a heart attack in a booth and wondered how this had happened and if he really was going to tell her why he'd come back and asked her out. "Something like that, yes."

They were half way through their lunches, during which he hadn't given her a clue about what he was thinking as they'd small talked, when out of the blue, he asked, "Monet, why do you go to church?"

She finished her bite, watching his moss green eyes. "To worship God. To fill up my spirit pitcher, to learn the doctrine, see my friends, and be obedient. God has asked us to. Why? I like church. Why do you go to church?"

He watched her in return and said, "To find out what you know that I don't. Have you always been obedient?"

"No. I was a pill as a teenager. You were ten times more obedient than I was then, I'm sure. I gave my mother gray hair. I take it you haven't always gone to church."

"My grandfather used to take me. I had kind of gotten out of the habit."

"So, how's the quest going?"

He shrugged. "I feel guilty now about touching girls that I'm not emotionally involved with."

Monet nodded without smiling. "That's a start."

"And I'm starting to wonder if it really is possible to forgive and forget and move on. Or be forgiven and forgotten and move on."

Jaclyn M. Hawkes

"I believe it's possible to forgive and be forgiven. But sometimes it's not easy. And your sins are forgotten, but God doesn't ever forget any of his children."

He looked at her and wiped his mouth with his napkin. "Geez, I was mad at you. Sometimes I'm still mad at you."

She looked at him, not at all sure where this was going. "I guess honesty is good. Is there a way to make you stop being mad at me?"

"Not that I can figure out."

She chewed another bite and swallowed. "So, then why did you come back?"

He looked at her over a sip of his drink and asked, "You want to know the truth?"

"Yes."

"I want to know about your skeletons. I left feeling like such a low life. Like I was hopelessly unworthy. Then I got wondering why you always say you're a failure when you're obviously gifted at what you do. It finally occurred to me that maybe the problem isn't just that I'm eminently untrustable. Maybe part of the problem is that you're hopelessly not able to trust. I want you to tell me about 'Frank the perpetually unfaithful Johnson'. I want to know why you have no faith anymore in men. I want to know if I'm truly a hopeless case or not."

It was all Monet could do not to be openly horrified. She stopped chewing for a moment, her face frozen. Talk about your emotional bomb. She carefully schooled her face, took a deep breath, swallowed, and said, "Or if I'm the truly hopeless case. I'm sorry I made you feel like a low life. You're so not. Please forgive me." Looking down, she inhaled and asked, "Who told you about 'Frank the perpetually unfaithful Johnson'?"

184

"Barry only said something in passing one day about how 'Frank the perpetually unfaithful Johnson' was the reason for your titanium clad cynicism. I'm assuming he's the ex."

She nodded. "He's the ex. The ex I put behind me. That I don't want to talk about. He was a pathological cheater. I was a pathological fool. That's about the story." Nick looked long at her and she fought the urge to squirm.

Finally, she shook her head. She couldn't. Not to Nick. Not yet. Instead, she said, "I guess it would be fair to bare my skeletons, so you don't feel like I was giving you less credit than I gave myself, because I certainly wasn't. But no. I can't face you and tell it. It's still too hard to admit the depth of the failure. Maybe someday. For now, you'll have to believe me that I truly am a world class disappointment. Both personally and professionally. Sorry to chump. Ask my mother sometime if you want to know. She can tell you. You were right. The trust issues are absolutely all mine. That's another of the things I figured out this last month."

"Do I have your permission to ask her and you won't be mad if she tells me?"

"It's not a great story, just a tale of stupidity. But you have my permission."

"So *are* your trust issues *hopelessly* yours? Is there any point in my coming back? Or should I just try to tamp down my guilt and go back to modeling?"

"What do you mean *go back* to modeling?"

"That's not the issue, Monet. Is there any point in my coming back here? Is it that I can't be trusted? Or that you can no longer trust?"

Monet sighed. "I don't know, Nick. I'm sure you're fine. Who in the world am I that I can label someone hopelessly anything? My skeletons are all mine.

I told you what happened that day with TG and how offended I was on your behalf. I'm sure there are millions of women who would trust you. I don't think melding your career and a marriage is ever going to be easy. But my hang-ups are definitely not any prettier. You're going to be fine."

"So that last day in the yard was what?"

"It was a failed divorced marriage counselor's inept opinion."

Nick looked at her for a long time, then put a hand across the table as if he was going to touch her, changed his mind and pulled it back as he said, "I'm sorry, Monet. I'm sorry I put you on the spot like that. I didn't mean to make you sad."

She shook her head and looked down at her plate. "It's okay. I've been divorced for almost two years. I should be past it by now. I think I am. I just . . . It's a boring story anyway." Sighing, she looked up with a stiff smile. "You were going to tell me what you meant about *going back* to modeling."

He looked at his watch. "No, I was going to hurry to get you back to your three o'clock clinic."

"My mom is going to take it."

He pushed his plate aside and seemed to settle into the leather of their booth, then looked across at her. After a moment of studying her, he said, "You look good, Monet."

"Thanks."

"How have you been?"

She wondered how to answer that, because it had been a ridiculously lonely month, but she simply said, "Fine."

Still studying her, he asked, "Are you being honest?"

She hesitated and then admitted, "No."

He seemed to take a moment to assimilate that, but didn't ask what she meant. Instead, he smiled at her and said, "At least you're honest about that. Was that one of those too vulnerable questions?"

"Yes."

She pushed her own plate aside and picked up a couple of crumbs, tossing them onto it before picking up the paper that had covered her straw. She began to wrap it around a finger. Slowly, Nick reached across the table to finish wrapping it, and then run his finger around the wrap and hers. He was watching her and she resisted the urge to pull her hand away, wondering what he was doing.

Nonchalantly, he said, "I was thinking about you, and your weirding out at my touch the other day. Can I tell you something?" She nodded because she had no idea what else to say. He went on, "Do you know that I've never in all my life held a girl's hand."

Pulling her hand away, Monet looked at him and felt her forehead crease in confusion. Trying unsuccessfully to keep the skepticism from her voice, she said, "Sure. You've had sex with scads of women, but never held one's hand. How does that work, Nick?"

He shook his head with a sad smile. "Uh, uh, uh, sister. Practice what you preach. Listen right before you accuse me of lying to you. Or accuse me of anything. Sex with scads of women? Isn't there supposed to be some Holy Spirit in there somewhere letting you know whether what I'm saying is truth or not? You honestly think I'm going to look you in the eye and flat out lie to you? Is that really what you think of me? I'm not Frank."

The confusion was compounding and she said, "I could never confuse you with Frank. Not even close. But aren't some things just too implausible to even wonder about? To have conquered as many final frontiers as you have and not held hands, was there no emotion involved at all for you? No romance?"

He suddenly looked as confused as she felt and asked, "Monet, exactly what final frontiers are we talking about?"

"Nick, for a guy who's been photographed wearing nothing but chocolate, acting innocent isn't going to work."

"The guy in the chocolate wasn't even me, Monet. I guess you couldn't tell because . . . Well. Never mind. What are you accusing me of? You think I've had sex with everyone I modeled with?"

As gently as she could, she said, "I'm not accusing you of anything, Nick. What you do is your business. Not mine. But can any male of any species be that disconnected from their body that they can be there but not be there at all? Maybe you didn't get more deeply involved with all of them, but even one percent of the girls would have been scads. Nick, I was a marriage counselor. Come on. I had to actually study how the male anatomy and psyche work."

He shook his head and gave a humorless laugh. "Geez, I can't even believe I'm having to defend myself about this." He leaned forward and became very earnest. "Monet, on that first day, did I really seem to be so animalistic that you truly believe I have no self control whatsoever? You were there. What went on there? Exactly when did the sex with that particular girl occur? And what? Did we do it on camera? Or did the other people there just turn their heads? Get real. Was my male anatomy working according to your psych professors? Come on yourself. You've been around me. Do I really seem out-of-control sex crazed?"

188

"No." She shook her head and let out a breath and said quietly, "No, you absolutely don't. I'm sorry. I'm being cynical again. I'd forgotten how detached you were after. Please forgive my assuming."

He reached across and touched her hand again and said gently, "It's okay, Monet. I understand. I honestly do realize that some male psyches aren't a whole lot more advanced than one celled organisms. But we're not all like that. I even understand that with your career, and with what I assume you've been through personally, being cynical has to be a given."

His voice softened and he leaned closer. "I wasn't lying, Monet. I'll admit that I've touched a lot of girls. I'll even admit that I've touched them much too intimately, but I swear. I've never held a girl's hand. And I've never had sex with any of the models. Not one. You can take that to your Holy Spirit and double check whether you can trust me. I'm not lying."

She nodded, truly trying to sort through her feelings and preconceptions. She especially needed to sort through the effect his hand was having on hers to be able to listen to the Spirit. She wasn't sure she was doing that great at listening, but at the very least, her feelings were warm and peaceful and she finally gave him a tired smile and said, "Okay, I believe you. At least I'm doing my best to through my titanium shell. But titanium's tough. You may have to be patient."

"Patient I can do. Do you think someday you'll let me hold your hand? You'll have sole ownership."

"Sole ownership I can do. And I'm sorry I'm a cynic."

He smiled as he got out his wallet, "Cynics can heal. Sometimes it just takes lots and lots of good 'speriences."

In the car, for some reason, Monet was thoroughly nervous. The conversation inside the café had been just a shade too controversial to be comfortable. But the real problem was, why had he spoken of holding her hand? He'd asked her out to lunch—not that big a deal, except that it was a right angle deviation from their instructor student relationship. And then he'd casually touched her just enough to send her frission meter into orbit. And then he'd ventured into the possible hand holding territory. Way, way out of their normal, no touchie comfort zone.

Somehow, their direction had changed and Monet wasn't sure how or when that had happened. And not only was she weirded out, she was energized, which scared the very starch out of her. She had no sense of what he wanted from her, really. Well, other than to hold her hand. But what did that mean?

She looked across the car at him as he drove, and he seemed to sense her look and her confusion because he said, "You know, Monet. I'm at a bit of a loss with you. Because, when you're upset, I have no idea how to comfort you. My natural tendency would be to squeeze your hand, or touch your shoulder. Something touch. But then I don't want to weird you out. So, then, I feel like I'm leaving you hanging nervous. How does a decent person deal with you?"

He was half smiling as he said it and she thought to herself, *At least he's an excellent communicator. He doesn't hesitate to try to deal with things.* She might as well be perfectly candid back. "Sorry, but I don't know how to fix me. You're right. Touch should work, but I truly am hesitant. But I'm fine."

He gave her a grin and said, "Boy, I'll say."

That made her finally laugh and she smacked him on the thigh. As she did, he reached down and caught her hand and looked over at her as he gave it an almost imperceptible squeeze and said, "Thanks for coming with me today." He ran his thumb softly over her knuckles. "Relax back into the seat, Monet and take a big, deep breath. Take two. A horse trainer I once knew taught me that it's calming. Close your eyes. And I'll take you home."

She did as he recommended, but even several deep breaths didn't take away the frissions coming from his fingers. He may not have held someone's hand before, but that didn't mean he didn't pick up a very sensuous technique fast. Or maybe it was her closed eyes that was amplifying the sensation, or that the car felt so luxurious, and smelled just like his neck had earlier when he'd held her.

Whatever it was, every time he ever so gently let his thumb stroke her fingers, the skin on her neck tingled. It even made her heart speed up and her breathing shallow. The center of the universe narrowed down to a space of about four inches in diameter where his strong brown fingers wrapped around her smaller ones. *Oh brother.* It was like she was fifteen all over again. And fifteen had been a little nerve wracking the first time.

At her house, even though she knew there was no way he would kiss her, it still felt like her very first date. He came around to open her door, then watched her eyes as he casually took her hand once more to walk her up to her house. His thumb touched her knuckles again and she literally felt butterflies in her stomach. It made her roll her eyes at herself even though he couldn't see. This was crazy!

At the door, he turned to her and didn't say anything, just looked at her for a long moment that felt longer. Finally, he gave her the smallest hint of a smile, gently squeezed her hand, then let it go and turned and walked away. She watched him slide into his very red little car and look up at her for another long moment before starting it and pulling away.

She finally took a deep breath that had oxygen in it as she turned to walk into her house. *Holy Copernicus.* What in the world were they thinking?

Chapter 16

At seven o'clock Tuesday morning, Nick hoped it was late enough and called Monet's cell phone. When she picked up, he said, "Good morning, pretty girl."

He could hear some sleepiness still in her voice as she replied, "Hi, Nick. Good morning. What are you up to?"

"Actually, I'm calling to find out if I can have my old lesson times back."

She paused for just a moment and his heart dropped, wondering if she was actually going to tell him no. Instead, she said matter-of-factly, "Nick, you don't need lessons anymore. You're nearly as good on a horse as I am. Just come ride with me for today. And talk to me. I couldn't sleep all night for trying to figure you out. We'll decide what we want to do about lessons when you get here. I can't take your money in good faith anymore unless you want to get really serious about showing or something."

His first impulse was to argue about whether she could take his money, but instead, he simply said, "I'm sorry you couldn't sleep. I'll be there at four. With boots. How much time have you got? Can we go to the waterfall?"

He heard the regret in her voice when she said, "I wish. But I already told my parents I'd barbecue with the family. Should I tell my mom you'll be there as well?"

He considered that, but wasn't sure he wanted to face them in case Monet told him to permanently hit the road. Which he knew was actually a pretty good possibility, knowing her. Instead, he said, "No. I shouldn't intrude. Just tell her I said hi. I'll see you this afternoon."

"See ya, Nick."

He pushed end and then decided he was going to go out to Healing Creek early and see if Marni happened to have a moment. He still wanted to know about 'Frank the perpetually unfaithful Johnson'.

Turning to get back to the stuff on his desk, he thought about holding Monet's hand yesterday. It had been so amazing. After all the touching he'd done in his nine year career, nothing had ever been as sensual as holding her hand yesterday. Just the touch of her small hand in his had been fantastic. It made him want to leave right now to go to her just so he could see if it was as incredible today. Who would have ever thought that being emotionally invested could make such an amazing difference?

He absently picked up the photos that Marco had taken the other night at the beach after Nick had thought they'd all gone home. They were just of him, alone with the surf, and the sea, and that phenomenal lavender and apricot light, but they were incredibly evocative images. Suitably respectable images. Maybe Monet had a point in him staying clothed and keeping his hands to himself. Some of his best stuff had happened just since Monet had uprooted his life.

He pulled one out and studied it, then set it aside, and printed a copy of a photo he'd taken of Monet on one of her jumping horses to give to Marni.

It may have been happenstance, but then again.

Maybe the shoots had become more evocative as well because his heart was truly, finally invested. He really hoped things went well with Monet this evening.

When he knocked on Marni's door at two-thirty that afternoon, she answered it in an old paint stained button down shirt that had to have once belonged to Landon and with a paint brush in her hand. Her eyes lit up when she saw him and she invited him in, gave him a one armed hug and said, "Nicholas! Oh, it's good to see you!" She called over her shoulder, "Landon, Nicholas is here!" Back to Nick she said, "He's home doing estimates today. Makes him entirely grumpy. He said he saw you yesterday. Come in. Come in. Come back and see my latest work. You can talk to me while I clean my brushes."

As they were walking through to where she had her easel set up in front of the sliding glass doors in the dining room, Landon came in with his phone to his ear, waved at Nick, then disappeared back into his study again and Marni laughed. "Poor man. He has that phone glued to his ear these days. I really wish he would retire. What are you up to, Nick? We've missed you here. Have a seat and tell me about life."

Once she was all settled back at her easel, he sat down in a padded dining chair and said, "Life is good. A little chaotic right now. I've been changing a few things up, and it's busy. But busy is good. How have you all been?"

"Good! Well, mostly good. Barry's in the middle of an awful case that he can't talk to anyone about much, and Monet is uptight, but maybe if you start coming back around that will get better. Are you going to start taking lessons again?"

Nick grinned. "If she'll let me. She says she can't take my money anymore unless I get serious, and you never know with Monet. She may just tell me to go away."

Marni frowned. "Well, if she does, Nicholas, you just ignore her and come anyway if you've a mind to. She's not the boss she thinks she is. And if she was she'd be miserable. No woman wants a man she can push around. Even if they think they do. You have a good mind of your own. Just use it and let her stew."

She indicated her canvas. "What do you think of this landscape? Landon thinks the colors are too muted."

He studied it for a moment and then said, "I actually like them. They are muted, but they set a mood. It's understated and peaceful. I don't think it calls for brighter colors. I love the light and shadow. They totally draw the eye."

"Oh good. Ambience was what I was going for, but Landon always likes more color. It's nice to have a fellow artist's opinion. How are you doing with your photography?"

"Well, actually." He handed her the envelope that had the photo of Monet in it. "This is for you. The photography is going well. I'm trying to slowly shift more from modeling to being behind the camera. The money isn't as good, but the respectability is far better."

Before opening the envelope, Marni looked at him and said, "Respectability is often in the eye of the beholder. If you act respectably—and respect yourself, you could be the sewer treatment plant janitor and still be respectable. It's a mindset, Nicholas."

Marni took the photo out and looked at it for a long moment and then looked up at Nick with tear bright eyes and whispered, "Oh, but she's a beautiful thing, isn't she? You should have seen her the day she was born, Nick.

More precious than you can imagine. And has blossomed all these years. Even with that mess with Frank she's stayed strong, handling such an ugly hurtful situation with such charity. Although it took the joy out of her. The trust. Someday, maybe that sparkle will come back. She's a treasure. I couldn't have asked for a better, sweeter, more beautiful child. This just catches her grace. Thank you. It's lovely."

"You're welcome. She is a beautiful treasure. Tell me about 'Frank the perpetually unfaithful Johnson'. Would you mind? She gave me permission to ask you. She wouldn't tell me herself. Said it was too boring. But she said you could."

Marni's eyes got big. "Really? You two were talking about Frank?"

"No. We weren't. That's why I'm asking you. She said she can't go there. But I was hoping it would help me understand her distrust and cynicism. Do you think it's something I shouldn't know?"

Marni shook her head hesitantly. "No... No, but . . . She doesn't go there. I mean she really doesn't go there. It rocked her world. Her whole world. It wasn't just that her marriage had gone south. As huge as that was. She'd also spent six years building a career in hopes of helping people to have joyful marriages. Like she'd seen growing up with Landon and me. She took Frank's complete and total lack of any vestige of character as her direct failing. Both in choosing him without realizing he was a compulsive liar and cheat, and in failing to fix him. Which would have taken nothing short of divine intervention—if he'd have even accepted that, but Monet felt it was all her coming up short."

Marni shook her head sadly, "He'd been cheating on her even when they were only dating and it never got better. Only none of us realized until it was too late and they were married. Then, we slowly kept discovering ugly little lies and things. He'd acted like such a good Christian man. Always pretending to be the most righteous. Fooled us all—except Barry. And with women who weren't even marginally worth losing Monet over, but he didn't seem to be able to stop himself. It was an addiction. He was on dating websites, going to singles bars, even using prostitutes. It was downright grisly.

"Only two months into her marriage, Monet realized she had to get an AIDS test. I think that was the worst thing of all for her. Made her feel so trashy. That's when the sparkle left. Then she was left with her own vows, a dangling career, and a husband she couldn't love or respect, but felt she couldn't leave. Even when Monet realized she couldn't fix him, she was willing to just endure rather than go back on her word to God."

Nick shook his head. It truly was an ugly, hurtful story and Nick wanted to cringe inwardly at sweet beautiful Monet going through it. He waited in silence, almost dreading whatever was coming next. If all of this hadn't been enough to make Monet kick the guy's butt out, whatever had been must have been terrible.

Marni continued, "The last straw was an eighteen year old girl with a baby who showed up at Monet's own house looking for Frank. He was the father. The girl thought Monet was his housekeeper. And dear sweet Monet. Rather than raining all over the girl who apparently hadn't even known Frank was married, Monet invited her in to wait for Frank to get home. The poor innocent thing sat on the couch holding her new baby and crying, while unbeknownst to her, Monet was loading Frank's things into his luggage.

"When Frank finally got home, Monet showed them all three and the luggage to the door and set them out. Much as she pitied the poor, naïve girl, Monet figured that baby needed a father and hoped and prayed that a daughter would do what a wife couldn't and make Frank straighten up. Who knows if it worked? Probably not, but at least Monet could finally feel justified in booting him. Thank goodness they'd never had any kids of their own."

Marni sighed. "Only Monet also felt like she had failed in her career and had to walk away from it. That's been harder to watch than her divorce. At least with Frank, Monet could try to rationally see that the problem was his. But with her work--she just thinks she was a failure. She wasn't. She was fabulous. But you'd never in a million years convince her."

Marni shrugged. "Maybe it's all for the best. Dealing with all those hostile marriages. Now at least she knows she's doing some good with the children. It's much less stressful, I believe."

Turning to Nick, Marni smiled and put both hands out as if she didn't know what to say next. "So, you see, it's easy to understand the distrust and cynicism. She'd thought she was doing everything right and making wise choices. It's *overcoming* the distrust and cynicism that is the mountain in the road."

He nodded thoughtfully. "I can only imagine." This was going to be bigger and deeper than he had understood.

Smiling, Marni brightened. "But she's tough, Nick. She's the strongest woman I know. Time will smooth the hurt. Time and goodness from someone else. You'll see. Don't count her out. I truly believe that, deep down, she knows she is a daughter of God and knows she's of infinite worth, no matter what this life brings."

Marni waved her paint brush. "That's the key to raising children, Nicholas. Help them to never forget who they are. Help them to know that it doesn't matter what they look like, or how smart they are, or even what mistakes they make. They are always children of the living God. Always of worth, just because He created them. Then when the chips are down, they'll understand that, no matter what happens, they're equal to the task.

"As long as they remember who they are, they'll make it through the big waves. And Monet knows. She just needs to catch her breath. And to remember how much the Savior valued women. Christ was the ultimate example of how to treasure women. Even the one's who had lost their way and forgotten their worth. That really helps women when so much of the world objectifies or denigrates them."

Nick was still trying to fit his brain around all Marni had told him. Half thoughtfully, he said, "Yeah, but sometimes we mortals can help immensely when we know what to do. That's a big question for me right now. Especially for someone with such feet of clay as mine. What do I actually do to help find her sparkle again?"

"We all have equally mortal feet, Nicholas. But we also all have our own gifts. In my opinion, you have the perfect gifts to help Monet. You are wholly gifted in the art of reassurance. The art of peace giving. You have the gift of balance. Harmony. That quiet, calming, sweet comfort and encouragement that even the animals can feel. That ability to bring serenity with nothing more than a soothing tone and a gentle touch. What in this life could be more rare and treasured than peace? And yes, I know that Monet worries about just how smoothly charming you are, but that is exactly what I'm talking about. She just needs to find the faith to relish your gifts rather than suspect them. It may take time, but it will come."

What she said next sounded so much like what Landon had told Caroline, only with different wording that it made Nick smile. "It takes time to dilute the negative with positive. Just be consistent and persistent. And remember that Monet has always been a very tactile person. Touch is her love language. She's always been very affectionate physically. She's even taken a number of classes about the energy of touch to try to understand its power. Something about how all of the human body runs on electricity and touch helps to transfer the energy." Marni waved her brush airily. "Something like that anyway. I don't understand it except to know that she's right. Touch is vital to the human spirit."

Nick shook his head at that. Physical touch was Monet's love language. But his nemesis with her. Even as he understood that her mountain in the road was exponentially high for him, he also believed Marni was right. Monet needed touch and it would eventually help her. Eventually was the key word here.

He stood up to go and Marni stood with him and he put out his hand and took hers. "Thanks for helping me to understand, Marni. I can see why she didn't want to go there, but it will be good to be able to understand and support her better."

Marni patted his hand and said, "You're a good man, Nicholas. The world could use more men like you."

Jaclyn M. Hawkes

Chapter 17

Nick thought about Marni's comment about him being a good man as he walked across the stable yard. No one had ever said he was a good man before. It was a whole new concept and his gut reaction was to doubt it. But then he didn't think Marni would have said it if she didn't mean it. That was one thing about these McLaughlin women, they didn't hesitate to say what they meant, but they didn't say something they didn't believe either. On the one hand, it could cut like a knife, but on the other, you could believe them. Maybe he was a good man. Or could be, with a lot more of making over his life.

Looking around, he wondered where Monet was. Gingersnap and another horse were tied to the hitch rail, and Monet's saddle was hanging over the rail nearby. He wandered into the tack room and got his saddle and took it out to the rail as well, and then put a head into her office to see if she was there, but she wasn't. He could see into most of the barns from where he was and there was no sign of her. He headed for the indoor arena. Maybe she still had a clinic going inside.

She wasn't there either and he went into the barn that had an alley he couldn't see into to search for her. She had to be here somewhere. As he walked down the alleyway, he heard a crash from the other wing of stalls and realized that this must be where they had moved the outlaw stallion. Then he heard her talking. "All right. All right. I can see it."

He came around the corner to see her standing there in the alleyway outside the big brown stallion's stall in the riding breeches that he so loved on her because they made her look absolutely classy and absolutely sexy at the same time. She was looking down inside the horse's stall from safely outside the heavy wire mesh that had been installed across the stall openings and Nick asked, "What's up, Monet? What are you looking at? Do you still have time to ride?"

She looked up and gave him a smile of genuine gladness that made him feel all warm and fuzzy inside, until he heard her say, "Oh, he's just knocked his water bucket down and spilled it and seems to think he can't survive without a drink. Yes, I have time."

Nick finished walking up to her and asked, "Well, can he? I thought you said that they can go without food for a while, but they needed water in front of them all the time."

"I did. I'm just being facetious. And dreading dealing with him to get in there and hang it up again so I can fill it."

At that, Nick shook his head. "You're not going in there, Monet. Let the guys handle him."

She smiled sweetly at him. "That was sexist. I was always taught that the boss should be willing to do even the worst jobs."

"They're just bigger. And stronger. I'm not trying to insult you. Why does his owner even keep him when he's so dangerous?"

"It's not a case of stronger. Now it's who's smarter. We've figured out to lure him outside with grain to work in his stall. And he's a world grand champion dressage horse. He's insured for more than half a million dollars."

"Geez, how do they even ride him?"

"They don't anymore. He was too much of a pain. Kept acting like he wanted to eat his competition. So they've retired him and are going to use him for stud. It's just the wrong time of year yet, so Burt brought him here while he's abroad."

"How are they even going to use him as a stud? They'll probably have to sedate him. Can't Cal water him for you?"

"Cal has the afternoon off. It'll just take a second. I just have to go in and hang the bucket again. I can fill it from out here once it's hung."

Still skeptical, Nick said, "Tell me what to do and I'll do it for you."

"Actually, can you put a scoop of oats into the feeder outside in the run and then call to him? Just watch him. That's actually the most dangerous part because of how we've had to beef up the enclosure. You have to climb the fence to be able to put it in and the top section is barbed so be careful. When he goes out, I'll slip in and hang the bucket."

He nodded. "You watch him, too. And take a pitch fork in with you just in case. Be fast. I'll try to divert him."

Taking the measure of oats, Nick walked to the door of the barn and outside to the stallion's run and carefully climbed the fence. Reaching over, he dumped in the grain, then dropped to the ground outside the run, stepped back and called out to the horse. Almost instantly, the huge brown beast came barreling out into the run, ears pinned back and teeth bared. He hit the end of the run, waving his head in threat and then grudgingly put his muzzle into the feeder to take a bite of the grain.

From inside the stall, there was a soft clang from where Monet was hanging the bucket, and Nick was horrified to see the stud spin away from the oats and charge back toward the stall. Nick yelled at him and kicked the metal railing of the run to get his attention, but the stallion ignored him. At that, Nick took a giant step onto the second rail of the enclosure, climbed one more, vaulted the top barbed wire into the run, and sprinted for the stall door with only the heavy plastic grain scoop for a weapon.

Before he even made it halfway down the run, he heard Monet scream. At the door, he could see that the stallion had bitten her on the top of her shoulder and literally picked her up and was shaking her viciously with his teeth. She was helpless to try to save herself. She had taken the pitch fork into the stall, but it was now lying on the stall floor, almost under the horse's feet and was useless.

Without hesitating, Nick ran straight at the horse and booted it under the belly as hard as he humanly could, hoping that male horses had the same problem with being kicked in certain places as male humans did.

It worked. The horse dropped Monet and she staggered and fell against the side of the stall and the beast turned on Nick, albeit slower than he'd been moving seconds before. Wielding the grain scoop like a shield, Nick lunged for the heavy rubber water bucket that was still lying on the floor of the stall and in the same movement swung it with everything he had. It hit the horse on the top of the head but only slowed the stud down a split second and then he turned on Nick with his ears still pinned back and teeth bared.

Without really even thinking, Nick punched the stallion in the side of the muzzle barely missing his snapping teeth and the horse made a grunting sound that was half pain, half fury as Nick instantly stepped sideways to get between where Monet still clung to the wall and the stallion. The horse reared, and taking a chance, Nick swung the bucket hard once more at its exposed under belly and connected solidly again. The stud made a deep almost gulping sound and spun away from him.

As it spun, it whipped its head around and Nick wasn't even sure what happened next. Somehow in its vicious fury, momentum carried the huge beast over backward and to the side. As it scrambled for footing, the top of its head slammed into the cast concrete doorframe with enough force to actually rattle the building and then it floundered against the doorframe and fell to the floor with nearly as much violence as the attack.

All four hooves began kicking and its head flailed back and forth. Even as it finally ended on its side, it kicked wildly, and Nick lunged to Monet to drag her out of the way of its thrashing. With an eye on the struggling horse, Nick literally hauled Monet to the stall door and fumbled with the latch for a frustrating second, before he was able to get the door open and carry her out.

Safely outside, with the stall door latched, he took a deep breath and looked down to where she clung to him with one arm. The other hung limply in a ghastly spatter of blood that covered her whole shoulder and dripped down both the torn front and back of her shirt. He could see the pain in her face and shook his head sadly as he carefully pulled back the collar of her shirt to see where the stallion had broken through the skin. Even bones appeared crushed. The beast had done frighteningly deep damage to both sides of her shoulder and up towards her neck. Man, he'd never seen an animal behave like that.

From inside the stall, there was a deep, slow groan. Nick looked over the partition to see the stallion twitch for a couple of seconds and then finally go motionless, its stillness seeming strange for an animal that had just been so savage. Wondering if the horse was dead or just knocked out, Nick turned away from it and smiled sadly at Monet and then gently put a hand beneath her knees and under her back, picked her up and said, "The grain was a good theory. You up for a ride to the emergency room? You might need more than a nose splint this time."

He carried her to his car and loaded her in as carefully as he could and then peeled out for her house to get some pillows. On the way, he called Marni and then drove faster than he should have, but the sooner Monet got something for the pain, the better. That shoulder was scrambled.

Monet gritted her teeth as Nick turned out the gate and she wondered how a car that had driven so silky smooth just one day ago could have suddenly gotten so rough. Nick accelerated through the turns and Monet was surprised that she didn't care although she wasn't wearing her seat belt. Even Nick's gentle hand on her leg didn't register through the pain that throbbed through her whole chest and left shoulder.

That trip was interminable, but at least she'd felt like she was accomplishing something. Finally sitting in a little cubicle in the emergency room, she was reminded about how slowly the wheels of medicine could turn as they worried first about getting her insurance information and only then began the process of finding a surgeon who could start putting her back together.

When they peeled her shirt away from her shoulder, she didn't have the heart to look down at her own flesh. She'd known even as that outlaw had latched onto her that the damage was going to be extensive. She was just glad Nick had been there to rescue her. Who knows what would have happened had he not been around when she tried to water the stallion. She hoped the horse was dead. Even Bert would be better off with the insurance money and not having to handle him.

The nurse inserted an IV and then a doctor put something in it that made Monet feel immensely better almost immediately. That warm swoosh washed through her and she finally took a deep breath, closed her eyes and loosened the death grip she had on Nick's hand with her right one. She didn't even want to think about how she was going to run a therapy stable like this.

Nick stood at her side during the entirety of it and stayed patient and gentle, even as he tried to get those wheels turning faster for her. She leaned into his quiet strength and was more grateful for him than ever when the surgeon finally did show up and began examining her. As Monet rested her now throbbing head against Nick's solid chest, she noticed that once again, being injured made the whole no touchie zone a non-issue. Who knew? Maybe this and her broken nose were God's way of helping her get over her weirding out at Nick's touch thing. He was incredibly comforting to lean against.

They put something else into her IV line and she began to feel sleepy and strangely disconnected from the whole situation. It was an unsettling sensation, but it beat the heck out of the pain that had taken her breath away. She closed her eyes and breathed in Nick's smell and tried to focus on his nearness and not how much everything hurt.

From a distance she recognized her mother's voice and opened her eyes to smile tiredly as her mom tried to hide her sadness at Monet's condition behind cheerfulness. Her mother came to stand beside Nick, and Monet figured between the two of them they had everything under control. She closed her eyes again, and tried to zone away from the pain.

A few minutes later, Nick leaned close and whispered, "I'll be right back." He gently kissed her temple and left, and Monet looked up at her mother in surprised confusion at both his kiss and at her reaction to it. It hadn't weirded her out even a little that time. It had to be the medicine.

With him gone, the nurses around her began to cut her out of her clothing. They asked her mother to remove even her jewelry and watch, and it took her a moment to understand that they were prepping her for surgery. The thought of surgery wasn't as troubling as it should have been for some reason, but she was glad that Nick wasn't there to see her being undressed. He must have left to give her some privacy.

He was very considerate when you thought about it. Considerate and handsome. She yawned and closed her eyes again, hoping that he'd come back and hold her hand one more time before they put her completely under. He was wonderfully comforting sometimes.

Chapter 18

The sense of anxiousness surfaced before full consciousness did. It took a while longer to wake enough to realize that she was having an anxiety attack. She'd only studied them before, never experienced one, and it took even longer to come around enough to acknowledge that she couldn't do a thing about any of it. It was horribly troubling and when she could finally make her body obey, she turned her head in frustration and then moaned in pain from the movement.

Almost immediately, she felt a gentle hand on her forehead and heard Nick's voice. It was unbelievably soothing. She tried to take a big breath and felt some of the angst ease. Nick was beside her. She would be okay.

Struggling to open her eyes, she tried to look up and focus and he gave her the sweetest sad smile and said, "I'm right here. You're okay, Monet. They think if you can wake up a little you'll be able to relax and shake the worries. How are you feeling?" He smoothed her hair back off her cheek.

She tried to take another deep breath and could actually feel herself start to calm knowing he was right there. Tiredly, she said, "Fine. I feel fine." It wasn't true. She felt like she'd been mauled by a grizzly and she was insanely uptight, but he didn't need to know that.

His brow creased in concern as he reached to hold her right hand. The left one was trussed up in some kind of sling. She realized she probably hadn't really fooled him, but she still didn't want to whine. She closed her eyes again to try to relax and sighed. He was far too patient and sweet to torture by complaining.

Several times she felt herself fading in and out of that frightening thick mist to realize on some level, that Nick or her mother was there beside her and was reassured enough each time to relax back into sleep. Finally, she felt herself waking up with less of the worry, and not feeling that way-too-much-cold-medicine feeling. She opened her eyes, tried to move, and then almost wished for the too drugged sensation. Almost. The pain was over the top, but she still preferred that to being stuck in the bizarre gray clouds in her head.

Nick was there again and she tried to concentrate to figure out why. This time he was asleep in the chair beside her bed, his thick black eyelashes resting on his cheek just above a dark five o'clock shadow. He was still wearing the button down with her blood spatters on it and even in his sleep, he looked exhausted. Handsome as the devil, but exhausted. She needed to make sure that he went home and rested—just as soon as she felt a little better. He'd been a godsend to help her through the anxiety.

Before he woke up, a nurse came in, took her temperature, and said a touch too brightly, "Oh, good. You're awake. The physical therapist has been in to see when she could start working on that shoulder. I'll tell her you're awake."

Knowing just enough about physical therapists to be wary, and in just enough pain to be thoroughly irritable, Monet glanced down at the slings and wraps that harnessed her ridiculously sore shoulder and arm, groaned and said tiredly, "Let's keep it a secret for a while.

Huh? I'm sure she has plenty of other victims to entertain for the day. Maybe tomorrow."

The nurse gave her an understanding smile. "We can try. But honestly, she's tough. Getting people back to a hundred percent is her mission and I've never seen her let anyone skate yet. But maybe she's gone home for the day. We can always hope. I'll bring you some more pain medicine just in case."

That pain medicine came in very handy when less than an hour later, a therapist who was a direct descendant of Attila the Hun wandered into Monet's room saying, "Shoulders have to move or they freeze up." Monet, Nick, and the nurse all three lost in the battle of wills against her. She began to maneuver Monet's shoulder and neck and even with the codeine, tears came to Monet's eyes with the movement.

Once she was gone, Monet relaxed back onto her pillows and closed her eyes again. Nick stood beside her to smooth her hair away from her brow and gently assure her, "It'll get better. Just give it some time."

She opened her eyes and he was so sweet that the tears that had threatened spilled over and Monet swiped at them stubbornly. "I know. I don't doubt that. I'm just feeling whiny. I hurt and I hate having to accept help. I should be home doing chores. And I'm sure you have a million things to do other than babysit your riding instructor."

He only smiled patiently. "Give it a minute, Monet. And let that stallion owner pay for the extra chores you're missing. If he can afford the crazed horse, he can pay for what it trashes. He ought to put it down."

Monet looked up at him. "He wasn't dead then?"

Nick shook his head. "No, but I hoped he was. Your dad said he was pretty out of it when they moved him. The owner flew back into the country and your dad insisted he take him somewhere else. Actually, what he said was that the owner had twenty-four hours to have him moved before your dad called the vet to geld him. Apparently it was a good threat. He's gone. And the guy was pretty upset about what happened to you and has agreed to pay for anything you need and damages."

Monet let out a breath and admitted. "Much as I love horses, that stud was beginning to take it out of me."

Nick sat back down in the chair and reached for her hand again. "Your dad is handling everything. And Barry is dealing with the owner. So relax." He grinned. "Just enjoy the complimentary therapist. Pretend you're at the spa."

She sighed. "Spa. I've never even been to a spa. Never had the time or the need, but I know it's not like this. How long do I have to stay here?"

He smoothed the hand he held with his other one. "You *get* to stay here another day or two, depending on how you do. Your doc wants to make sure that the pain is manageable and that your tummy gets started working again."

"Why would my tummy not work?"

He shrugged. "Apparently sometimes after general anesthetic, it forgets what it's supposed to do. Are you hungry yet? It's been about twenty four hours since you've eaten. Is it telling you anything?"

She gingerly shook her head. "Only that I didn't realize I'd been out for so long, and that my shoulder is hammered. What does the doctor say about it?"

Nick leaned forward in his chair. "That you're one tough lady and that shoulders take a long time to heal. He said it's the only joint in the human body that can move in all directions like it does, held in place by multiple

214

ligaments and tendons. That horse tore a lot of them and broke your collar bone. You're a project."

She felt herself wanting to actually grin at his tone. "A project? A surgeon actually said that?"

"Something like that. He'll be back sometime to tell you himself. In the meantime, he said I was in charge and that you're to behave yourself."

"You're making this up."

"Maybe."

"Did he give an actual time period for how long it will take to heal?"

"Monet, I'm trying to tease you into not asking that question. Would you cooperate please and not ask yet?"

She tried to straighten up and winced. "How long, Nick?"

"Six weeks in the slings with therapy. Then another four before you can lift anything or ride to speak of."

Monet groaned. "Six weeks. Ten weeks. Holy Copernicus. My head's too fuzzy to think. Isn't that like Christmas? He wasn't kidding a long time. Can I get it shortened for good behavior?"

He grinned at her lame joke. "I don't think that's really how it works, Monet. But I'm sure good behavior would be appreciated."

Yawning, she said, "Well, you're in luck. I'm too tired and sore to be poorly behaved."

He squeezed her hand. "Go back to sleep, Monet. There's no point in fussing anyway."

At first, all that registered through the pain medicine again was the low murmur of voices, but as she became awake, she recognized Barry's voice. He and Nick were having an almost whispered conversation. Without opening her eyes or being fully awake, Monet tried to figure out what they were saying. Something about going to church. Nick wanted to know about Barry's church. What time it was. No. Where it was. Something. In her haze it didn't make much sense and she realized she must be dreaming. Why would Nick wonder about Barry's church anyway? She quit trying to figure it out and relaxed back into the medicine fog.

The next time she heard them talking in her dream, Barry was saying something about Nick pushing past her comfort zone. About touch and energy and love languages. It was disjointed and made no sense. Like her own brother would want a guy to pressure her for a more physical relationship. These narcotics were something else.

Still, when she next half woke and Nick was there, she reached for his hand that was so tenderly stroking her arm. His touch was incredibly comforting.

Later, deep in the haze of sleep, she dreamed she heard boots and then TG Alder's voice sounding almost a little threatening as it said, "You again. I shoulda known. What? Do you think you being here gives you some kind of ownership?"

Nick's hand tightened slightly where it held hers and his voice had a touch of steel to it when she dreamed she heard him smoothly reply, "She's a young woman, not a piece of property, TG, but I get your drift, and yeah, I'll stake a claim here and then some. You have a problem with that?" Nick's sweet possessiveness made her want to give a happy sigh, but she was too tired. TG didn't reply, but the boots walked out of her dream.

When she heard her dad's voice, there was no mistaking him and she struggled to wake her befuddled brain and open her eyes. It was dark out. He was there, sitting beside Nick, talking about business of all things. Business valuation. Depreciation and taxes. Writing off losses from unusable images. Business ethics. Home office expenses. It was more disjointed than ever to her counselor's mind, but she really didn't think she was dreaming this time. It was hard to focus with the medicine. But then if she had had too much medicine, why did she hurt this much?

Nick must have noticed her trying to open her eyes and leaned forward to stroke her hand and whisper, "Your face is going to get stuck like that. Are you okay? Your dad is here." His long look from those marvelous eyes helped her to wake out of the haze.

Her dad came to stand next to her bed and smiled his kind, patient smile, touched her cheek and asked, "One too many tangles with that outlaw, huh? How are you feeling?"

She began to fumble with the bed controls. "All right."

Nick helped her raise the head of her bed as her dad shook his head and said, "I'm your father, Monet. You don't have to give me a line. How are you really?"

She fought to keep from tearing up as she admitted, "I'm sore, Dad. Big boo boo."

He nodded and softly said, "I know, sweetheart. And I'm so sorry."

She blinked and nodded. "I kept trying to prove I could handle him, when I should have just insisted that Herb move him. My stubborn head."

Her father grinned at her. "You have a stubborn head? Where in the world would you get a stubborn head? Not from your mother and me. Well, at least not from your mother." He put a hand on her good shoulder.

217

"Don't you regret that stubborn head, girl. It's been a pain at times, but it's also helped you get through some stuff. God knew what he was doing when he gave it to you. It's made you strong."

"Strong is only good if it's wise." She shook her head sadly. "This time, it definitely wasn't wise. At least it was me that he got."

He shook his head. "He's gone, Monet. Let's draw a line and put it behind us and zero in on getting you feeling better and out of here. If you can start eating, they'll let you leave in the morning. You'll have to drive in to therapy every day, but at least you'll be home. How about some robust orange Jell-O?" He held up a single serving container from her rolling table. "Sugar free even. Can you beat that?"

Monet groaned. "They're trying to kill me. It's a vast left wing conspiracy. First Attila the therapist, and now this. Get Barry in here. I'm going to need legal representation."

"He's been and gone. Said not to wake you."

Monet looked over at Nick. "Barry was here? I dreamed he was, but . . ."

Nick grinned. "He said to tell you you looked awful in that color of hospital gown."

Monet glanced down at the faded blue print gown and nodded, "He's probably right. They design these things that way on purpose. They make you look even sicker, and then they charge you more. Is sugar free Jell-O my only option?"

Nick held up a plastic cup from her table. "Water, ice, apple juice, or the Jell-O. Don't worry. I'm sure if they go down easy, they'll let you have a pizza."

The nurse came in the door just then and heard the last of the conversation. Without skipping a beat, she said,

"No pizza. Would you like some sugar free Jell-O?" The nurse held up the Jell-O just like her dad had.

Monet accepted the carton. "Ahah. Just what I've been craving.. You do realize that people have been eating sugar for thousands of years and the race has seemed to survive quite nicely. It wasn't until the sugar substitutes appeared that we all started dropping like flies from cancer."

The nurse glanced at Nick, did a long double take, then looked at her dad and asked, "Is she irritable? Or teasing? Or just going through sugar withdrawal?"

Nick chuckled and opened the Jell-O for her and her dad pushed her table closer and said, "I'm sure it's just the sugar, and not the fact that she's badly hurt, and then had surgery without the benefit of the odd pizza. Just ignore her. She'll come around."

Monet picked up the spoon and tried to get a bite of the Jell-O, but the carton scooted across the table before the spoon broke the rubbery surface. Nick snagged the carton and held it back toward her and she managed to scoop out a bite. Putting it in her mouth, she closed her eyes and dramatically said, "Mmm. That is undoubtedly the finest sugar free orange Jell-O I have ever had the pleasure of eating in my life! Mmm mmm mmm! Better than Momma's fried chicken! I do declare!"

The nurse rolled her eyes and went out and Landon sat back down as he said drily, "Your mother doesn't make fried chicken."

Monet gestured with the spoon. "Don't tell the conspiracy. Why orange? I didn't know they even made orange Jell-O. It tastes like cough syrup."

She took two bites and then hesitated, suddenly wondering if it was indeed going to stay down. She shouldn't have thought about cough syrup. At her hesitation, Nick handed her the little cup of apple juice and encouraged. "Maybe this will taste better. Or just some water. Take a couple sips and see how it goes for a few minutes."

Nodding gingerly, she pushed the Jell-O aside and said tiredly, "I think that's an excellent idea. What time is it?"

Nick looked at his chunky gold watch. "Eight-thirty-two. On Wednesday. In the evening."

"Wednesday." She thought about shaking her head and decided against it. "I've lost a whole day. Our horses aren't still tied to the hitch rack, are they?"

Nick shook his head and her dad said, "The horses are fine, sis. Everything is fine but you. The only thing you need to worry about is healing. We've got the stables handled."

She tried to move just enough to ease the bone deep ache in her shoulder and closed her eyes. She really should have listened to Nick about not going into that stall.

Chapter 19

It must have been late when she next woke from the blood pressure cuff on her arm doing its inflation thing. The lights were dim and though there were buttons blinking and weird noises coming from all the machines around her, it was relatively peaceful.

Nick was still there. He'd changed his bloody shirt and shaved and he looked positively sexy sitting there clicking away on a laptop. There ought to be a law against someone looking so good when she felt too thrashed to even try to comb her hair. When had he gone to shower? He'd been there every single time she'd woken up.

She studied him as he worked. He was completely focused and remarkably engaged for a man who seemed to have put aside his own life to stay with her. It was no wonder he was working this late. She'd totally interrupted his schedule. He left the keyboard to touch his screen and she noticed how the muscles of his shoulders stretched the fabric of his shirt as he moved. It made her want to sigh except that she wanted to keep watching him without him noticing. What was up with him? What was up with *them*? He'd shown back up in her life two days ago and hadn't said much, but something had changed. Something had changed with both of them. Only she had no idea what it was.

She blinked sleepily. He was so sweet to stay with her. What did he want from her? They hadn't ever made it to the talk she'd planned on having as they rode yesterday.

What did she want from him? For all this time, she'd been so sure that he wasn't the kind of guy she would even consider caring for, but then what had happened? And when had it happened?

The cynical psychologist in her wanted to give herself a world class lecture on being realistic, but somehow, her heart or her soul—something—had gone neatly right around that inner skeptic, and had begun to trust him. Completely strange, considering their backgrounds, but somehow it felt incredibly safe and right. It was positively unexplainable. And absolutely comforting. Even with her shoulder trashed for who knew how long, there was an inexplicable sense of all being right. If she'd had the mental energy, she would have been thoroughly worried.

Instead she looked over at him again. He had been so gentle with her through this. He'd been so gentle with her always. And patient. Amazingly patient considering some of the wicked honest conversations they'd had. It was a miracle that he would even still speak to her after some of the things they had discussed. She watched his strong brown hands as he worked. He had marvelous hands.

He was definitely a worker. If he went at the rest of his life the way he'd gone at learning about horses and riding, then it was no wonder he'd become so successful in spite of doing it all on his own at such a young age. His work ethic was phenomenal. And his natural competence only added to that. And to his attractiveness.

She blinked again. He was insanely attractive sitting there beside her. It made her frission meter go haywire. Yeah, she weirded out about them touching, but that didn't mean that her body didn't literally tingle when he was around her. Just watching him sit beside her made it hard to breathe sometimes. Like now. It was crazy.

It must have just been whatever they were giving her for pain. She definitely wasn't like this usually. Which wasn't actually true where Nick was concerned, but she wasn't going there tonight. No, she definitely wasn't delving there when her defenses were drugged. It was too hard to think rationally as it was, with him sitting there exuding guardian of the hurt and defenseless. It was too easy to think irrationally about how nice it was when he held her hand. Who would ever have thought that holding a person's hand could be that sensual? But then he did have the most incredibly strong masculine hands.

As she thought about his hands, they stilled on his keyboard, and she looked up from his hands to his face to find him looking at her. His face was every bit as hypnotic as his hands. In fact, more so because of those liquid green eyes. In this light, it was impossible to see the brilliant color that she knew was there, but the magnetism was definitely fully intact. It wouldn't be hard to drown in those eyes.

She slowly blinked again, wondering if she was dreaming, but he was still there, still sexy to the core, when she opened them back up. He closed his computer and reached his strong hand towards hers and she felt that insane little twist in her stomach that only Nick could induce. It made her breath catch.

He took her hand and did that simple thumb caress that turned her skin inside out, and she did sigh this time. She couldn't help it. Holding his hand was the most insanely evocative thing. This had to be the medicine. She wasn't a sigher. She wasn't a drown in green eyes kind of a girl.

He moved toward her and leaned down to push a tendril of hair away from her cheek, watching her like he needed to make sure she was okay. Yeah, those eyes were molten. She could smell his aftershave and it melted her brain. He leaned even closer, and she closed her eyes as he tenderly kissed her cheek bone. Okay, so she *was* a drown in green eyes kind of a girl. How was a person supposed to get enough oxygen in these hospitals anyway? There was definitely not enough oxygen this close to Nick DeGrassi.

Opening her eyes again, she could see the color of his, even in the dark, because he hadn't pulled back much. He ran his other thumb tenderly over her cheek bone, still watching her and then softly said, "You're awake."

She nodded ever so slightly. "Yes."

"How are you feeling?"

Breathless. "Fine."

He gave her that half smile that reached his eyes lately. "Fine again?" She nodded and he gently touched her face one more time, smiled bigger and whispered, "You're right. You do feel incredibly fine." She rolled her eyes and he asked, "Fine, as in you'd keel over before you'd complain?"

"No. Finer than that. Just not pain free, lets go play racquetball fine."

"Mmm. I see. You play racquetball?"

"Sometimes. Not tonight."

"Well, the courts *are* all closed until morning."

He hadn't moved back away from her and she couldn't help watching his mouth as he spoke. His lips had been firm but soft on her cheek and she wondered what they'd feel like on her mouth. Or what they would taste like. That thought set the butterflies off in her tummy again, and she glanced back up into his eyes, only the intensity she saw there made the butterflies frenzy.

Surely he wasn't imagining the same thing she was. Even if that was what she thought she was seeing in his eyes. He glanced down at her mouth, and back up and the liquid green went back to molten. Then again, maybe he was. She couldn't pull her eyes away from his and the slight caress of his thumb only added to the spell. *Drowning might not be a such bad way to go.*

Some kind of a beeper went off and it finally broke the tension. Both of them turned to look at the television screen above her bed, and she felt her face heat when she realized it was her pulse monitor that was sounding a warning. The line on the screen had gone exactly as crazy as her heart had when she'd been held captive by his eyes. *Oh brother.* She tried to take a deep breath and relax and the line on the screen began to slow down.

A nurse came in the door, looked at the screen, then at the two of them, and back at the screen again. She reached up to push the reset button, glanced Nick up and down, then said, "She's a patient, Romeo. Try to keep that in mind."

Nick let go of her hand to raise his in a defensive gesture. "Hey, I didn't do anything but look at her."

The nurse only shook her head and said sagely, "I 'magine with you that's all it takes. If her heart does that again, stop looking and turn around. You'll make her chest burst into flames." With that, the nurse went out and Nick turned back to Monet in confusion as she tried to laugh right out loud without moving her shoulder. Like his turning around would be any better. That nurse obviously hadn't seen the way he could wear a pair of jeans.

He shook his head. "Geez, what did I do to deserve that?"

Monet only laughed softly again, squeezed his hand, turned it loose, and closed her eyes. At least he was humble about his dangerous charisma. He didn't seem to have a clue that he could spontaneously combust a patient, or drown someone with only his eyes.

He settled back into his chair and picked up his computer again and Monet took more deep breaths and listened to the click of his keyboard. In some ways, she wanted to know exactly what was going through his head as he worked, and in some ways, their friendship seemed to go much smoother without any discussion about it. She wasn't sure what to think about that. It was directly juxtaposed to her nature to just give in and go with the flow, but maybe that would be best. Although, considering the circumstances, she felt like she ought to have a minimal idea about what was going on here.

At length, she opened her eyes and gingerly turned her head toward him. When he looked over at her, she studied him for a long moment and then softly asked, "Nick, why are you here? Why have you stayed with me this whole time? You don't have to sugar coat it."

He held her eyes as he considered her question for what felt like a good minute, and then said just as softly, "Because I love you, Monet."

He didn't look away as he said it and Monet was blown away as she tried to process his answer. *Loved her? Holy Copernicus! So was that sugar coating it? Or totally not sugar coating it?* It only took a moment for the heart monitor to go off again.

The same nurse came in, punched the reset button and muttered under her breath. "I'm sure you only looked at her again, Valentino. Seems we're gonna need to set the alarm range higher in here. We can't be calling the nurse with every glance." She adjusted something on the monitor and went out and Monet looked back over at Nick, wondering if she'd heard right.

He set his computer aside and moved toward her again, still watching her eyes. Finally, he gently asked, "Are you okay? Or did that freak you out?"

Monet wasn't sure how to answer that. She finally gave the barest hint of a smile and said, "You saw the pulse monitor. With that thing hooked up, I'm about naked emotionally."

He didn't smile back as he said, "Yeah, I'm thinking about keeping you connected indefinitely. I can use all the insight I can get with you. But is your heart going crazy good or bad?"

She honestly didn't know the answer and tried to shrug, but it hurt. "You tell me. You're the Romeo. I'm just the heart racee."

Leaning close, he picked up her hand again and asked, "Well, was that happy racing? Or anxious racing?"

He wrapped his warm fingers around her two littlest ones and caressed the back of her hand with his thumb and Monet was lost for a moment in the touch and couldn't focus on whether she was happy or anxious. Mostly, she was just feeling monumental physical attraction. His stupid little tiny touches were making her warm from the eyes down and completely confused from there up—if she even had that much gray matter frission free enough to think tonight. Which was questionable.

Finally, she admitted, "I don't know, Nick. Honestly, I'm not nearly anxious enough about you. Which is frightening in and of itself. I think it must be the pain medicine that's confusing me."

He leaned in close and used his other hand to smooth her hair back as he looked into her eyes again. He brushed a finger slowly along her brow bone, let it barely

227

brush down the side of her cheek, and then ever so lightly touch on her ear lobe.

She watched his eyes the whole time and knew he was going to kiss her and surprisingly, it was exactly what she wanted. He leaned even nearer, paused for a long, anticipation filled second, and then ever so gently kissed her lingeringly on the mouth. His lips felt way better there than they had on her cheek. Way, way better.

Even though it was a sweet, gentle kiss, her frission meter went crazy. So did the heart rate monitor, and Nick reluctantly pulled back and sighed as he stood up to push the reset button.

He sat back down in his chair and picked up her hand, but didn't lean back over close again.

It was probably a good thing. Monet had loved being kissed, and it was happy racing, not anxious, but she would probably hate herself if she kissed Nick a lot in the hospital when she was just a bit looped from narcotics. That would have ruined it and he must have sensed that.

Instead, he leaned back, closed his eyes and began a soft, gentle exploration of every little inch of her hand with his. It was slow and chaste and reassuring, and insanely sensual. She closed her own eyes and relaxed into his touch, hoping for this moment to last. Forget drowning in his eyes, she'd rather drown in his hand on hers. It was the most romantic, compelling thing she had ever felt.

Several minutes later, when she was almost asleep from his touch, without opening her eyes, she quietly asked him, "Nick?"

"Mmm."

"Why did you kiss me?"

She heard the smile in his voice as he answered, "You're the psychologist, Mo. You tell me. Why does a man kiss a woman?"

While she thought about that, he moved his attention to her wrist and softly stroked the tender skin on the inside of it with one feather soft finger that gave her chills all the way up her arm. After a moment, he asked, "Why did you let me kiss you, Monet?"

She considered that. She wanted to give him the obvious answer and say something about why a woman would let a man kiss her, but she couldn't. It would be too flippant and he'd given her an honest answer in a round about way. A kind, generous, reassuring answer. It felt incredibly nice to have someone say that they wanted to kiss her. It had been a long, long time. Too long. Nick's kiss had been absolutely worth the wait.

Eventually, she just tiredly told him the truth. "I don't know why, Nick. Maybe I love you, too."

Jaclyn M. Hawkes

Chapter 20

Barry and her parents showed up the next morning to help her home from the hospital. Nick was still there, although he was in a different shirt again, and looked clean-shaven and crisp, and she wondered if he'd somehow gone home and cleaned up in the middle of the night.

After the doctor released her, Monet was a little puzzled with the way that both of her parents and even Barry deferred to Nick to let him wheel her out and load her into his car. They even let him pay for her prescription at the pharmacy on the way out. That was bizarre.

She knew in the last few days, something had happened to change her and Nick's friendship, but she still didn't understand what that something was, and she certainly hadn't spoken to her parents or Barry about it. So what was up with her parents? Heck, what was up with her and Nick?

He was his typical gentle solicitous self, and when he got her to her mom's house, her mom helped him to take her inside and put her into a recliner in their family room. He tucked a throw around her, pulled out the foot rest, and then handed her a glass of milk with a pain pill before plunking himself down on her mom's couch beside her.

It almost made the sliver of feminist she owned want to rebel because she hadn't asked him to stay, but that sliver couldn't get past the woman who was still mixed up emotionally about him, but was thoroughly grateful for his care anyway. She looked over at him, noticed that he looked fabulous and definitely at home in her mother's house and decided she was going to sort through all of these feelings later when she felt better. Right now she just wanted to close her eyes and relax and think about him kissing her last night. That was about the nicest thing she could ever remember.

That afternoon, she woke to hear him on his cell phone negotiating with someone about something to do with photo copyrights. It made the niggling doubts that she'd been trying to bury for days about being involved with a model push uncomfortably to the surface, and she felt the worry that had been nonexistent in the hospital drop into the pit of her stomach. She consciously tried to think of something else to push it away, but she fell asleep again before she quit worrying.

While she dozed, she heard him back on his computer working away at something. Several times she heard him talking on the phone, and the low steady tone of his voice was still somehow comforting until she'd hear some bit of conversation about images or design work, then she'd begin to wonder just what she was doing again.

Much as she hated it, she needed a good reality check about just what kind of a guy Nick was—that she had known from literally the very first day. It wasn't like she could delude herself that she didn't know better. She knew perfectly well. Then she'd look over at him and remember his tender care these last days and try to push the worries to the back of her mind again. She decided again to indulge herself in enjoying him at least for a little while, now when she was under the weather. When she felt stronger, she'd be more responsible with her heart.

In the early evening, her mom offered to bring them dinner in the family room, but Monet asked to try to eat it at the table. It had only been a couple of days, but she was already sick to death of lying around and feeling lousy. It made her feel irritable and even more lousy.

Nick hovered as she got up to walk into the dining room, so he was right there beside her when she saw a new eight by ten framed photo sitting on her mother's piano. It was of Monet on her white horse, Normandy, neatly going over a fence out on the hunt course.

She picked up the photograph. At first, she was enthralled with the grace of the image. It was evocative and lovely, taken just at that ultimate moment of uplift as the horse and rider were in perfect air-born harmony. The peace of the image was huge, the balance excellent, and the colors of the light on the white horse and green of the course were vibrant and dynamic, the background of Healing Creek Stables beautiful in its serenity. Overall, it was an incredible photo.

Then she noticed that it was taken from the side and back with her in her form fitting riding jodhpurs, boots and blouse. It was, frankly, an excellent study of the female posterior anatomy. When she thought about, it became apparent that it was quite simply a picture of a woman's very attractive body, even if she did say so herself.

It made her mad. He'd taken a photo of her, just like they took photos of every other nasty babe he posed with. All the worry that had been waiting in the wings of her mind over falling for a man like Nick seemed to drop into the forefront. All the questions she'd pushed to the back of her mind about how she was going to deal with his vocation, came front and center.

233

It was thoroughly galling to be dumped into his pot of trashy women. And she hadn't even realized that he'd taken it.

She turned the frame over and began to try to take the print out. She would be darned if she was going to be just another one of his snake charmed bodies. She couldn't get it out one handed and Nick asked, "What are you doing? Here, let me help you."

Almost snapping, she said, "I'm taking that photo out of the frame, Nick. What do you think?"

Obviously surprised, Nick asked, "What's wrong, Monet? Why are you upset about the photo?"

Marni had stopped just inside the dining room door and was watching the two of them with a look of concern on her face as Monet said starchly, "I'm not one of your trashy models, Nick. You're not going to take a photo of my . . . Of me in tight riding breeches and add it to your repertoire."

Nick's eyes widened and her mom said, "Excuse me. I'm just going to go grab a fresh tomato to serve with this salad."

She left through the back door and Nick asked, "What? You think it's a picture of you in tight clothes? You think I took a photo of your butt?"

Disappointment rolled over the discouragement that she'd been struggling with over her shoulder injury and it made tears threaten her composure as she turned on Nick. "You know exactly what it's a picture of, Nicholas DeGrassi. Don't play stupid. I'm not just another one of your girls."

He shook his head and calmly said, "It's a beautiful image, Monet. I gave it to your mother for Pete's sake. It's a tasteful, respectful image of a beautiful girl, on a striking horse, in a lovely setting."

Still unreasonably frustrated and hurt, she challenged back, "Don't you dare dump me into your pile of surgically augmented thong dolls who don't have the brains to even realize they are being used!"

Nick looked honestly shocked and it made her wonder if he realized at all that he had cheapened her by taking the photo and making her just another of his models. Her tears spilled over. She wanted him to understand and added sadly, "I'm not some poor tramp who doesn't know who she is. Who's willing to bare it all to the highest bidder to sell something. I do know who I am. I'm a daughter of God."

With an infinitely gentle tone that made her cry harder, he said, "I know. I know that, Monet." He put his arm around her and pulled her gently to him and went on, "That knowledge is actually what makes you the most beautiful girl I've ever known. Easy, Monet. I wasn't trying to insult you. Or use you. I swear it. Take one of those deep breaths you taught me about. Relax."

He put his other hand under her hair at her neck and gently massaged it and soothed, "I know your body is a temple, honey. That you're the furthest thing from a tramp. But just because humans have cheapened the human body doesn't change the fact that bodies are beautiful. You're created in the image of God. The respect you demand makes you more exquisite than ever. And you are pretty. You're beautiful. It's not my fault. It's not a fault at all. It's a gift."

He hugged her a bit tighter and said sadly against her hair, "And don't judge the girls, Monet. Leave judgment to God. Most of them didn't set out to be trashy. Someone taught them they were objects. Someone taught us all. Someone on the adversary's team. It's not right, or fair. But people—especially little girls learn what they are taught."

Monet wiped at her tears and nodded. "Okay. You're right. And I'm wrong to judge. But don't sneak around here with a camera. Tell me. I didn't even know I was being photographed. It's like paparazzi or something."

He gave her his half smile. "Get used to it, baby. You're in a relationship with a photographer. And you're far too beautiful not to shoot. Photography is an art. A gift. Don't begrudge me that. Hey, it's the most respectable talent I've got. Don't knock it."

She sniffled and shook her head. "I'm not knocking it. You do have a gift. But I can't be like the other girls. I can't."

He held her close again. "Oh, Monet. You're such a nut. You're like no one else on the planet." He pulled back and tipped up her chin so that she looked at him and he said, "I'm so sorry that I offended you. I didn't mean to. I swear it. You were just beautiful. Is it really that bad? Your mother loved it. Do we have to take it away from her?"

She shook her head again. "No. I guess not. But I'm not the other girls."

"You're not the other girls. I promise. In fact, what other girls are there? I didn't even realize there were any other girls than you, Monet."

She looked up and felt some of that anxiousness settle into her heart again. "Now you're burying yourself, Nick. Stop while you're ahead."

He put an arm around her waist and nudged her toward the dining room. "Come on. You'll feel better with real food in your tummy. I've heard that homemade soup makes troubles shrink exponentially. Even only perceived ones."

She let him seat her at the table as her mother

hesitantly came back in, but all his kind words didn't shrink the angst she was feeling. He was sweet. And beautiful. And smart. But she'd known all along that she shouldn't fall for a muscle bound Italian girl charmer.

It was a long, not very restful night. What sleep the pain from her shoulder didn't interrupt, dreams of Nick with the girls from his website did.

Then both Nick and TG arrived at the same time to visit her the next morning. The posturing was over the top and although part of her wanted to climb onto Nick's lap and rest, another part of her was frankly too tired and sore to even deal with them, and she went into her mother's guest room and laid down and let her mother entertain them. Actually, she needed to add cynical to tired and sore. What was she going to do about Nick?

He knew that something was bothering her. It was probably something he could fix if he told her about selling off the more graphically romantic side of his business and working from behind the camera now instead. Even letting her know that he was firmly back involved in church would probably help, but he kept hoping she'd have enough faith in him to just trust him.

It was silly, but for some reason that was important to him. He wanted her to be able to see and feel the changes he'd made, without him having to prove everything to her. Not that he wouldn't stick with her even if he did have to prove something, but he'd been working so hard to show her that he had faith in her working through her own baggage that he wanted her to do the same thing for him.

She was still too reserved with him ever since that stupid photo incident. He was working to get back to her being comfortable and trusting with him like she'd been in the hospital, but he knew it was going to take some doing.

The second morning after she got home, Nick knocked on her door to pick her up for physical therapy, and hoped it went more smoothly than it had gone in the hospital. She answered the door and the very first thing he saw in her face was gladness to see him, but then that shadow came into her eyes again. At least the gladness had been there. He bit back a sigh. He'd known she was cynical and that she was strong. And she was worth it.

Smiling, he said, "Hey, pretty girl. You ready to go get that shoulder back on the road to perfection?"

She nodded almost resignedly, but then she smiled as well and said, "Absolutely. Thank you for coming to take me."

Meeting her eyes, he said, "My pleasure, Monet." He casually took her hand. "I just hope you don't get Attila the therapist again."

"I won't. I made sure when I made the appointment. My guy is supposedly a long haired young guy with a genius for shoulders. The receptionist said he looks about fourteen, but he's the best."

"Then perfection is nearly in the bag." He opened the door and helped her into his car and they headed out toward the city.

She didn't say much on the drive, so he just left the radio on low, and focused on touching her hand. She was funny about her hand. It seemed to be completely non-threatening to her, but if he worked at it, he could get her to unwind beautifully just by touching it. The thing about it though, was that after getting her unwound, he was sometimes completely wound up just from touching it.

Sometimes his reaction to their relatively casual relationship amazed him. Whatever their relationship was. Who knew?

At the physical therapist's office, she was still a tad distant to him until they got working and her shoulder became more painful. For some reason, when she was vulnerable and he helped her, she was more trusting of him. It made him all the more grateful that she allowed him to be there for her, although he'd have given anything to be able to go back and rethink that day.

When they were finally through with her exercises, her eyes were teary from the pain and he wrapped her in a hug without thinking twice about it and she hugged him back. He held her for a long second and breathed in the smell of her shampoo and felt her relax against him. Sometimes the strength of the emotion he felt for her surprised him. He hadn't been just talking when he'd said that he loved her.

When she eventually looked up at him, he could see the strength of her own emotion in her eyes and it gave him hope. She hadn't been just talking when she'd said that maybe she loved him back either. And he knew there wasn't really a maybe about it. She did. It was there in her face and in her most basic reactions to him. He also knew she still wasn't comfortable with that, but she felt it anyway. He leaned and kissed her silky hair. Then took her hand and headed to his car. They were working on her getting more comfortable. She just needed enough good 'speriences.

Back at her house, he helped her in and then went to check on things at the stables. The stallion owner had agreed on a settlement to help her while she was injured, and Landon was overseeing things with Cal and Miguel, but Landon still had a business to run as well and welcomed the help.

Nick fed and watered the two front barns, put the yearlings on the walker, fed all the broodmares, then went back home to work in his office. He could have actually worked from Monet's living room, but had decided she probably needed some space from him. Maybe if he backed off a little she'd let herself come more to him emotionally. At least it seemed that way lately. He'd thought it was only guys who didn't want what was offered, but did want what they couldn't have; but maybe that was just human nature. At any rate, he was going to keep trying to find a way to break down the barriers to her heart, no matter how long it took.

Chapter 21

Monet heard her cell phone ring and tried to wake up enough to answer it. When she saw that it was two-forty-five in the morning, for a moment she felt a sense of panic as she groggily said, "Hello."

Her dad's voice cheerily boomed over the line. "Your black mare's finally gonna drop that colt. You wanna come out here and supervise? Or stay in bed and nurse that shoulder like a responsible patient?"

She kicked out of her sheets. "I'll be there in two. Uh, make that five. It's hard to dress one handed." Hanging up, she barrel rolled the way the therapist had taught her to get up. Man she hoped this baby arrived here safely. She'd been trying to get this mare settled in foal for four years now. It was why she was foaling in the middle of the summer. A late foal out of a champion mare was much better than no foals at all.

As she got up, she thought about calling Nick. For some reason, she wanted him here to share this with her, but then when she thought too much about it, she'd question her sanity. She was so torn right now between worrying that she should back away from him because of what he did for a living, and simply following her heart and letting herself fall more in love with him.

Struggling to brush her hair back, she slipped on a head band, picked her cell back up, punched up Nick's number and pushed send. His voice when he picked up was adorably sleepy.

Trying to think past the attractive huskiness, she said, "Would you be interested in taking some photographs of a mare foaling? I have a mare who is going into labor."

That seemed to wake him right up and he said, "Absolutely. I'll be right there. Thanks, Monet."

"You're welcome. Hurry. Horses aren't like humans. This goes quick."

She heard the smile in his voice as he said, "I'll see if I can find a fast car. See you in a few."

She held the phone for a moment after the call ended. Dang he had a sexy voice. She pocketed her phone. Well, he'd talked about doing more journalist type projects. If he was serious, this one would be a great one.

Six minutes later, she walked into the broodmare barn, still trying to button her fleece jacket. Twelve minutes later, Nick walked in with another man. They were both carrying a boatload of camera gear. Monet recognized him as the man who had been shooting the photos that very first day. He looked tired and yet entirely competent. Nick introduced him as Marco and Monet shook his hand wishing she had known Nick was going to bring him. She would have spent a little more time trying to tame her hair.

Within just a few moments, they had quietly set up an impressive amount of gear to both film and take still photos of the mare that was just now alternately kicking in irritation and pacing her stall. Occasionally she would be lay down and roll. She was wearing an elastic belt that had instruments on it to record what her body was doing, and Monet pulled a canvas lawn chair out of the way to sit on and keep an eye on the video screen. She had spent a fortune on this horse foaling monitor set up, but one healthy champion baby would more than pay for it. And

242

it wasn't like she could do much to assist her dad one handed anyway.

The mare finally laid down for a longer time, and Monet could tell from the monitor that her labor was getting stronger. Her dad was quietly watching from outside the stall, while Nick and Marco silently filmed and shot still photos from where they had cracked the stall door. Feeling completely left out, Monet got up and went to stand between her dad and Nick as they looked on. She didn't feel so hot and should have taken a pain pill before she came out, but it was remarkably soothing to stand between these two men she adored, and watch this sleek black mother deliver a new little life. Births were always amazing to her.

After a long, low groan, the mare finally expelled part of what looked like a clear, liquid filled balloon, and Monet could only hold her breath. These next two minutes were of paramount importance. If the foal was going to make it, it had to be safely born, and start to breath within just a couple of minutes now.

With another groan, the mare gave a final push, and the foal was born, still wrapped in the slippery clear membrane, except for the tips of its tiny front feet, that had broken through the bag near its nose. Beside her, Monet heard Nick softly breathe out, "No way."

Instantly Monet's father quietly went into action. He took one of the clean towels he had stacked nearby, and slipped into the stall to kneel near the foal and tear the bag away from its nose. Then he began to quickly wipe away any fluid and clear its breathing passages.

At his brisk treatment, the baby began to move and Monet felt herself take a huge breath of relief. The baby was at least alive. Now if they could just get momma and baby through to where the baby would stand and nurse, everything would probably be all right.

When the nasal passages were good and clear, Monet's father stepped back out of the stall to let the mare and colt be for a time. The blood would pump through the umbilical cord for a few more minutes if they both just lay still, and the baby would be stronger for it, as long as it wasn't having trouble breathing.

For several minutes the four of them watched quietly, the only sound that of the cameras, and then, finally, the baby began to kick and move and try to roll to where it was resting on its belly. When it began to fuss, the mare carefully sat up as well and gave a long, groaning sigh and then got to her feet. As she did, the umbilical cord tore from near the foal's belly.

The little, dark, slippery baby startled as it did, and the mare put her nose down to sniff it, making a low, wickering noise to it as she gently nuzzled it. Monet started to cry. She did it every time. This whole birth thing was the most amazing, touching, beautiful thing in the world, even if it was a thirteen hundred pound smelly old race horse that was doing it.

She took a deep breath and Nick glanced sideways at her, then dropped one hand from his camera to gently squeeze her good shoulder, then go back to shooting photos. As he touched her, Marco looked up from his eye piece and over at them and then glanced from Nick to her and back again a couple of times, before getting a confused look on his face and going back to his video camera.

With her good hand, Monet picked up another clean towel from the pile, wiped her eyes with a corner of it, and then she and her dad went back into the stall to begin toweling off the foal and checking it over. Her dad daubed iodine on the baby's raw umbilical cord, pulled more of the sack away and they began to scrub at the little guy as the mother looked on in concern.

Monet knelt beside the tiny stud colt and began to softly talk to it, just the way her father had taught her when she was a little girl, as she gently dried off its face and ears. Her father had always insisted that early and gentle handling was the key to a good, steady, gentle horse, and over the years Monet had come to truly believe him. These babies that were handled within moments seemed to always be the easiest to work with when they got older.

After another several minutes, Monet slipped back out and then her father did as well, and they watched from the outside again. The baby was getting more and more active and the mother more vocal as he stumbled around trying to figure out how to make his long, long legs cooperate so he could get up. He made a handful of attempts that all ended with him landing back in the straw at his mother's feet before he finally, very tentatively managed to get all four feet under him to stand.

Even then, he only lasted twenty or thirty seconds before tumbling over again, but he was strong. And so was whatever that stubborn little will was that newborn horses have, that makes them keep trying until they finally figure it all out, and stand long enough to wobble over to their anxious momma, and find a warm drink.

When they finally heard that sweet soft telltale sucking sound, Monet exhaled another sigh of relief and felt the tears in her eyes again. Another black with three white feet and a half moon on its face. It was going to be a beautiful baby. And hopefully another horse that lived to run like its mother had. There really wasn't anything as beautiful as a healthy, happy race horse.

Nick set his camera down, and turned to her to wrap his arm around her gently again. She turned her face into his chest, put her good arm around his waist and let the tears come. He understood how sweet this moment was to her. He understood how many dreams this little champion baby entailed for her. And he would be thrilled right alongside her to watch it grow and reach its potential. He'd know just how she felt about it all.

He leaned his cheek against her hair and softly said, "Thanks for calling me, Monet. This has been awesome! I've never seen anything like it. We got some great film. Thanks." She nodded against him without saying anything. It was a pleasure to share her passions with him. And it was so sweet to have him enjoy them as much as she did. Not to mention having him hug her when she was emotional.

How cool would it have been to have found him when she was in college? How different could things have been if she would have had him in her life earlier, instead of taking some of the other paths she had? So many aspects of her life could have been so much more fulfilling.

She pulled back from him and wiped at her eyes and whispered, "Sorry."

He only shook his head and leaned to tenderly kiss her temple. "Don't be sorry. It's okay. It was great. Wasn't it?"

"It was." She gave his forearm a squeeze and turned to her dad. "Thanks, Dad. For everything. I probably shouldn't have come, but I wanted to be here. If I go back in, can you and Nick take it from here? Just ask Cal to mop up. You know Mom will be out here first thing as well." She went onto her tip toes to reach up and kiss him. "I love you, Dad. Thanks for teaching me to love baby horses."

With that, she waved to Marco and headed out of the barn. She heard Nick's footsteps behind her and turned back to him in the dim light of the alleyway and said, "Thanks for not being mad at me for waking you up."

He reached for her hand and pulled her to a stop in front of him. "Are you kidding me? That was the coolest thing I've ever seen. I wouldn't have missed it."

She nodded even though he probably couldn't see her in the dark. "It's definitely cool. There's something about a brand new baby anything that is unbelievably sweet, isn't there? Sorry it makes me a little emotional."

He ran a hand gently up her arm and to her hair. "I love you emotional, Monet. Especially when you're emotional. How much you invest in what you love is adorable to me."

"That's weird, Nick."

"Not weird. Unusual. It's very unusual for a woman to care deeply about things anymore. Well, about things that matter. It's incredibly refreshing."

She smiled tiredly in the dark, "Whatever you say. I'm still embarrassed. Your friend probably thinks I'm a nut. Would you walk me back to my house?"

"I would. And my friend probably thinks you're cute. Not a nut. He's as stoked about tonight as I am. This will make a great story."

They turned and began to walk and Monet snuggled over against his arm in the cool of the night air. He put his arm around her and pulled her close and asked, "You cold?"

"Not now. Thanks. Your body is warm."

When they got to her porch, there were moths flying around her porch light and she reached in and clicked it off before turning back to him. She had been only going to say goodbye, but as her eyes got used to having the light off, she could see the intensity in Nick's eyes again that had made her heart race the other night in the hospital.

She was instantly torn between being wise, the way her cynical side pressed her, and being kissed, the way her body pressed her. The cynical side was probably a better idea, but Nick's attractiveness won out and she looked up at him, glad that there wasn't a monitor that was going to start beeping about her heart rate again.

He stepped closer, cupped her good shoulder with a hand that was warm right through her shirt and glanced at her mouth. He watched her eyes and she watched his for the whole day it seemed to take for him to bend his head. Finally, she felt his mouth on hers and she closed her eyes and took in a breath as her brain short-circuited with pleasure as his mouth moved over hers.

At first it was sweet and gentle again, but then he hugged her tighter and became more intense. Man, she had forgotten how nice it was to be thoroughly kissed. Or maybe she'd never known it could be like this. It had never been like this that she could remember.

She felt herself make a small moan and slipped her one arm around his waist, fisted his shirt and stood on her tiptoes to press herself closer. When she did, he wrapped his arms around her even more tightly and made a sound of his own as he kissed her with an intensity that made her brain completely shut off. She didn't think, just let herself revel in the feelings welling inside her. That breathless heated pleasure felt incredibly sweet here in the cool of the night breeze.

For a few moments, Nick kissed only her mouth, his lips seeming to feed off her feelings—off her need. Finally, he gave a nearly inaudible sigh and pulled his mouth away from hers to move it to her cheek, just in front of her ear, and then to that incredibly sensitive hollow below her ear where his warm breath and the slight scratch of his whiskers made her skin turn inside out.

She fisted the hand in his shirt tighter and tipped her head back and to the side to bask in it. No one had ever kissed her neck like this before and she'd had no idea it would make her nearly lightheaded with pleasure. She couldn't help the sigh that was almost a moan. At the sound, Nick's arms tightened again until he was hurting her shoulder, but for a second, she didn't even care. She just let him nuzzle that sensuous spot on her neck until her breath completely caught from the chills.

Finally, when her shoulder became too uncomfortable, she pushed him back just enough to ease the ache and then she buried her face in his neck and took a deep breath to try and even her breathing. She could feel his chest heaving as well, and for some reason it made her feel more secure against him. He had been as affected by their kissing as she had been.

She put her lips right against his collarbone, nearly tasting his skin, and breathed in the scent of him that she'd come so recently to love. It was a mixture of aftershave and his car and some other scent that was uniquely him, and it went clear into her brain. Somehow, it killed all the angst she felt about him occasionally, and only heightened the incredible attraction she felt toward him. The skin of his throat against her face felt cool, and smooth, and warm all at the same time, and it was incredibly evocative. It brought pleasure like she had never known from a simple kiss.

Content to stay right where she was forever, she let the weight of her head rest on him and took one more deep breath, wishing that she didn't have to tell him goodbye, and send him home soon. Or ever.

As she breathed back out, he let out a ragged breath of his own, and took a slight step back from her. He looked down and into her eyes and then gently kissed her on the mouth again, for a second softly, then more firmly, then incredibly softly again. Still breathing slightly fast, he whispered almost against her lips, "Monet. Girl, you taste like heaven. Your mouth makes me crazy." He looked straight up and took a deep breath, then looked back down at her. "I'm so sorry I hurt you, baby. I didn't realize."

She shook her head and gave him a tremulous smile. "It's okay. I didn't notice. Not for a sec."

His voice was husky when he said, "Yeah. I was right there with you." He brushed his chin against her hair. "Sorry. I wasn't going to kiss you. Really, I was just going to make sure you got in safe. I keep worrying about crowding you." He paused and then breathed out, "But then your lips made me forget."

Turning her head, she nuzzled his chin and whispered, "Sorry."

He closed his eyes and let her keep nuzzling and asked, "Yeah?"

"Mmm, no."

"Me neither." He leaned down to kiss her one more long, lingering time. "Goodnight, Monet. I'll come and take you to therapy again tomorrow. Get some sleep."

"Good night, Nick."

Back in his car, on the way home a while later, Marco casually said, "So, is this where you disappear to occasionally lately?"

Nick nodded. "Occasionally."

"It took you a while to see that girl home. She live far away?"

"Oh, a stone's throw across the yard."

"She just had a hard time getting her key to work."

"That lock does need some work, I'll tell you."

"She's a class act."

"Very."

"She didn't seem as comfortable with you that first day as she was there tonight."

Nick tried not to smile. "No. No, she's gotten a tad more comfortable."

Marco shook his head. "She's what happened. Isn't she?"

Nick looked across the car at him in the dark. "What's that supposed to mean?"

Marco shook his head again, and looked out the window and mumbled, "Leave it to you, Nick. Ten million hot girls do nothing for you. So you fall for the princess. I guess I should have seen this coming." Turning back to Nick, he asked, "You gonna marry her?"

"You think I have the guts to ask a girl that classy to marry me?"

"You have the guts to do anything you set your mind to. I know you. And I saw the way she looked at you."

"I'd marry her tonight, Co."

"You're gonna ruin my whole career, you know. For a girl."

"She already happened and your career's better than ever. What are you talking about?"

Marco looked out the window again. Finally, he softly admitted, "I used to believe that some day I'd find a decent girl who would look at me like that."

Jaclyn M. Hawkes

Chapter 22

Nick had been taking her to therapy every day for a week, when on the way home, out of the blue, he casually said, "Monet, I need to go out of town for a few days. Well, for ten days, actually."

Turning in her seat to look at him, she struggled to keep a placid face. Ten days. Man, that seemed like a year to her. Stoically, she asked, "Where are you going?"

"Iceland. Marco and I are going over to do a shoot."

For weeks now, Monet had been trying to ignore his occupation and not let it bother her. When he was with her, treating her so well, she was somehow able to push it to the back of her mind to justify how much she wanted to be with him. At his announcement, reality came rushing back in a hurry. She nodded woodenly. "So when do you leave?"

"Day after tomorrow." She nodded again, but didn't say anything. What could she say anyway?

They drove the rest of the way in silence, then when they pulled up in front of her house, he turned in his seat and asked, "No comment? None at all?"

Looking up at him, she reached her hand across to put it on his arm and admitted sadly, "I'm going to miss you. Ten days sounds like forever."

He unclipped his seatbelt. "It does, doesn't it?" Getting out, he came around to let her out, paused beside her and said just as sadly, "I'm going to miss you, too. Now I wish I hadn't agreed to do it. It seems crazy long to be away from you."

She watched him, wanting to burst into tears, but suddenly feeling like such a fool to be this attached to him and wondering how they'd gotten to this place. For weeks now, she'd felt safe, but suddenly she had to question if she was being insanely foolish. She wished like ninety that they could have a gut honest talk about exactly what their relationship was. Holy Copernicus but she was out of her mind.

It only made her more confused when he came closer, backed her up against his car and then leaned in right in broad daylight to watch her face for a second and then bend to kiss her.

It wasn't a tender sweet kiss this time. It was firm and hot, almost demanding, and made the skin on her neck tingle as he put both hands gently into her hair and pulled her to him. At length, he pulled away, and swore under his breath and she looked up in surprise at him.

He shook his head, looked down and swore softly again, and she said, "Nick, what? What's wrong?"

He shook his head, more slowly this time. "It's all wrong. It's all wrong, Monet." He gestured between the two of them. "What's up with us?"

"What do you mean?"

"I mean, do you have any idea what my biggest life's dream is?"

She looked at him in confusion and hesitantly asked, "What are you talking about?"

"Or how many kids I want? Or where I want to vacation?"

"You want to go to Yellowstone in September to see the leaves and the geysers. I didn't even know you wanted kids. Why are you asking this?"

"No. I want to go canoeing in Maine and eat lobster." He took her hand and walked from the parking area into her yard, and then into her house, where he finally stopped and turned to her again. He looked at her for another long moment, then surprised her by leaning to kiss her once more, just as desperately as he had beside the car. She was completely confused, but couldn't help kissing him back anyway.

When she did, his kiss only deepened. It was passionate and intimate, but something was wrong. He seemed sad, or maybe even angry for some reason, and there was almost a desperation to his sudden need for physical affection. While she thoroughly enjoyed it, she finally broke away from him to look up at his green, green eyes in confusion and asked hesitantly, "Nick, what's going on? Are you okay? You were fine ten minutes ago. What made you this upset?"

Evenly, he said, "You did."

"How?"

With an overtone of bitterness, he said, "You and your perfectly controlled counselor titanium shell that you back yourself right into when anything threatens to go anywhere near something vital or important."

She shook her head. "What are you talking about?"

Sounding completely frustrated, he asked, "Monet, what do you want from me?"

She narrowed her eyes. "Okay, Nick. Just start at the beginning and tell me what I did to make you so mad at me. I'll try to fix it. I'm sorry. I don't even know what I did."

"Monet, I just told you that I had to go to Iceland for ten days."

"I know that. I heard you. Why did that make you ticked at me?"

"Because you didn't say, oh that sounds fun! Or holy Copernicus, I'm going to miss you. Or do you have to? Or even, why Iceland, of all the places on earth? And certainly not, can I come with you? No, instead you pull this counselor calm face and safely put all of your emotions neatly back into your shell where they can't be reached by mere mortals. It frustrates the daylights out of me."

"Apparently."

He rolled his eyes and again asked, "What do you want from me?"

"Are we talking do I want you to open doors for me? Or do I want you to communicate with me? What?" She paused for a second and then hesitantly added, "Or are we talking like the commitment word? Or the intimacy word? What are you asking?"

"Yeah. You tell me, Monet. What do you want?"

Crud, what was he asking? She shook her head. "I don't want anything from you. We're friends. Very good friends. Do I have to want something?"

He backed her up against the wall and put both of his hands on either side of her head, kissed her hard again and said almost silkily, "You had better be lying to me, lady. Tell me that this is just one of those poised moments where we don't talk about what matters."

Her eyes widened. "Are you threatening me?"

"Of course I'm not threatening you. Don't be stupid."

She put both hands on her hips. "Don't be rude. We are perfectly capable of having . . .

He interrupted her by kissing her soundly for another long minute again and then saying, "The truth, Monet. Were you lying? What do you want?"

"Nick, why are you asking me this today?"

"The truth, Monet. Be brave enough to step boldly out of that blasted titanium shell and level with me." She put her hand to her forehead and sighed and he added, "And don't give me that too vulnerable bit again. We're both well into the vulnerable realm. Be honest."

At that, she stood up taller and said almost defiantly, "All right, Nick. Let's do be honest. And what exactly is it that you want from me? Let's start with that."

"Chicken." He leaned and kissed her neck again, then gently bit her earlobe. It made her suck in a breath before he continued, still half angrily, "Fine. I'll be honest. I want it all. I want the rest of your life, Monet. I want commitment. I want marriage. I want eternity. I want you in my bed every night. I want your heart. I want your mind." He kissed her hard again. "I want your body. I want to have babies with you. Six of them. I want to walk into our house at night and smell homemade spaghetti sauce and have a handful of little kids come running to the door to hug daddy. I want to wake up in the morning all tangled up in your skin. And have you pat me on the butt the way your mother does your dad when she thinks no one is looking. I want to laugh with you as we try to figure out what our grandkids are trying to tell us before they can talk very well. I want to hug you when you cry when that baby colt that was just born, dies of old age. I want your triumphs. I want your heartaches. I want your passion. I want it all."

Oh, it was such a good thing that she wasn't hooked up to a heart monitor! She watched those sparking green eyes in wonder, and had no idea how to dredge up the type of courage it would take to admit to him the kind of things he had just admitted to her.

Wow! He really wanted all those things from her! She felt herself begin to smile. Finally, she put up a hand to softly touch his mouth and quietly said, "Dang, you are an eloquent man. Forget visual arts. You should be a poet." She moved into his arms and gently kissed him on the mouth and he kissed her back, a little stiffly at first. Then, when Monet moved to press her body close to his, he pushed her back against the wall and fairly pounced on her.

Several minutes later, he tenderly bit her lower lip and said, "This is a very persuasive diversion, honey, but you didn't answer me. And I'm still mad at you. I still want the truth. Temptress though you may be."

She smiled and moved to nuzzle his ear and he made a small sound of pleasure before pushing her away. "You're good, girl, but the shell has to go. It's making me nuts."

Sighing, she took his hand and led him to the couch, then climbed right onto his lap and leaned her good shoulder against him where she could still look up into his face. "All right, Nick. But are you up to really being honest? Because the shell isn't the problem. The shell is just protection from the issues. What I want isn't the problem. If we added a few things, your list could easily be my dreams come true."

"What aren't you saying, Monet? What are the added few things?"

"Even the added few things aren't issues. What about the things you left unsaid? Those are the elephants in the room."

"Things I left unsaid? I said quite a bit. What did I leave unsaid?"

She sighed and looked down, wondering how to proceed, and he said, "Just be honest, Monet."

She shook her head. "No. That's exactly what you said the last time we talked and it ended in a ball of fire, buddy. Remember? You left me."

"No. That was the second to last time we talked, and I came back. I am here."

She kissed his jaw line, then snuggled closer. "You are. But that was an awful month."

His voice softened and he ran his fingers through her hair. "But we worked it through, Monet. That had been a brutally hard, honest moment, but we figured it out. That's good. That's what healthy relationships do. So tell me."

"Have we figured it out, Nick? Or have I just been being too tempted by your delicious hunky body to be halfway smart, and keep my distance?"

His forehead wrinkled and he asked, "We're talking about you not weirding out when I touch you. That serious talk. Right?"

She nodded, "Mmhmm."

The wrinkles turned into a full blown frown. "So, you haven't been totally passionately kissing me because you're emotionally invested in me? You've been kissing me because my body tempts you?"

She smacked him. "Oh, stop. You know darn well that I'm emotionally invested. Why else would I even be tempted? What I meant was, even if I am in love with you, shouldn't I still be weirding out because you touch so many girls as your vocation?"

He met her eyes and paused for a long moment, then asked quietly, "So, you're in love with me?"

She looked back at him and then suddenly got up and said, "We shouldn't be having this conversation, Nick.

We shouldn't even go there. You're just going to get upset with me and go away for a month or whatever and . . . We should stop now, and just walk around the elephant in the room like we've been doing."

He reached for her hand and pulled her back down onto his lap again. "Whoa. Easy, Monet. Back up for a second. What was that all about? Hyper drive into the shell or what?"

She shook her head and leaned back against his shoulder and sighed. "I earned the shell for a reason, Nick. We're just demonstrating that. Of course, I'm in love with you. Are you telling me you don't realize that?"

He tipped her chin up so he could look into her face and said gently, "I've been hoping, Monet. But sometimes you're hard to figure out. Why do you think I'm straight up asking you today?"

Bitterly, she said, "Because I didn't react properly to your announcement that you're going off to Iceland to pose with some bimbo in not enough clothes. Forgive me." Tears started into her eyes. She was suddenly exhausted and asked, "Can we be done with this conversation, please? I'm sorry I'm not saying what you want to hear."

He pulled her head over to lean on his shoulder and gently said, "Don't cry, baby. Please don't cry. We can stop talking. But can I just ask you one question?"

She nodded. "Sure."

"Tell me why you're sad right now."

The tears started in earnest and it took her a minute to finally whisper, "Because I'm an idiot. I have a master's degree in psychology and I'm still a complete romantic fool."

"Honey, that's pretty harsh negative self-talk."

She sniffled and nodded. "But true." She leaned

into his neck and cried for a second and then said, "I want you to go now, Nick. I think I'm just going to go try to rest for a while."

He rubbed up and down her back for a moment and then said, "Monet, I need to tell you something. Have you been on my website lately?"

With her face still buried in his neck, she said, "No. Of course not."

"Why?"

She leaned up and looked at him. "Are you trying to get me to tell you I don't want to see you anymore?"

Patiently, he said, "No, Monet."

"Why would I want to go on your website? What woman would want to be number thirteen-hundred and one?"

"Go get your laptop."

She leaned back down against him and said almost petulantly, "No. You know it weirds me out. I just want to be foolish and a romantic idiot and keep my head in the sand."

"Monet, if you could change something about me. Anything. What would you change?"

"I swear you're a masochist. Take a tip from a failed marriage counselor and never ask people questions like that."

"Okay, let me give it a whirl and you tell me if I'm right. You'd change my vocation so that I'm not snuggling with bimbos, in not enough clothes, that I care nothing about. How'd I do?"

"You're spot on. And you're still a masochist."

He rubbed her back. "What else?"

"What else are you beside a masochist? Insane."

"I'm not. Just tell me."

"What makes you think I would change anything else?"

He put a hand up into her hair and ran his fingers through it. "What about getting back close to God? Wouldn't you recommend that?"

"Nick, who in this world doesn't need to get closer to God? That's a no brainer."

"I know, but you knew I'd gotten lazy about religion. I thought you'd want me back on track."

With a completely softened tone, she said, "Nick, I'm not your mother. Or your judge. You've already told me that you knew there was a problem. Your heart is good and I have no doubt that you'll figure it out. Where you're at isn't as important as where you're headed. That one is between you and God, not you and me."

"But the modeling with the girls is between you and me?"

She looked up at him, mad again. "Darn you, Nick. I've been struggling for months to try and deal with your stupid nasty girls. Why are you trying to make the elephant bigger than it already is? It's plenty big enough. Is this whole thing just some twisted way of dumping me? It doesn't have to be this convoluted. Just tell me you're out of here!"

"Go get your computer, Monet."

She sat all the way up. "I told you no, Nick. I want you to go home now."

"Monet, trust me."

She closed her eyes for a second and then opened them and admitted sadly, "I'm trying, Nick. I am. But seeing you mostly naked with scores of women isn't going to help. I can promise you."

He pushed her off his lap and stood up beside her, then pulled her back into his arms and kissed her, but she tried not to react to him. For a little while, it worked. Until he left her mouth and went to that tender sensitive spot under her ear again. There, it took him about three seconds before she felt herself breathe out a soft sigh and lean into him. A moment later, he came back to her mouth and she kissed him more than willingly.

Later, when he pulled away, he hugged her for a minute, then took her hand to lead her in to her kitchen desk where her laptop was. When the screen came up, he leaned over and clicked on her search engine. Pulling out the chair, he motioned for her to sit.

He typed something into the toolbar and a moment later his site came up, complete with the whole 'Baron of Romance' banner, and the rows and rows of far too intimate images. Something deep in her chest began to shrivel. Beside her, Nick said, "What the heck?"

He leaned down to stare at the screen and then clicked on refresh and said, "Sorry about that." He stood back up, and exposed a new home page that was vastly different than the one she'd just been looking at. It still said 'Images of Romance', but the whole look of the site was changed. There were still photos, but the tone had changed drastically. They were tasteful shots of Nick or a handful of other very masculine, heroic looking men, or just striking shots of beautiful scenery. But there were no girls. None. Not a one.

Monet felt her heart stall for just a moment and then she slowly turned to look up at him in thrilled surprise. Still wondering what was going on, she asked, "When did you do this?"

He only smiled and asked, "What do you think?"

With tears filling her eyes, she whispered, "It's beautiful. This is incredible. I love it." Turning back to the screen, she scrolled through pages and pages of the same kind of images. All tasteful. All respectable. All fabulously laid out.

When she got to the end, she put both hands over her face and began to cry harder, but he said, "No, baby. That's not all." He leaned down to type something else in and another website came up. This one was 'DeGrassi Images.com' and was all manner of unromantic photos and the articles that went with them.

Monet clicked through them, and then stood up and turned, but she couldn't look up at him. He came close to her and pulled her face up and said gently, "I told you to trust me. You should have known I wasn't trying to hurt you. I love you."

"I was trying to learn to just trust you in spite of everything. But it made me sad. And worried."

"I know. And I needed you to trust me, just like I trust you." He kissed her teary eyes. "I love you. I need you. Didn't you realize that I would do whatever I needed to to help you know you could trust me? I'm going to Iceland to do a documentary on their geothermal steam systems. And I want you to come. With your own hotel room."

She searched his eyes and he hugged her to him and said, "Monet, if I promise never to touch another girl, would you promise not to ever go find that old website again?"

She nodded against him, but then asked, "Why would you promise never to touch another girl?"

Leaning, he kissed that spot on her neck and said silkily, "Because I found out about the secret faithful rule. I'm trying to be worthy of the only girl who matters. I want to marry her."

She looked up at him for a long moment and hesitantly asked, "Do I know her?"

He bent to give her the most sweet, warm kiss of her dreams. "Intimately." He kissed her again. "She keeps my pilot light perpetually lit."

Feeling tears well again, she tried to smile and asked, "Is that what that light is in your eyes?"

"Yes. It's coming from my heart. I finally found the love of my life."

She leaned into his chest and wrapped her good arm around his waist and sniffled. "My mother would say that was the most romantical thing she's ever heard."

"Well, you should trust your mother. She's incredibly wise."

Half laughing, but still teary, she said, "I don't know. She actually believes those romance novels come true."

He considered that for a second, then kissed her for another long, long moment and said, "Sometimes they do, Momo. Not very often. But sometimes they do."

The End

About the author

Jaclyn M. Hawkes grew up with 6 sisters, 4 brothers and any number of pets. (It was never boring!) She got a bachelor's degree, had a career as a cartographer for the federal government and traveled extensively before settling down to her life's work of being the mother of four magnificent and sometimes challenging children. She loves shellfish, the out of doors, the youth, and hearing her children laugh. One daughter is now married to a wonderful young man. Jaclyn and her awesome husband of 23 years, their remaining three children, and their happy dog now live in a mountain valley in northern Utah, where it smells like heaven and kids still move sprinkler pipe.

www.jaclynmhawkes.com.

266

Author's Note

This book was the result of a very entertaining lunch meeting with my publicist. You see, there really are people, (ridiculously muscle-bound men in various stages of undress, often found in frightfully compromising situations with lots and lots and lots of similarly clad lovely women), who make their livings being models for romance novel covers. I kid you not!

If they weren't just a hair—or sometimes several hairs, scandalous, they'd be thoroughly compelling. And since I choose to crack up over the complete over-the-topness of it all instead of going the "they are going to burn in hell for their promiscuity" route, I tend to laugh a lot—as I blush when I happen onto this type of thing as I'm struggling for book cover ideas. (Whew, that was a sentence!)

At this point, I have to admit that I love those all pecs and beefy shoulders and voluptuous bosoms hanging out covers. I often think they're beautiful and I love the sense of history and rich colors and bold type fonts, not to mention the sense of almost primal romance they depict. Most of them definitely wouldn't fly for the kind of romance I write, but I usually think they're great! Usually.

However, because they are sometimes the aforementioned scandalous, and are often insanely and yes, ridiculously outrageous, I have to admit, that I have been known to roll my eyes and shake my head, just as Monet did when she first discovered Nick's website at the start of this book. I mean, really people. Hundreds of different snuggle partners? That's hard for a faithful and proud of it girl like me to even wrap my little mortal brain around.

Anyway, back to that silly lunch. It took place soon after I had discovered these book cover models existed and I mentioned it to my publicist. She laughed just like I had at the whole deliciously scandalous idea. (She and I have a tendency to laugh quite a bit at times, actually.) That's when she said something about, "Wouldn't it be funny if you wrote a book about a hyper refined heroine who found herself attracted to one of those guys?"

Things snowballed from there to the point that it turned out I went home with a few great plot ideas in mind. It was a good thing it was mid-afternoon and the restaurant was mostly empty. Hey, it was all her fault. She has this amazing laugh.

The weird thing is, as I was doing research for this book, I discovered that a huge percentage of marriage counselors are divorced. Not only that, but it would seem that more often than not, marriage counselors aren't necessarily interested in healing marriages. It appeared that many want to help their clients free themselves from the "unfortunate and misguided" idea of marriage.

Really? I'm sorry, but that's just weird. In my obviously innocent and naively romantic little world, a strong marriage is the goal. After all, our families are the basis of Heavenly Father's plan, and strong families are founded upon strong marriages. Plus, if you can't keep your own deal together, I'd imagine you probably shouldn't be offering how-to advice to anyone else. Especially not for a gazillion dollars an hour. And even more naively, isn't the whole idea of getting marriage counseling usually so you can work things out and stay together?

I'm so out of style, bless my heart. Can you say that about yourself? Anyway, I had fun writing this book. I hope you enjoyed it. I wish you all a truly happily ever after marriage. Shop well and then work hard and I promise you that great marriages can come true. To me, 23 years into this marriage thing, it's the most fun of all!

Jaclyn

www.ingramcontent.com/pod-product-compliance
Lightning Source LLC
Chambersburg PA
CBHW070326260626
47160CB00003B/962